If It LOOKS LIKE a Duck

FRaNK MaLLeY

WHISPER PUBLISHING

WHISPER PUBLISHING
www.whisperpublishing.co.uk
info@whisperpublishing.co.uk

1st Edition

Paperback ISBN: 978-1-7395943-0-5
eBook ISBN: 978-1-7395943-1-2

For Carole and Michael, and in memory of Nan.

'No man ever steps in the same river twice, for it's not the same river and he's not the same man.'

Attributed to Heraclitus

ACKNOWLEDGEMENTS

A big thank you to the mighty river running near my Bedfordshire home. I've spent many hours enjoying its tranquil beauty, walking along its picturesque banks and, on occasion, observing its swollen menace, wondering what secrets it must hide. One particular stretch inspired *If it Looks Like a Duck.*

Many thanks to the team at Whisper Publishing, in particular editor Wendy Wilson, 'nit-picker in chief', whose shrewd observations, meticulous attention to words and grammar, and tireless enthusiasm made the publishing process so enjoyable.

Most of all, love and gratitude to my family. To my son, Michael, for his support as always, and my wife Carole for all her encouragement, draft reading, constructive criticism and all-round enthusiasm, not to mention endless tea and coffee. Love you lots.

If you enjoy *If it Looks Like a Duck*, the author would appreciate a quick review on Amazon, Goodreads, or your favourite book website. Reviews are vital – a few words matter.

If it LOOKS LIKE a Duck

PROLOGUE

If Johnny knew that in little more than an hour he'd confront death for the first time in his brief, pampered existence, he would have stayed in bed. Instead, he slouched off the mattress, pawed the curtains and blinked at the gathering haze forming in shimmering ridges over the back cornfields despite the clock having not struck 10.

Another day of relentless heat. Another day of news bulletins banging on about record temperatures and global warming, offering tips on surviving the summer holidays. Wear loose-fitting cotton clothes. Freeze your sheets. Stay out of the sun between 11am and 3pm.

Johnny's mum knew that made sense. She told him so after he'd negotiated the stairs, moaning that his cornflakes were too soggy. Recently, Johnny complained a lot. A cereal complainer, according to his mum, although the joke went over his sleepy head. Quite how she ran a house and held down a job before he turned 14 was a mystery.

"Why don't you offer your services to NASA, Johnny? I've heard the latest Mars probe's in danger of missing its landing spot."

She spooned on the sarcasm, wondering how her *darling boy*, who once hung on her every word, turned into a teenager who knew more than the Dalai Lama. In his imagination, Johnny threw a sneer, telling her she was funny, but knew nothing about anything. Buttering toast, she shook her head in resignation.

"Well, I know about swimming in cold water on hot days and it can take your breath away, so be careful."

"Mum, I'm not a kid. I can look after myself."

An hour later, stripped down to knee-length swimming trunks, Johnny sat on a wooden bridge spanning the River Lex. Legs dangling over the side, he debated with two schoolmates, Chris and Karl, whether they should dive or drop eight feet into the murky water.

There'd been a late change of location. They'd planned to swim at Lexford lido, part of the picturesque lake complex in the town's park. Official lifeguards supervised there, while the facility offered deckchairs, changing huts, and food kiosks. In hot weather, bodies rammed the pool, small children constantly needed the toilet, and mums with disapproving looks and sharp tongues scolded teenagers for doing what teenagers do in swimming pools.

"Stuff that," said Karl.

Chris's verdict also included an F and a U. Johnny went with the flow.

By the time the boys reached the wooden bridge on the river, 500 yards from the park but screened by a tight bend and a row of tall willow trees, Johnny's mobile clocked 11:10am. Had the boys carried a thermometer, it would have signalled 34 degrees Celsius. Sizzling hot, but at least the venue proved private and peaceful.

A kingfisher twitched along the reeds lining the riverbank, and two dragonflies simulating fighter jets darted back and forth. Ripples formed on the calm water, where basking fish brushed the surface, while in the distance a chain saw whined.

"Summertime," Johnny sighed, throwing back his mop of wild hair and marvelling at a vast, cloudless sky. He hummed the opening bars of his mum's favourite song. He didn't know who'd written or sang it, but who cared? Living couldn't have been easier on such a blissful morning.

"Come on then. Who's going first?" said Chris.

"Me." Karl was eager.

Skinny, ginger, spotty, a willing nature compensating for his lack of physical prowess, Karl inched to the edge of the wooden platform, carved crudely by swimmers in bygone summers. He held his nose, squealing before plummeting, legs scissored. The splash forced a plume of water high into the sky, showering cooling drops onto Chris and Johnny.

Karl surfaced, affecting a curious doggy paddle. "It's freezing," he gasped, beckoning the others to join him.

Chris's bulkier frame propelled a higher fountain skywards.

Last came Johnny. He didn't stand, preferring to squirm to the edge of the platform. A nervous swimmer, he hadn't admitted as much. It was his secret, he'd never told his mum. He could handle a few widths of breaststroke in the safe confines of an indoor pool, but swimming in the sea, a lake, or river, all manner of creatures wriggling and darting around his extremities, generated a sick feeling. Letting his mates down would make him feel worse, which is why he breathed in courage and slid off the platform, striking the water awkwardly. A belly-flop.

Gasping and thrashing, Johnny sucked water deep into his lungs. Thunder filled his ears, eyes stinging as he squinted through algae and floating debris soup. He broke the surface and hyperventilated. Someone shouted, but he sank again, taking in more water. Green, foul tasting sludge. His right foot snagged on what he thought was a submerged tree branch. Panic turned to terror. Johnny kicked out. Nothing budged. He thrashed again, strength draining from his limbs as blood fled to core organs.

'Swimming in cold water on hot days can take your breath away.'

The warning. Oh, why didn't I listen to Mum?

Frantically, Johnny stretched down, touching a clump of fine vegetation attached to the obstacle trapping his leg. Coarse, slimy, the texture of seaweed. He pulled with all his strength, muscles burning, lungs about to explode. At last, the obstruction loosened and lifted. Rising with it, Johnny's head bobbed above the surface, eyes still shut. He sucked in oxygen, grabbing what felt like a branch with one hand, clutching the apparent floating weed with the other, gripping, spluttering, desperate to pump air into his sodden lungs.

Johnny opened his eyes and blinked away green gunge. The bearded face of a man came into focus, inches away from the end of his twitching nose. A man who stank to high heaven. With good reason. He was dead. Johnny screamed. A short, shallow shriek of terror. Shaking one hand free of the stiff's shoulder-length hair, he released his grip on the dead arm, feeling all remaining strength dissolve. His body relaxed, mind floating to a place of peace and calm, as if studying the surreal scene from his earlier vantage point on the bridge platform. Gazing down on the spooky stirrings of a ghost, with straggly hair and shaggy beard, who'd risen from a tangled lair in the depths of the Lex. To rescue him with perfect timing.

If Chris and Karl hadn't reached Johnny and dragged him to the bank, he would've sunk once more into the murk and disappeared. Perhaps forever.

1

The war-strewn cities of Syria were Dan Armitage's preferred workplace, throwing up acts of heroism, tales of fighting, destruction, and lamb kebabs to die for. They made a reporter feel truly alive. Pity, because Dan was sitting in an office on sleepy Lexford High Street in England's comfortable Home Counties wondering where his front-page lead was coming from.

Dan was fed up with this latest long summer. Tired of garden fetes, tea parties, and photographs of toddlers with ice cream smeared faces masquerading as news. In recent months, the nearest the *Lexford Journal* editor had come to a proper news story involved a neighbourhood whistle-blower catching the town's vicar breaking the nationwide hose pipe ban.

Vicar lands in hot water

The paper's corny headline screamed from the front page, Dan offering a prayer of thanks when the circulation manager reported a five per cent hike in sales of the print edition. Sitting with his back to the newsroom window, Dan playfully crushed an empty cola can, absently pondering. How might he explain to the proprietor that he was about to lead the newspaper on a grandad whose fame extended to making dog shapes out of cigarette packets? The telephone on the adjoining table rang. Normally, the acting news editor would answer, but a lunchtime sandwich had tempted Jasmine Sharkey away from her desk and everyone else on the news floor was busy.

Jumping up, Dan took the call. "Hello, you're through to the Lexford Journal news desk. Dan Armitage speaking. How can I help?"

"Is Johnny's mum there?"

"What? Who?"

"Johnny's mum. Mrs Mercer. She needs to come quick."

Concerned and intrigued by the panic in the boy's tone, Dan guessed the caller was between 12 and 15. Half a century younger than the average reader who called the *Journal*.

"Okay, calm down. Tell me who you are and what the problem is."

"I'm Karl, Johnny's friend, and he's not very well. I'm on his phone. He nearly drowned. I think he's okay now, but he's been sick and there's a man in the river and he's dead. Johnny said to ring his mum. Is Mrs Mercer there, please?"

Dan stood and peered over a backdrop of heads, eyes trained on computer screens, proofreading stories, checking adverts. The *Journal* hit the streets on Thursday afternoon on the considered basis that the week was mature enough to have generated fresh news and issues, while a long weekend lay ahead for readers to absorb and dissect.

At one end of the open-plan room, a low partition separated editorial staff from advertising and accounts. On the far side of the partition, Dan spied Sharon—*the* Mrs Mercer—blonde hair tied in a bun, busy chatting to a colleague. Sharon was a fixture and fitting, having progressed from a copytaker in the dying days of clickety-clack typewriters, to the accounts department. A vivacious personality and work ethic ensured she became a popular member of staff. She also brewed a delicious cup of tea.

"Okay. Listen, Karl. I'll find Mrs Mercer for you, but two questions. Are you sure there's a dead man in the river? Have you called the police or an ambulance?"

Karl had never seen a dead body in real life, but the man was floating head down in the river and hadn't stirred when Johnny screamed blue murder in his ear. It seemed a safe bet. "Yes. No."

Dan motioned to Jaz Sharkey, who'd returned to the office. She detected the urgency in his demeanour as he pointed to chief reporter, Pete Rainford. Seconds later, all three huddled around the news desk phone.

Dan spoke into the receiver, tone gentle but infused with composure and authority. "Here's what we're going to do, Karl. You're going to tell me exactly where you are and—"

"By the wooden bridge on the river, close to the park. Behind Hendos supermarket. About half a mile from where all the boats park up."

"That's great. Now, I want you to stay with Johnny and make sure he's okay. I'll phone for an ambulance and the police. And I want you to stay on the phone until …"

The line went dead.

"Damn. Sod's law. Probably ran out of battery. Right, Pete, get down there. I'll call an ambulance and the cops. Make way for a new lead. If this stands up and there *is* a body in the river, it'll make a great newsy splash. Bad choice of words, but you know what I mean."

Craning his neck, Dan checked Sharon was still at her desk before dialling emergency services to relate the details. Because a minor was involved, the operator assured him they'd treat the call as a Code 1. Blue light and siren response. Dan omitted to report the body in the river. He knew from experience that ambulance staff alerted police to all incidents of sudden or unexpected deaths. If police arrived before Pete, there'd be scant prospect of getting close enough to file a detailed report. Dan reasoned another few minutes wouldn't hurt. The man would be a long time dead. He replaced the receiver.

Jaz quizzed him. "What about the dead body? Should I ring the police?"

Dan pulled her close. "I'll do that. Can you explain things to Sharon and take her down to the river? Even if Johnny's okay, he'll be upset and want his mum. And she'll need support. No doubt he'll go to hospital for a check-up."

"Okay."

He watched Jaz's easy, rhythmic sway heading down the office, honey-blonde hair framing an elfin face, a warm, ready smile never far from her lips. There was something caring and compassionate in the way she carried herself. Everyone loved Jaz for that, especially Dan, which is why he'd asked her to marry him. She'd said yes, but they were in no rush. They were good together. Comfortable. Relaxed.

As Sharon absorbed the news, hand shielding her open mouth, Dan noted the shock and concern on her face. She and Jaz hurried down the back stairs. From the office window, Dan saw them half-skip, half-run to Jaz's red car and drive toward Lexford Park. He waited another minute, then called the police.

It took a few anxious minutes for Jaz to reach the spot behind Hendos, where cars parked in a dirt and gravel clearing allowing access to the path along the riverbank. The ambulance was there, although no sign of paramedics. There were no formal directions to the wooden bridge on the river, but the route was obvious. Down a narrow weed-strewn path, across a clearing, then along the towpath. Around 200 metres. Despite the humidity, Jaz and Sharon ran most of the way.

They found Johnny sitting on the grass wrapped in a blanket, two paramedics fussing over him. The male checked Johnny's heart and vital functions on a mobile monitor. The woman treated a cut to his right foot, sustained while lashing out to free himself.

"You'll have a good story to tell your mates at school, won't you, young man?" she said.

Johnny nodded, shivering under the blanket, contemplating the humiliation awaiting him when school resumed, courtesy of Karl and Chris. *Little Johnny Mercer can't swim. Little Johnny Mercer smells of fish poo. Little Johnny Mercer hugs dead people.* He felt sick again, looking sheepish when he saw his mum.

Sharon burst into tears and reached down to hug him. "Oh, Johnny. What were you thinking coming down here? I told you cold water's dangerous."

"I know, Mum, I know. I'm sorry."

Jaz left Johnny and Sharon in the paramedics' care and headed to the arched wooden bridge, where Pete interrogated Karl and Chris.

Pete was 22 going on 52. Young enough to be abreast of new technology, but curiously steeped in old school journalism, a legacy emanating from his dad and grandad. Both worked on the editorial desk of the *Daily Express*, in the days when the profession's gravy train steamed along at full speed. His questions were precise, shorthand, meticulous. No fancy digital recorders for Pete. The old ways were still the best. At least, that's what his dad told him. His notebook filled up with an account of Johnny's plunge into the murky depths, the struggle to surface, his encounter with the corpse, and Karl and Chris's alertness and courage when dragging him out. Page one material for the *Lexford Journal*. A modicum of spin, a few dynamic pictures, and the story may even sneak into the

Daily Express. Karl and Chris continued to tell their tale, heroism embroidered a fraction.

Jaz listened until a suitable pause presented itself. "What happened to the dead man?"

Karl's head recoiled, a nauseous grimace contorting his features, as if he'd opened a fridge and met an ancient kipper. He pointed to the wooden slats of the bridge below them. "Down there, stuck in the rushes."

Jaz craned her neck, studying what first resembled rotten river debris mixed with green algae. Closer inspection revealed a big man, fully clothed in white T-shirt and khaki shorts, head and body flipped to one side, torso trapped against a floating tree branch. The corpse bobbed up and down as water lapped against the bank.

Jaz took her phone and snapped pictures of the body and immediate surroundings. She crossed the bridge, edging down the bank to grab closer shots. Though gruesome, the work was engrossing. She didn't hear the police officer until he was almost upon her.

"Excuse me, madam, what do you think you're doing?" The tone was gruff, disapproving.

Jaz retorted with a disarming smile. "My job. My editor phoned you guys."

"You shouldn't be taking photographs. This could be a crime scene. I'd like you to leave right now, please."

"But—"

"No buts. Move. Now!"

Thank God Dan had the nous to give the paper a head start, Jaz mused, sauntering back up the towpath, studying the photos. Long lank hair. Beard. Broad shoulders. White T-shirt sporting an emblem. Jaz fiddled for a few seconds with the zoom function to expand the picture. Although perspiring from her exertions in the afternoon sun, a chill slithered up her spine. The image of an anchor and, to remove doubt, *The Anchor* printed underneath.

The long hair and logo solved the enigma. Jaz was certain the body was that of Roger Mansell, landlord of The Anchor pub. Renowned for charity fundraising, his face was familiar to readers of the *Lexford Journal*. The logo wasn't the only striking characteristic. From the middle of his white T-shirt, a gaping, near round, red-stained hole stared back at her.

Although Jaz had no experience in such matters, she wondered if a shotgun made such a hole.

2

Next morning, Detective Inspector George Cross paid Dan a visit. Though unsurprised, Dan didn't relish the meeting. Since assuming editorial command at the *Lexford Journal*, Dan regularly sparred with the inspector. Not in a good way. More in the way India and Pakistan periodically contest Kashmir. Uneasy peace, punctuated by sporadic bursts of conflict.

Dan saw his job as gathering and disseminating local news with speed and accuracy. Informing readers on crime, education, and council policies, though he hadn't endeared himself to Lexford's rulers by running a poll to find the best collective noun for a group of councillors. In at number one, an incompetence followed by an impotence. An indecision, Dan's favourite, trailed in third.

Reviewing theatre shows and musical events was also the paper's priority, as well as taking a spirited stance on spiky topics, such as the recent erection of controversial speed cameras on the local bypass. Motorists complained road signs were confusing, random speed limits arbitrary, while police officers lurked in unmarked cars training long-distance radar guns on unwary drivers. Readers dubbed it 'sniper alley.' Dan's regular column suggested the purge had gone beyond safety, accusing police of a cynical, money-making campaign. When readers claimed they'd spotted officers hiding behind lorries and under tarpaulins with radar guns, Dan said police tactics verged on entrapment rather than enforcement.

Pigs in blankets

Dan deemed his first headline accurate, but too explosive. He toned it down, although a school of thought suggested his finished article appeared more provocative.

The Police v The People

The editorial stand hadn't endeared Dan or the *Journal* to the local constabulary. In recent weeks, when the duty reporter phoned the police station seeking information with a cheery, 'Anything for us?', they got a surly tone and sneering response. 'Only contempt.'

Dan considered such criticism evidence that he was doing a good job, a conclusion reinforced by a supportive postbag. In the circumstances, his handshake with Inspector Cross was firm and as friendly as both could muster.

The inspector's shuffling gait and suspicious nature matched his job description. The ageing process had kicked in. Not that he was old—probably no more than 50—but his movements, clothes, and demeanour seemed old. Perhaps responsibility and daily exposure to life's evils has that effect. At least, that's what Dan mused, detecting the faint hint of a sneer as the inspector cast eyes over the office desk. Six copies of the *Journal* were open at different pages.

"Bit dramatic this morning, I thought," Cross said, viewing the front-page headline.

River of death

A strapline running along the top of the page contained more information:

Schoolboy saved from drowning after macabre embrace with corpse

Perched above the story, Pete Rainford's bold byline, while inside pages included copious quotes from Karl and Chris relating Johnny's fateful plunge from the bridge and details about the body's discovery. A portfolio of Pete and Jaz's photographs lent the story colour and movement.

Dan had excluded graphic shots to stay within the realms of taste and decency for a local rag. Mysterious stories about dead bodies sold newspapers. Pictures of the mess that was once Roger Mansell didn't. Also, at the time of printing, no one had formally identified the corpse. Jaz was almost sure of her identification, but 95 per cent wasn't good enough. Not for Dan, especially not before police informed relatives. He hadn't allowed speculation about a gunshot wound.

Dan didn't react to Inspector Cross's opening remark, instead behaving like any other experienced, resourceful hack fishing for information. "Any idea how the body came to be in the river?"

"I'll ask the questions, if you don't mind. I want to speak to the reporters first on the scene." Cross's accent carried lively sing-song vowels, at odds with his dour demeanour.

Dan beckoned Jaz and Pete. Normally, they wouldn't work the morning after print day, but neither wanted to miss the potential of intriguing follow-ups for online editions.

They sifted through the previous afternoon's timeline, from receiving Karl's phone call to finding the body, while one of Inspector Cross's assistants, a pasty-faced constable who looked 18 but was probably 25, took copious notes. After a laborious series of pedantic questions, Dan glanced at his watch, drummed his fingers softly on the desk and teetered on saying, *Don't you read the newspaper? This is all in there.*

Fortunately, Dan restrained himself, masking his frustration and launching into another fishing expedition. "Can you confirm the body is Roger Mansell, landlord of The Anchor, and can you confirm he was shot?"

Inspector Cross coughed. Rough. Raspy. A smoker's cough. He cleared his throat and turned to face Dan, whose finger curled around a pen, poised to note information, although he'd actually been sketching a caricature of the inspector's face. Sunken eyes, riverbed lines, big Roman nose. The doodle proved unflattering on two counts. Dan was no Picasso. Inspector Cross no George Clooney. The inspector assumed his most formal delivery.

"Mr Armitage, what I'm about to tell you is completely off the record and not for reporting until we officially release the news, probably late this afternoon. Is that understood?"

Dan nodded, Jaz and Pete squirming forward in their seats, eager to receive the scoop.

"We believe the body in the river is that of Roger Mansell, landlord of The Anchor pub. Right now, everything points to his death being a tragic suicide."

"Suicide?" Jaz couldn't hide a tone of disbelief.

"Yes."

"Suicide?"

"Please don't say that again."

"Not murder?"

"You're right. Suicide's not murder."

Striving not to rise to Jaz's doubting response, Inspector Cross sucked in a long, deep breath through a mouthful of wonky, gritted teeth. "For your information, and again, it must go no further at this point. We've discovered a suicide note on the landlord's boat, moored upstream from where he was found. The note's signed by Mr Mansell, the signature verified. Tragic though it is, suicide in Great Britain isn't uncommon. I looked up the statistics. Almost one hundred men a week take their own lives. It would appear that Mr Mansell was battling psychological and personal problems. It really does look like an open and shut case."

Jaz had heard that phrase recently, while watching an old detective series on TV. The case turned out to be neither open, nor shut, complex clues identifying the murderer as the policeman who started the investigation. Her eyes narrowed, looking at Inspector Cross in a different light.

"So how did he shoot himself? With what?" she said.

"Who said he shot himself? I didn't."

"So, what made that bloodstained hole in his chest? The one I shot from every conceivable angle. I know little about guns, but it looked to be the size of a shotgun barrel to me, and if it looks like a duck, swims like a duck, and quacks like a duck, well—"

"Then it's probably a duck, or in this case a shotgun, is what Jaz's trying to say," Dan butted in.

Inspector Cross didn't hide his derision. "Ah, the philosophical duck test. I've heard that trotted out once or twice down the years, usually from people who think they know more than the police. Do you know what I say?"

"Go on," said Dan.

"I say, John and David are walking along a foggy street when they spot a man coming towards them. John says, 'Looks like our friend Nobby.' David says, 'He certainly walks like Nobby.' When the man reaches them and says, 'Hello,' John and David see it isn't Nobby, but his twin brother, Ned."

Looking at Jaz, Inspector Cross affected his most patronising tone, difficult to do in his sing-song accent, but he tried hard, eventually succeeding. "What I'm trying to say is, it's never wise to rush to judgement solely on evidence of looks or sounds."

Jaz's eyes glinted fire. "Or on the evidence of a suicide note?"

Turning away from Jaz, Cross addressed Dan. "It's true we haven't discovered the weapon used, but we're currently searching the river in the area surrounding Mr Mansell's boat. Due to recent weather, the water's murky, but our divers are experienced in such conditions and we expect to discover the weapon sooner rather than later. I think that concludes our meeting. Thank you for your cooperation."

Inspector Cross rose from his seat and gestured towards Jaz and Pete. "We'll need you both to come down to the station to give witness statements, and we'd like to study the pictures taken of the scene and the body. We have our own, of course, but in the interests of completeness, yours could prove useful as you were first on the scene. Is that okay?"

Dan stood up and shook hands with the inspector. "No problem. I'll ask Pete to collate and send them to you electronically if that suits."

"Yes." Cross shuffled out of the office, his assistant trailing a couple of paces behind.

Jaz half-expected them to stop at the door, Cross to scratch his head and mutter, 'Just one more thing,' but he didn't. She watched for a few seconds as he ambled through the air-conditioned newsroom—a slight limp from a troublesome hip impeding his progress—to the stairs leading onto Lexford High Street and another day of simmering heat.

When he'd gone, Jaz turned to Dan. "What a condescending so-and-so. Made me feel like I was something nasty on the bottom of his sole."

"I'm pretty sure he has no soul."

"Exactly what I was thinking. He's an annoying little man. Fancy calling your son George when Cross is your surname. I mean, you wouldn't. Would you?"

Jaz smiled. "Bet he has a sister called Victoria."

"And a brother called Chris. But it doesn't make him wrong."

"No, but something smells fishy about this. Can Trish and I have a snoop around for a couple of days? Oh, go on, Dan. Say yes. Please say yes. Only a few days. I'm sure there's more to this than meets the eye. At least the eyes of Inspector Cross."

Dan looked down at Jaz with a resigned expression. If he said yes, it would likely be an expense the paper could ill afford on its current tight budget, as well as sour further the delicate relationship with Inspector Cross and his not-so-merry band of plods at Lexford police station. If he said no, the paper may miss a story that demanded telling, and he'd disappoint the woman who had, for the first time since the death of his beloved wife Annie, brought joy and love back into his life. There was no contest.

"Oh, all right, but just a couple of days."

"Love you." Jaz hugged him, then kissed him on the cheek, adding with a chuckle, "And who the hell in the twenty-first century calls anyone Ned and Nobby?"

3

Trish Parker wasn't a gardener. Rolling cigarettes as a teenager was as close as she got to horticulture, although, to be fair, she knew a bit about grass and weed back then. Nowadays, she didn't know which end to hold a spade, but here she was in her small front garden, busy fingers pruning a bunch of geraniums. She wasn't dressed for gardening. Crisp white blouse. Tight blue jeans. Yellow rubber gloves. White patent high-heel shoes and designer shades balanced on her head like a bee's eyes.

Jaz smiled and clambered from her car. *That's our Trish. Whatever she's doing, always looks ready for a stroll down the front at Cannes.*

On hearing a car door slam, Trish glanced up, deadheaded a flower with sharp secateurs, then waved a marigold hand. "Hiya, Jaz. Glad you rang. Haven't seen you for weeks."

Jaz opened the small iron gate and skipped up the path. The pair hugged, rocking back and forth, as students do after receiving unexpected, good exam results.

"What's with the gloves, Trish? Hardly suitable for gardening," Jaz chuckled.

"Maybe, but they aren't to stop thorns. I hate the smell of geraniums. You think they'll be so sweet, but the leaves are too earthy. Make your fingers smell like death. I hate that."

"Why have you planted so many, then?"

"Because I love them."

"You just said you hated them."

"No. I hate the leaves but adore the flowers. What I love even more is, throughout summer, they keep coming back week after week, month after month. Geraniums love giving joy, as if they've all been to enlightenment classes and learned that saying."

"What saying?"

"Oh, I don't know. Happiness is now. It isn't yesterday, it isn't tomorrow. Only today's flower can be enjoyed today. I can't remember it all, but it boils down to being happy now and you'll learn how to be happy always."

Jaz wrinkled her nose, a tad concerned. "Trish, you haven't been smoking something you shouldn't, have you?"

For a moment, Trish's eyes focused far away, head slowly rocking back and forth. Snapping out of her trance, she stripped off the yellow gloves with a flourish and let rip a deafening cackle with chuckles and wheezes that were heard down the street.

"Had you going for a while there, didn't I? Did you think I'd joined the Moonies or something? Come on, let's go inside and have a nice cup of tea."

If Jaz and Trish had been peas, they wouldn't have sat in the same pod. Not even the same field. Jaz was naturally shy, but possessed a sharp mind, intellectual rigour and a passion for academic learning. She answered questions on all the highbrow TV quizzes and bagged a first class degree in English and History reading the complete works of William Shakespeare plus an assortment of English classics. Jane Austen was her author of choice.

Trish's literature of choice was reading red-top tabloids, gossip columns, and celebrity snippets. She was ditzy. If you asked her the capital of Spain, she'd probably say '*S.*' It didn't matter. She was naturally streetwise, and the differences between her and Jaz these past two years only drew them closer.

Arm in arm, they wandered through Trish's hallway into a tasteful lounge decorated in pastel shades, a deep pile, cream rug languishing on a lacquered oak floor.

"Oh, you've hung the photo up at last. I love it," Jaz said.

In silence, they peered at the image, memories it evoked bringing a tingle to Jaz's forehead. Hairs rose on the nape. She remembered the day a year ago, when she and Dan accompanied Trish on her bucket list wish to climb Mount Snowdon in Wales. With a timer, Dan had taken the picture at the summit, where they'd met Bob Murphy and Bill Murdoch, two older fellow cancer sufferers. Murph and Bill couldn't climb, but had kept their promise and made the ascent via the rack and pinion railway.

Trish cherished that meeting, which is why she'd forked out to enlarge the image to poster size. The panoramic backdrop of hills and lakes all the way to the Welsh coast was a spectacular sight.

With her finger on the protective glass frame, Jaz traced the outline of each figure. "Have you heard from Murph?"

"No, nothing."

Jaz pointed to herself in the middle of the group, an arm around Trish. "Look at me with short hair. It was still growing back then, just like yours."

Jaz's careful grooming had restored her honey blonde hair to shoulder length, while Trish kept her dark hair, now flecked with striking silver, short. A stint of chemotherapy had temporarily robbed both women of their locks.

Jaz pointed to the wiry frame of Bill Murdoch, whose ambition to work as a professional comedian went unfulfilled. He'd kept them laughing on the car journeys during a month-long course of radiotherapy at the Barrett Bailey hospital. "Poor Bill. So sad when we heard the news his wife had slipped away. I cried. Wasn't Jean's funeral fantastic?"

Trish smiled, recalling the unconventional service six months ago when she, Dan, and Jaz made the trek to Bill's hometown. As a tribute to Jean's favourite comedians, Bill arranged for the congregation to sing Morecambe and Wise's version of *Bring Me Sunshine*. Some of Bill's mates even skipped out of church, imitating the funny dance that always ended Eric and Ernie's TV show.

Jaz and Trish couldn't help singing the first two lines of the theme tune, laughing and hugging as memories of their cancer battle—not as raw but still emotional—jostled to the surface. Trish broke the mood of introspection.

"We must pop in on Bill. Haven't seen him since his fall. Right, how about that cuppa?" Trish brewed two steaming mugs and joined Jaz at the kitchen table.

"How do you fancy a job for a couple of days?"

Trish sat up straight. "What type of job?"

"A bit of snooping around. Checking a few things out. Could be something or nothing, but you never know." Jaz explained the body in the river story.

"I read the reports in the *Journal*."

"What you won't have heard is the dead man had a gunshot wound in his chest. I know because I took the pictures. Pretty grim it was, too. The cops think it's suicide and it may well be, but Dan has agreed we can follow up the story for a few days. Even if there's nothing more to it, at least we should get a colour piece for next week's print edition."

Neither Jaz nor Trish were qualified journalists. Jaz had started as a secretary for the *Lexford Journal* a year earlier when Dan became editor-in-chief. A natural curiosity made her perfectly suited to identifying story opportunities. A grounding in grammar and literature allowed clarity and verve in her writing. It would have been stupid to ignore such talent. Dan didn't. He encouraged her and though Jaz's main duties involved sub-editing, checking stories for grammar and punctuation, and rewriting when required, she also showed an aptitude for composing features. Exploring the story behind the story. She'd become an asset on the news desk, even considered studying for her national certificate as a fully paid-up member of the journalist profession.

"Ooh! Sounds exciting. I'm a sucker for mysterious deaths and chalk outlines."

"They found the body in the river, Trish."

"Whatever. Dead landlord. Gunshot wound. Count me in. Better than watching sheep all night in a dark, wet field in the middle of nowhere."

Jaz raised her eyebrows at the reference to the last story they'd investigated together. A stake-out to catch sheep rustlers, which went awry when they found themselves 70 acres away from the crime.

"Timing is everything." Jaz remembered the not-so-near miss.

"The right place is everything."

"I'm not arguing."

"In fact, there's a time and place for everything." As always, Trish had to have the last word.

A burst of *Dancing Queen* on Jaz's mobile phone rang out. Dan.

"Hi. You were right. In the last few minutes, the police released a press statement. They've formally identified the dead body as Roger Mansell from The Anchor. It's online now."

Jaz switched to speaker so Trish could listen in. "Any news on the gun?"

"Not yet, but I asked Pete to go down to the river. There's a police dinghy and divers patrolling the water. Looks like they're still searching."

"Okay, see you later."

"Bye, Dan," said Trish, but Jaz clicked the red button before he could reply.

Jaz slurped a mouthful of tea and slung her bag over her shoulder. "Come on. No time to waste."

Trish insisted on freshening up, following her exertions in the garden, swapping jeans for a cool cotton skirt and sky-high heels for a more functional pair. She'd knocked off a couple of inches.

"Onwards to The Anchor, Trish. A good place to start."

4

For a pub whose landlord had recently surfaced from the murky depths of the River Lex, trade appeared brisk when Jaz turned into The Anchor, a charming coaching inn, with black and white Tudor façade, nestled on the banks of the river. To the east, a picture postcard bend in the river framed by weeping willow trees, lazy, drooping branches caressing the water, waiting to scoop a basking trout. To the west, a pedestrian butterfly bridge linking the inn and open fields around it, with one approach to Lexford Park.

Jaz squeezed into the only parking spot overlooking the river. From the vantage point, she spied half a dozen narrowboats moored to metal cleats on the towpath. People sitting at picnic tables took comfort under the welcome shade of huge black and white parasols or on the grass in full glare of the sun. Some enjoyed a cooling pint, watching children run up the grass bank, then rolling down amid joyous squeals.

"Such a perfect day. Why would anyone living here want to commit suicide?" said Jaz.

"Beats me," said Trish.

A news report came through on the local radio. Jaz turned up the volume. The first item confirmed Dan's news. Police had identified the body in the river as Roger Mansell, the well-known landlord of The Anchor pub. No further details other than police inquiries were continuing.

Jaz and Trish exchanged a knowing look and stepped from the car, into the sunshine and down stone steps onto a gravel path leading to the pub's front entrance. An enticing aroma of hamburgers and frying onions filled the air. Trish slipped off her sunglasses. Jaz's eyes took seconds to adjust to the comparative gloom of the interior. Dark wooden beams gave a rustic appearance and an artistic someone had splashed walls in cool pastel shades and hung prints of horses and pictures of riverboats. Save for a couple chatting in an alcove, and a fluffy black cat sprawled on the floor disguised as a mop, the main lounge was quiet.

The pair strolled over to the bar, Trish's heels clip-clopping on wooden floorboards.

"What can I do for you, ladies?" the barman said.

Priding herself on first impressions, Jaz thought the man had an honest face, his smile exuding warmth and kindness. Deep blue eyes twinkled, blond hair thick, lustrous and long, neatly cut. Early to mid-thirties, she thought. "Two orange juices, please."

The barman ducked under the bar to grab two bottles and glasses. "You'll be wanting ice, I'm sure." He spoke in a soft London accent.

"Yes," said Jaz.

Trish decided pleasantries had extended long enough. "I'm surprised you're open after the news about Mr Mansell."

The barman shrugged. Pragmatic, matter-of-fact, his only sign of emotion, a slight tilt of the head and raise of the eyebrows. As if death was little more than a side dish on the lunchtime menu down with soggy fries and greasy mushrooms. "Tragic, but life goes on. I've been in touch with the brewery, who said it was best to go ahead as normal. We had a big boat party booked for today. The brewery bosses didn't want to let anyone down."

"When did you last see Roger?" said Trish.

"Excuse me. Who are you exactly, and why do you want to know?" A wide smile still formed a pleasing shape on the barman's face, blue eyes dancing from Jaz to Trish, but his tone held a modicum of suspicion.

Jaz answered. "We're from the Lexford Journal. I helped to find the body. Poor Roger. He must have been in a terrible state to take his own life."

"That's what the police said. I'm Logan, by the way. Logan Sharp. Several officers came down yesterday evening asking questions. Spoke to some regulars. I'm not sure I should be talking to you."

"I still think it's surprising they allowed you to open up with this being Roger's home. When did you last see him?" Trish said.

"Oh, no. Roger didn't live here. He hadn't lived here for a couple of years. Not since he and his wife split. He lived on his boat."

"His boat? One of those outside?"

"No. The Artful Roger. A narrowboat moored on the river about half a mile away. All mod cons. He didn't want to live on the job anymore. Did enough hours as a landlord, or so he said."

"How long have you worked here, Logan?" Trish pressed.

"You're sounding like the cops again."

"Sorry, we're trying to piece together the full story."

"Okay, no problem. I've been here about eighteen months. I run the bar. We employ a couple of barmaids who do shifts when it's busy, and Brian, the chef. Makes a mean hamburger. Roger used to take care of all the stuff with the brewery, organising special offers, funeral receptions, quiz nights—that type of thing. Sometimes I helped with ordering, but really, I just pull pints."

"And look pretty," said Trish.

Logan's smile widened. "If you say so."

"You didn't say when you last saw Roger."

Logan grabbed a towel and wiped down a beer tap. "The police asked me that, too. I'm pretty sure it was last Sunday. I remember, because the day before, he'd told me he was going away for a few days and asked if I could hold the fort by myself. Sunday's our busiest day with lunchtime roasts, so he said he'd go away that evening after the rush was done."

Jaz looked puzzled. "In his boat?"

"Don't know. Didn't say. I presumed so. He never got over his marriage break-up. Seemed sad and preoccupied."

Logan nodded at a bunch of noisy boating folk approaching the bar, discussing the efficacy of the lock they'd navigated by a weir half a mile downstream. He gave one of the dazzling smiles Jaz realised he doled out freely to all comers. "Sorry, ladies. Duty calls."

Jaz and Trish found a table opposite the bar. Jaz had visited the pub twice before. Once for drinks with Dan at the start of their relationship and again to look for her dad, who'd suffered from dementia and had wandered out of the house. That was two years ago, when she and Trish had forged their friendship while undergoing daily treatment at the Barrett Bailey. Jaz gestured to the far side of the lounge, to a snug bar with a swing-through door and panelled wood partition topped with frosted glass.

"Do you remember me telling you about Dad going missing one day and finding him in a pub? He'd got into an argument with two big guys and would've taken a beating if a bunch of bikers hadn't stepped in to save him."

"Yeah. Didn't Dan trip over, send tables and glasses flying, and didn't you all get barred?"

Jaz chuckled, putting a forefinger to her lips. "Shush, you'll get *us* thrown out. It happened over there in that little room."

Trish peered across at the snug, hearing the rise and fall of animated, deep-pitched conversation. "Sounds like a few guys arguing the toss right now. Come on, let's see what's going on." She stood up, motioning to Jaz with an eye roll.

They cradled their glasses and clip-clopped over. Trish pushed open the swing door and held it for Jaz. The hum of conversation ceased. A sad-looking man with a lumpy face, pasty but full of raised veins reddened by a lifetime of lunchtimes in places such as The Anchor, sat on a wooden bench under a redundant dart board. Beer glass half full, watery eyes suggesting the drink was neither his first, nor last. Death warmed up, crossed Trish's mind.

Three men sat at a table in the middle of the room, pints poised. They turned to check out Jaz and Trish, puzzled expressions suggesting women didn't regularly frequent the snug.

Jaz's voice was light and jolly. "Mind if we join you? It's cooler over this side by the window with the breeze from the river."

"Not at all. Sit yourselves down," said one man, pulling up a chair at the only other table in the snug.

Jaz thought two of them resembled farmers. Wide, powerful shoulders. Meaty forearms, doubtless developed by tossing hay bales and shearing sheep. On further inspection, that wasn't their only common feature. Both looked around 40. Both had thick, curly brown hair, distinctive hooked noses, and shifty, smouldering eyes, drooping eyelids, making them too narrow, as if afflicted by a permanent squint.

Trish was thinking shifty, too, but was more struck by their similarity. "My God. You two are identical. Must be brothers. Am I right?"

"Twins, actually," said one man in a slow country burr. "I'm Joe and this is Victor."

"Hi. I'm Trish and this is Jaz."

"Sisters?" said Joe.

Jaz deemed the twinkle in Joe's eyes both mischievous and disconcerting.

Trish laughed, pointing at her dark hair and touching her little beaked nose. "Seriously? Do we look like sisters?"

Joe shrugged, and Trish glanced at the third man, expecting him to introduce himself. Affording her the merest nod, he raised his pint to his lips and took a long slurp of beer. Sporting a ginger goatee, spiky hair, and tombstone teeth that wouldn't look out of place galloping around Aintree, the man looked younger than the twins, his expression sullen, disinterested. He put his glass on the table, biceps rippling under his short-sleeved shirt, revealing a striking tattoo of a swan rising out of the water, wings spread, neck straining. The hem of the man's sleeve partly obscured the top of the tattoo, but, for a moment, the detailed drawing transfixed Jaz as she recalled similar artistry adorning her late father's back. The memory brought a warm glow.

Joe gave a throaty chuckle. "Oh, don't mind him. That's just Crime. He doesn't say much. He's shy. Can't talk to the ladies. Never could."

"Crime?" said Jaz.

"Yeah, that's his nickname. He's always been called that, hasn't he, Victor?"

Victor stammered. "Yeah, we all used to play in the same village cricket team. Crime was a cracking fielder and a handy batsman back in the day. Joe was the opening bowler and Roger the wicketkeeper."

Jaz's heart raced a little faster. "Roger Mansell?"

Joe nodded. "Yeah, tragic business. You must have heard, he's the landlord here found dead in the river. Logan told us about it. We're all in shock. Looks like he topped himself with a shotgun and fell in the river."

"Really?" Joe surprised Jaz. She knew the police had spoken to Logan but thought it unlikely they'd have given details at this early stage before searchers had found the weapon. Seemed she and Trish had stumbled on not only regulars but a group of the landlord's friends. Jaz sensed a follow-up story and divulged their identities. "Actually, we work for the Lexford Journal. We received the call at our office from the young lads who found Roger's body and want to make sure the story's as accurate as possible by talking to his friends and family if we can."

Jaz had gambled. The revelation could have prompted the men to clam up or perhaps seen Jaz and Trish turfed out of the pub. Fake news, phone hacking. In recent years, neither had enhanced the reputation of journalists, whether in the White House in Washington or The Anchor in Lexford.

Joe and Victor didn't hold that view. They were enlightened. Saw the bigger picture. "That must be worth a round of drinks, at least," said Joe.

Trish rose to her feet, looked at Jaz, and both nodded. Minutes later, Trish returned from the bar with three foaming pints. She threw in three packets of cheese and onion crisps. *After all, the Journal's a classy publication.*

5

The twins raised their glasses. Crime grunted, which Trish took as a sign of approval. Victor swigged beer, licked his lips, then wiped away leftover froth with the back of his hand.

If Roger Mansell's cricketing comrades were in shock, as they claimed, there were few signs. No crying in their beer. No mawkish mourning. Quite the opposite. Victor and Joe seemed energised, light-hearted even, though Crime remained sullen and distant, making a meal of opening his crisps.

Something didn't feel right, Jaz decided. Of course, it could be the alcohol masking reality, taking the edge off grief. Allowing the men to booze on regardless, despite their friend and former teammate lying in a mortuary, having apparently blown a hole in his chest.

All three hurled another measure of ale down their throats, mesmerising Trish. "Do you always drink so fast?"

"Everything in moderation, including moderation," said Joe, sitting back sporting a satisfied grin, allowing Trish to absorb the breadth of his wit.

Jaz punctured the moment. "I think you'll find someone famous came up with that line."

Joe fixed her with a steady gaze. "Fame's overrated, don't you think? Money trumps fame in my book. All any man needs is a good woman, loyal mates, a friendly boozer, and a good few quid in his pocket."

Jaz sensed the drink had loosened tongues. She seized the opportunity to probe further. "Was Roger a loyal mate? Were you all close to him? By all accounts, he was a popular guy."

As she spoke, Jaz studied Crime, and could have sworn his lip curled and his eyebrows raised a fraction, but Victor dived in, garrulous despite his stammer.

"Well, I don't mind telling you for the record. Roger was a good guy. Great cricketer. Generous. Heart of gold. Always sponsored the Lexford marathon each year. Until recently, he used to organise two quizzes a week, all proceeds going to charity. I think he got nominated for landlord of the year a few years back. He didn't win, but probably should have done. If it hadn't been for his shoulder problem—"

"What caused that?" said Jaz.

"Started years back when he had that bad injury, didn't it, Joe? Dived full length to make a catch. Held on to it too. Against Kimbolton, think it was. Hard pitch. That summer, when there was a hosepipe ban like now. Don't you remember?"

"Mm, yeah," muttered Joe.

The three men raised their glasses and glugged once more in perfect harmony. The action fascinated Jaz. *How do they do that? Synchronised drinking. Must take lots of practice.*

Victor went on. "He busted his shoulder and needed an operation. Had problems for years. Used to say global warming was melting the polar ice pack, so how come his shoulder was frozen solid? We saw him popping pills behind the bar, washing them down with whisky chasers just to get rid of the pain. Last twelve months it got so bad he could hardly move his arm. He certainly couldn't haul crates around. That's why he got Logan in, wasn't it?"

Joe shrugged.

"But what really knocked him most was when his wife left him. Don't think he got over that. It was the kids, you see. He missed them. Got down about it all."

Jaz scribbled in a notebook, intrigued by Victor's stutter triggered by the K sound, but not on every occasion. A selective stammer. She made a mental note to research speech impediments on the internet.

Trish also hung on every word. "Why did she leave?"

A pause. Joe looked at Victor. Trish sensed a connection between them. A twin thing. A burst of telepathic electricity that had the effect of altering the flow of conversation. From open to shut. Like turning off a tap.

Victor's tone was quiet, more serious. "Don't know about that. What goes on between a married couple is private and Roger kept it that way. That's how it should be. It's a mystery to us why he'd want to top himself and we want to know why, but there are two sides to every story. All I know is, you'd go a long way to find a more decent, upstanding bloke than Roger Mansell."

"Too true." Joe nodded in agreement.

Crime choked into his beer glass, uttering something indistinct through gritted teeth and a venomous hiss. One word. Jaz couldn't be sure what he'd said, but *was* sure it wasn't complimentary. Sounded like shithouse.

"Ignore him," said Joe. He lifted his glass to drain his pint. "Same again?"

Victor and Crime nodded. Joe made to go to the bar. "Would you ladies care for a refill?"

Trish was ready to accept when she caught Jaz's eyes motioning to the door. "No. Apparently we're leaving."

Joe held the door open to the main lounge. Jaz and Trish ducked under his arm. Something bothered Trish. She had to know and turned to face Joe before he could traipse to the bar. "Tell me, Joe, why do you call him Crime?"

Joe chuckled. "Because he doesn't like putting his hand in his pocket. Never gets a round of drinks in."

"But why Crime?"

"Because everyone knows crime doesn't pay."

Trish stifled one of her trademark cackles and she and Jaz wandered outside. The scorching heat had dissipated, but the temperature still hovered around 28 Celsius. Blouse-clinging clammy. They walked to the car, Jaz fanning herself with a notebook, musing over what she'd learned about Roger Mansell and his regulars. She pressed the key fob, heard the expected clunk, then a sound she didn't expect.

"I don't believe it. I don't fucking believe it."

Jaw jutting, Trish spat out the words, craning her neck to peer around the low-lying branches of a tree. She gaped across the car park, smouldering eyes fixed on a couple striding arm-in-arm into the pub. Curly black hair flecked with grey, distinctive round shoulders, the man looked in his early forties. Perhaps half his age, maybe younger, the petite woman skipped to keep up with him.

"What is it, Trish? What's the matter?"

Trish pointed at the couple, her tone bitter. "That bastard's back, that's what's the matter."

"Who's back?"

"Terry, my ex-partner. The one who ran off with my daughter the same week as my cancer diagnosis. I told you, remember?"

"I don't like to ask this, but—"

"Yes. That's my daughter's arms around him."

6

Bill Murdoch was a limping, wheezing, wisecracking health warning.

"Hips knackered, knees knackered, lungs knackered, and if the prostate cancer doesn't finish me off, the dodgy ticker will."

"Don't beat about the bush," Jaz smiled. She and Trish sat opposite Bill in the lounge of his Lexford home.

After leaving The Anchor to help Trish cool down, they agreed to check on Bill. He'd broken an arm after falling the previous week, and Dan, who'd looked out for Bill since his cancer treatment days, had taken him to Lexford Infirmary. Bill had insisted on being discharged even though he walked with the aid of a walker.

"Are you sure you should be home, Bill?" Trish asked, concerned.

Bill stretched his arm to show off his plaster cast, which already showed half a dozen signatures. "I knew it was bad. Soon as I got to casualty, I told the doc I broke my arm in two places."

"What did he say?" said Trish.

"Stop going to those places."

Jaz sniggered. Trish cackled. Typical Bill. Few aspects of life were immune from his quick-fire humour. Jaz and Trish missed him. He was trundling towards his eighties and getting frailer by the month, but he didn't seem old.

His conversation was fresh, vigorous. Mind interested and interesting.

"So, what have you two been up to?"

Jaz explained Roger Mansell's story and the bare essentials of their enquiries at The Anchor.

"Isn't that where you found your dad when he wandered off?"

"That's right, Bill, well remembered."

"These twins, Joe and Victor, they sound dodgy."

"Why do you say that?"

"I was reading an article in a magazine at the hospital called The Perfect Alibi. About identical twins who'd got away with murder."

"Really." Jaz looked intrigued.

"Yep. The cops were certain one of them had done it. There was even DNA evidence, but identical twins have the same DNA. There were no fingerprints and the police couldn't be sure which twin was the murderer, so both walked. Apparently, it's not a one-off. Happens all the time."

Trish threw Jaz a curious look. Victor and Joe had seemed normal. Hard-working, even harder-drinking farmers, but they had an intimidating physical presence. Add proximity and opportunity, throw in a history with Roger Mansell and the thrust of Bill's magazine article, and who knows what strange things may have happened.

Jaz knew what Trish was thinking and her guarded look spoke volumes. Where was the motive? Not to mention the will to shoot a man in cold blood. The twins spoke fondly of Roger. They sounded genuine. It was Crime who seemed less than friendly.

"I'm pretty sure these twins aren't partners in crime," said Jaz. "The police are convinced the landlord committed suicide. It's just me who thinks there's more to it."

"And me," piped up Trish.

"Thanks, Trish, but you don't have to say that."

Jaz went off to the kitchen to make tea while Trish caught up with Bill. During their cancer treatment, they'd been good pals, soulmates at times. More than once they'd spilled innermost thoughts and an unlikely bond had formed. It helped that Trish always cackled at Bill's brimming font of jokes.

Under Trish's interrogation, Bill revealed that since his broken arm reduced him to one fully functioning limb, he had carers three times a day. One to get up, another to serve lunch and prepare an evening meal, and one more to help him to bed. Sometimes the same carer performed two of those roles, sometimes three different carers turned up.

"They're a godsend at the moment. Can't even make myself a cup of tea. June gets me up most of the time and Karen makes sure I don't go hungry. And Pat from next door pops in too. She's wonderful. She was a good friend of Jean's, came to the funeral. I'm well looked after, but one carer is strange."

"In what way?"

"Couldn't help noticing she was staring at me the first time she came. I didn't want to be rude, so I let it go. The next day she was making lunch but, out of the corner of my eye, I kept seeing her stealing glances in my direction. Almost flirtatious."

"Did you say anything?"

"I didn't like to. But the next day it happened again, and I challenged her."

"What did you say?" Enthralled, Trish's mouth was agape.

"I told her I'd noticed all the looks and could she please stop. I found it disconcerting."

"Go on."

"I felt terrible. She told me she was sorry, but it struck her how much I looked like her third husband."

"How many husbands had she had?"

"I asked her that. She said two."

Trish's cackle brought Jaz running from the kitchen. They all drank tea and when the girls were ready to leave, Jaz insisted Bill must ring if he needed anything.

"You could get me a couple of crossword books if you don't mind. Something to keep the old grey matter churning. No rush. Any time you're passing. There's a tenner under the vase on the sideboard."

Jaz lifted the vase. Nothing. "Are you sure, Bill?"

"Sure, I'm sure. That's where I left it."

"There's nothing here."

"That's funny. I could have sworn. Never mind. Look in the drawer."

"No cash here either."

He rooted in his pocket for his wallet, took out a tenner and handed it to Jaz. "Maybe I'm losing it."

"I don't think so, Bill. But we all have our senior moments."

Jaz and Trish said goodbye, once outside agreeing how uplifting it was to see Bill again.

"He lights up a room," said Trish.

"Interesting what he said about the twins and DNA."

"You don't think they could have killed Roger, do you?"

"Don't know. Too early to rule anybody in, or out."

7

Dan wasn't a numbers sort of guy. He'd failed maths at school. Hated X and Y equations, with unfathomable conundrums. If you had three oranges and five apples in one hand and four apples and six oranges in another blah-blah. He'd cut to the chase and give his favourite answer. Very big hands.

In Dan's world, words trumped numbers. He'd always written about people's hopes and ambitions. Tapped into fears and emotions. For 20 years as a war correspondent with the *Daily News*, he'd travelled the globe. Meeting deadlines, living on sharp wits and generous expenses, he'd witnessed the courage and fragility of the human condition. He felt privileged to have done so, but had had his shot of fame and been shot at more times than he cared to recall.

The *Lexford Journal*, the hometown newspaper that taught Dan the profession's basics more than a quarter of a century earlier when it sold 35,000 copies a week, was supposed to be his idea of quitting the relentless competition inherent in the national agenda. Yet, here he sat on a stuffy Saturday morning, staring at columns of flickering numbers on a computer screen, all adding up to a circulation dip of 20 per cent on last year. The paper now sold less than 10,000 copies each week and, although the online edition raked in views, it didn't make money.

Not yet. No subscription service meant no regular income, with advertising rates online bordering on insignificant.

Dan knew the reasons well enough and sifted them in his mind while waiting for Thomas Henry, the proprietor. Readership slowly dying. Literally. Stand outside a newsagent and observe the few trudging out with a copy of the *Journal*, which is exactly what Dan had done before accepting his job. Most nursed dodgy knees, worn-out hips, or worse, as they shuffled and hobbled down the street. Many had silver-grey hair or none at all. Young people didn't buy local papers, full stop. Or anything with full stops if truth be told. Texting and social media had much to answer for.

To make things worse, it was a lazy, slow summer. Most of the *Journal's* regular readers had gone to resorts in Wales and Scotland or flown to banal Spanish timeshares once deemed a bargain, but now holiday millstones they couldn't give away. Long days. People out and about. Too many frothy, blank-page fillers. Not enough authentic news. The trade had a name for it. The silly season. But this was beyond silly. This was silly to the power of 10.

Dan ran his fingers through dark hair. Thick, glossy, impressive for a 50-year-old, even if flecked with strands of silver. Draining the gritty dregs of vending machine coffee from his plastic cup, he peered through the glass partition in his office, overlooking the editorial floor. He spied Jack Ashton, the paper's latest recruit, head bobbing behind a computer screen at the far end of the room. Dan had interviewed Jack nine months ago, the lad's passion coupled with wide-eyed enthusiasm making an instant impression, as did his command of grammar and knowledge of local politics. Sure, Jack's 19-year-old naivety surfaced when it came to writing intros and headlines, but Dan knew that would improve with experience. He could be knocked into shape.

Jack manned the busy online edition. Sub-editing, uploading changes, adding the occasional fresh story. A skeleton staff manned the paper's offices at weekends, usually one reporter, often the youngest. The graveyard shift. Today, as the office clock ticked towards 10 o'clock, Jack had company.

Not only was Dan in the office, but Jaz had driven in with him to write her follow-up to the body in the river revelation. As Dan absorbed the circulation figures, he also pondered on a headline for Jaz's background story on Roger Mansell, scribbling on the pad in front of him.

Heart of gold

Then a strapline with more details.

Tributes pour in for charity champion found dead in river

Dan bit the top of his pen in thought, toying for a moment before scribbling again.

River mystery deepens

The explanatory line this time zeroed in on a question many readers may be pondering.

Shocked regulars ask: Why would popular landlord kill himself?

Dan was debating the merits of both sets of headlines when Thomas Henry rapped on the glass partition and strode in. Dan rose and shook hands.

Thomas was beanpole tall, his military bearing ensuring every inch counted. A public school pupil, he'd attended Sandhurst College, passing out as captain and amassing six years' service in the Royal Engineers Parachute Division before making his fortune in the City of London. A punishing daily fitness regime had chiselled his face and body, not in the healthy way he desired, but saddling him with unnatural gauntness. He looked anorexic, yet everything about him exuded precision. Crystal vowels, gleaming shoes, sharp pin-striped suit, short back and sides, a smidgeon of gel perfectly plastering his black locks in place. Dan thought Thomas was the sort of 45-year-old who probably ironed his underpants. And socks. And sheets. Yet Dan liked him. Thomas had proved ramrod straight when he offered Dan the job.

"You won't get rich working for me, Dan, but *I will* give you my full backing on all editorial matters and *you will* make a difference."

For the past year that's exactly what happened. Thomas supported Dan at every turn, even when the new editor-in-chief confronted the advertising manager, whose story preference involved diary items, garden fetes, and pictures packing in as many children as pixels. The ad boss argued that at least the kids' relatives would buy the paper.

Dan's counter was blunt. "The *Journal's* a *news*paper. The clue's in the first four letters."

To Thomas's credit, he hadn't flinched when Dan demanded an increased expenses budget. Dan believed worthwhile stories emanated from knowing the right people, forging connections between reader and newspaper. Promoting trust. If trust arrived at the cost of the odd drink or occasional free meal, then so be it.

Dan sat, gesturing for Thomas to do the same. He remained standing, resting his hands on the desk. A giraffe drinking at a watering hole entered Dan's thoughts.

Thomas's demeanour was serious, his tone earnest. "Dan, I won't mess with you. We're in the shit. Deep shit. You've seen the latest circulation figures. Twenty per cent down on the year. That's unsustainable. I know it's been a strange time and we're still trying to establish an online presence that brings in significant revenue, but something has to change."

Dan's mind gyrated, a flush of anger surfacing even though Thomas had been careful not to imply criticism. Yet Dan knew Thomas spoke sense. No news outlet could survive such devastating circulation losses for long, but he also believed in his strategy. "What do you suggest?"

"For one, we need more stories like this body in the river, especially when he's a well-known landlord. I fully expect circulation to be up this week."

Dan's top lip curled, and he experienced another shot of heat. "Well, that's settled then. Every week, I'll arrange to find a dead landlord in the river with a bullet hole in his chest. How about the chap from the Three Tuns? No, forget that. Let's go for a number seventy-three bus mowing down Lexford United's top striker on the High Street. Better still, what about Lexford's mayor found hanging by his ceremonial chains with the ornamental mace stuck where the sun don't shine? Everyone likes a ceremony. That should sell a few papers."

"Don't be ridiculous, Dan."

"Right back at you, Thomas. Big news stories like dead landlords in the river take care of themselves. Building contacts takes time. We're getting there. When I took this job a year ago, the *Journal* wore flared trousers, kipper ties, and tapped its glittery platforms to T Rex. It was stuck in the seventies. Hadn't changed for half a century. These days, newspapers that don't change die. We have changed. We're turning it around. Uncovering more hard news while the postbags and forums have never been livelier. We need to hold our nerve. You need to hold your nerve. Things will get better."

Thomas stood up and two thoughts struck Dan. The first was random. He wondered if Thomas painted his ceiling at home and whether he could do so without a stepladder. The second thought was bang on the money, which was why it bolted from Dan's lips before he could rein it in. "Do you know the difference between a good news story and your backside, because it doesn't sound like it?"

"Be careful, Dan. Don't take that tone. I've given you all my support so far, but the board demand to see a plan of action. We need to cut costs. We want to see the *Journal* streamlined."

Dan knew exactly what that meant, but he asked anyway. "What are you saying?"

"Cuts, Dan. Significant cuts."

"How much?"

"Minimum seventy-five thousand off the editorial budget."

"Seventy-five grand? You can't be serious. The expenses bill for the entire department isn't five thousand a year. We're cut to the bone already and seventy-five grand amounts to a couple of senior salaries, at least."

Thomas's size 12s shifted uncomfortably, but his tone remained steely. "I'm talking three jobs, minimum."

Dan stood up. He consciously raised his shoulders, straightening his back to reduce the intimidating effect of Thomas's superior height. Dan stretched to 6ft, but Thomas still towered above him.

"I didn't come to the *Journal* to sack people. I've seen enough suffering in my time, and won't put people out of work."

Thomas fixed Dan with his iciest glare before turning to leave. He reached the glass partition, paused, and looked around. Dan detected a sad, almost desperate tone in his voice. "Dan, if we don't do something drastic fast, everyone will be out of work."

Sinking into his swivel chair, Dan watched Thomas walk past Jack and Jaz. They exchanged pleasantries for a moment before Thomas strode from the office.

Heart of Gold

Dan picked up his pen and struck a line through the words. "What this paper needs is hard news and tough questions. Headlines readers cannot ignore."

8

On Saturday afternoons, Jaz loved rummaging in the charming, cobbled arcades of Lexford. Off the High Street, hidden away in the tiny bookshop, she'd search for a paperback. Flicking through pages—not too thin, not too weighty—historical romance, her preference, but not a necessity. A book in which she could bathe her mind for a week or so.

She picked up *The Bridges of Madison County* and remembered watching the film version of the bittersweet tale of profound love. She found the opening sentence beguiling. All about songs, blue-eyed grass, and the dust of ages. Perfect mind-bathing material. She bought the book and a couple of crossword manuals for Bill and moved on down the High Street to the ironmongers. With its intriguing nooks and crannies, shoppers could buy anything from a piece of string to a full suit of armour. Picture hooks were Jaz's only requirement. After buying, she was ready to head home when muffled music rang out from deep inside her handbag. She found her phone on the fifth ring.

Dan's voice. "They've found the gun."

The line was scratchy, Dan's words indistinct. Jaz pressed the phone hard to her ear, stepping into the doorway of the nearest shop to shield traffic noise. A tailor's, the window full of suited mannequins. Jaz looked over the grey waistcoats and staid ties. Too formal and old-fashioned for Dan. "Say again."

"They've found the gun."

"Where?"

"No surprise. In the river."

"By Roger's boat?"

"No, about two hundred yards away."

"That's strange."

"Maybe. Maybe not. Anyway, the police are holding a press briefing at five-thirty. I'm sending Pete. Do you want to go along as well?"

Jaz glanced at her watch—4pm—then looked into the eyes of the nearest mannequin. It stared back blankly, and for an instant her mind wandered down a curious alley. *What sights had that mannequin seen on Lexford High Street down the years? What crimes had it witnessed? I wonder if it set eyes on Roger Mansell. What's a female mannequin called? A womannequin? A Julie? Or a Judy? Oh, never mind.*

"Yes, Dan. I'll be there. See you later." Jaz hung up and called Trish.

An hour later Jaz and Trish entered Lexford police station. For Jaz, it was the second time in 24 hours, having reported there with Pete Rainford to give witness statements the evening before.

They signed in at reception, the duty sergeant making a crack about Jaz being a frequent flier before guiding them through the number-coded door and down a long corridor to a small room painted with dazzling white walls. A single folding table and 12 plastic chairs completed the clinical look. Primarily used for interviewing suspects, the room also acted as an impromptu press conference venue on the odd occasion Lexford had news worthy of dissemination.

Despite Saturday being his day off, Pete had already arrived, as had a trainee reporter from the *Citizen*, a free paper, and the *Journal's* closest competition. Sitting in a corner, a long-haired blonde girl fiddled with a microphone lead protruding from a case of audio equipment bearing the words *County Radio—A Sound Investment*.

Jaz and Trish swapped small-talk with Pete until Inspector Cross entered the room, followed by his assistant. Cross sat behind the table, his assistant motioning everyone to take a seat. The radio girl came forward and placed a microphone on the table.

Cross waved the back of his hand at the microphone. An overly dismissive gesture, Jaz thought.

"None of that today. No interviews. Microphones and recorders off, please. This is a briefing only. A courtesy to the local press. We're awaiting tests, but I wanted to bring you up to speed on what we've found, as there appears to be considerable interest in this case." He fished a folder from his briefcase, fiddled with it for longer than necessary, then pulled out a piece of white A4 paper.

He studied the paper for another prolonged period. As *pedantic* came to Jaz's mind, Cross said that after a meticulous search of the River Lex, using dinghies and dredging equipment, police divers had recovered a shotgun. Ballistics experts had identified the gun. A 12-bore, double-barrelled model belonging to Mr Mansell, who owned a valid firearms certificate. Tests were underway to determine whether the wound and any gunpowder residue on the body matched the gun.

Cross reminded them that his team had also found a signed suicide note and investigations pointed to Mr Mansell suffering from depression and at potential risk of danger to himself. Jaz listened intently, but couldn't help thinking Cross delivered his findings with the same authoritative, disinterested tone policemen used to disperse onlookers. *Move along, please. Nothing of interest to see here.*

When he finished speaking, the inspector replaced the A4 paper in the folder, took out an A3 smug expression, and stuck it on his face. He popped the folder into the briefcase and rose to leave.

That arrogant look irritated Jaz. She didn't know why, but it did. Logic told her this case was straightforward. She knew the smart course of action. Allow Pete to write up the latest information while she went home to order an Italian takeaway, watch a film, and share a bottle of claret with Dan. But the capoeira, the fighting dance of Brazil, had begun. Right there in Lexford police station. That look struck the first chord, and Jaz sensed the slow, insistent beat in her ears.

"Inspector Cross, don't you think it strange that they found the gun two hundred yards from Mr Mansell's boat and, if my calculations are correct, even further from where his body surfaced under the wooden bridge? How can that be?"

Cross sat back, folding his arms with a false sympathetic expression verging on a sneer. "Ah, the duck lady."

Jaz's hackles rose.

"It's a fair question, but one with an equally fair answer. Mr Mansell was last seen late on Sunday afternoon at The Anchor, where he'd been supervising Sunday lunches. We believe he went from there to his boat moored on the River Lex. Sometime that night, we believe he shot himself with his shotgun. Accidentally or deliberately."

Trish had been listening in respectful silence and everything so far appeared reasonable, but she sensed a vibe emanating from Jaz. The time seemed right to run with it. "So, what are you saying? He staggered two hundred yards before chucking his gun in the river and jumping in after it?"

Inspector Cross rubbed his cheekbones with a thumb and forefinger, closing his eyes for a moment. A simple move, but it conveyed disdain, verging on contempt. Exactly what he intended. "No, we believe Mr Mansell shot himself while sitting on the side of his boat. He tumbled into the water, taking the gun with him, then floated downstream where his body became entangled under debris until disturbed on Thursday."

Trish remained puzzled. Her mystery-solving experience extended to the odd game of Cluedo, where she always struggled to match the weapon to the crime. At least there were no daggers, spanners or candlesticks in play here. "But surely the gun would sink, not float?" she said.

"Not if it went into the water attached to Mr Mansell, then became detached later. At this time of year, there's a lot of debris in the river. Another fact to consider is that on Sunday night in Lexford, this heatwave caused a thunderstorm. According to the Met Office, in a few hours, over two months' rain fell. The river would have been raging, making it easy for a gun to travel that far on the current, even if it wasn't attached to the body. In fact, under the circumstances, it's bordering on miraculous that we've found it so quickly."

"Will you be checking the gun for DNA?" the radio girl said.

"Good question. You must watch crime shows. Yes, over the next couple of days, we'll be analysing the gun for residue and ballistics markings. The chance of finding latent prints isn't good but not impossible and we can find DNA on items submerged after days in water, though the heat, algae, and the distance travelled isn't helpful."

"But it still all points to suicide?" said the girl.

"That's a decision for the coroner, but put it this way. I see no reason to divert more manpower to a case which, while not solved definitively, is no longer suspicious."

Grabbing his briefcase, Inspector Cross again made to leave.

"What about the suicide note?" said Jaz.

With a heavy sigh, Cross sat down, fixing sunken, exasperated eyes on Jaz. "Mrs Mansell has seen and read the note. She's confirmed the signature is that of her husband. We will pass it to the coroner as evidence before releasing to Mrs Mansell."

"Can you say how it was written?"

"What do you mean?"

By now, Jaz was making Inspector Cross well cross. His cheeks flushed, right eyelid twitched, and his knuckles turned white from clutching the case. Jaz was enjoying this briefing.

"Was it handwritten or typed? In pen or pencil? Freehand or capitals? That sort of thing."

"I don't see how those details concern you." Cross shrugged, refusing to make eye contact.

"What about the courtesy bit?" Jaz's tone was calm and even.

"Excuse me?"

"You said this briefing was a courtesy to the local press. You don't seem or sound courteous."

Drawing in a long breath, Cross's right fist clenched, but he ignored the remark. "All I will say is this. It was signed in blue biro and we found a pen matching that description on a desk on his boat. And, yes, before you ask, for the sake of completeness, we are analysing that too. Now I must go."

Cross strode towards the door, an irritable twitch contorting his features. In his haste to leave he forgot his briefcase and as he turned stubbed his toe on a table leg. "Jesus, Mary and Joseph!" He tripped, almost falling over. Probably would have done if his assistant's strong arm hadn't steadied him. For a few moments he tottered on one leg, grimacing, hissing indecipherable oaths, before limping out of the office without a glance at the reporters. Jaz rolled her eyes. Trish smirked.

"You can't keep a good man down, can you?" Jaz whispered.

"Or, in this case, a roaring dickhead," said Trish.

"I heard that."

They spun around to see the desk sergeant, who'd arrived to chaperone the press pack to the exit. His feigned annoyance immediately softened into a conspiratorial smile. Once outside, the radio girl and the lad from the *Citizen* sloped off together up the High Street and disappeared into a wine bar on the corner. Pete said he'd return to the office to post a new story online, detailing the discovery of the gun.

"Fancy a takeaway and a glass of wine, Trish?"

"Thought you'd never ask."

"Great. Then we can work out who really killed Roger Mansell."

9

Something about church on Sunday mornings appealed to Jaz. Nothing to do with religion. More about public service. She likened the Church to the National Health Service. There at birth 40 years ago, when christened Jasmine Annabelle Sharkey. There when they box her up and carry her off with a few comforting words. Many years from now. Hopefully.

In between, she could use both when the need arose. Broken finger, food poisoning, radiotherapy, weddings, funerals, Christmas carol service. All free at the point of delivery, even if both organisations increasingly attracted begging bowls. Religion wasn't everyone's cup of tea, Jaz conceded, scanning the beautiful interior of the Gothic parish church of St Anne's in Broughton Conquest. Including her and Dan, she counted a congregation of 11. The local bridge club attracted a bigger gathering on a Friday afternoon, but for Jaz, there was nothing not to like.

Marvelling at the intricate stained-glass windows punctuating thick stone walls and impressive balustrades, Jaz pictured stonemasons lifting such heavy objects, aligning them with meticulous precision at a time when the Magna Carta was still the compelling talking point of the day. She listened to the vicar's sermon, based on the parable of the talents from Matthew's gospel. She'd heard it countless times and the vicar's sonorous voice set her eyelids drooping, but the message resonated. *Use your gifts to the best of your ability.* Belting out, *How Great Thou Art*, Jaz concluded the sparse congregation lacked the oomph to do justice to such a rousing hymn.

She also indulged in the charming memory of Dan's marriage proposal by the effigy of Sir John Sewell, a knight of the fourteenth century. The image of Dan, scrambling around the stone floor on all fours to find the ring he'd dropped, never failed to bring a smile to her face or a flutter to her heart.

As the congregation meandered into the sunshine, the vicar shook each parishioner's hand, thanking them for coming. He had kind eyes, although his ruddy face and ample paunch suggested food and drink were specialist subjects.

On the gravel pathway, Jaz struck up a conversation with two regular churchgoers admiring pink and yellow wildflowers in the natural meadow garden. Enjoying the warmth, Dan hung around a little farther down the path, loosely studying tombstones in the garden cemetery. The passage of time fascinated him. Some stones covered in layers of moss and lichen dated back centuries. Dan suspected one inscription mentioned the fourteenth century, but a faded facia meant he couldn't be sure. Anyway, he reasoned, surely none were original inscriptions, not after 600 English winters battered unprotected stone. He felt a tug on his sleeve. The vicar, still in full-length black cassock but liberated at last from duties with his flock.

"Dan, how are things at the *Journal*? Nice garden fete picture last week, I thought, and thanks for the space you gave to the campaign for the new toilet block." His voice was soft, a touch pious, but that went with the job description.

"No problem, Gerald. It's a good cause. About time we dragged some parts of the church into the twenty-first century, and toilets these days are essential."

"Not sure about the headline, though."

Dan laughed. For some time, he'd pondered the picture Pete Rainford had taken of Reverend Gerald Ford clothed in vivid purple and gold vestments, standing in front of the historic church on the spot where the toilets would be housed. The obvious headline couldn't be ignored.

All dressed up and nowhere to go

The vicar chuckled at the memory. Then his manner grew sombre. "Terrible news about Roger Mansell. I believe the police think he killed himself. Hard to take that in. If there was one person I'd never have suspected of taking his own life, it would have been Roger."

"How well did you know him?"

"Not that well, I suppose. I've been here eight years, and he used to come to Sunday service most weeks with his wife and two children. He tried to get me to start an hour earlier. Said ten-thirty in the morning was too tight timing because he needed to get back to the pub to prepare for the Sunday lunchtime rush. He still came, though, until he and Cheryl split up two years ago. Or separated would be more accurate. Neither of them came after that."

Dan gazed at the cloudless blue sky, briefly considering the meaning of life and how things are rarely what they seem. As if to prove the point, a jet—silent, majestic—sketched a fluffy vapour trail of stunning beauty at 36,000 feet while polluting the world.

"To be honest, Gerald, I don't blame him for not coming. It probably wasn't the right time to hear that God is the most important relationship you can have. Or God can restore what's broken and transform it into something amazing. Or all you need is faith. No offence, Gerald. Religion can be comforting, but sometimes it can be suffocating. All Roger probably needed to hear was that he wouldn't lose his kids."

Gerald put his hands together as if in prayer. The habit of a lifetime. "No offence taken, Dan."

Jaz broke away from her flower admiration group, hugged Dan, then linked his arm. They bade farewell to the vicar and ambled to the car.

"How about a spot of lunch, Dan?"

"Where did you have in mind?"

"The Anchor?"

Dan knew better than to argue. Two of the things he loved most about Jaz were her cheeriness and tenacity. "You're like a dog with a bone."

"What sort of dog?"

"A Jack Russell terrier with honey blonde hair. Small and wiry, one of those that never obeys orders. Full of mischief. Quite annoying, actually. The sort that steals chicken bones from the kitchen bin and runs around the house taunting you with them."

"But highly intelligent."

"Yeah, if you count running off with my toothbrush and hiding it under my pillow."

Jaz laughed. "It sounds like you used to own a Jack Russell."

"I did. When I was about six."

"You never told me that."

"I just did."

They pulled up outside The Anchor. Still not noon, but the sun soared towards gas mark five and already quite a crowd had gathered. Forming an orderly queue, half a dozen boats hugged the riverbank, diners under parasols at most of the outside tables. Jaz smelled lamb roast and the sharp tang of mint sauce.

Dan swatted away a couple of wasps. "Let's go inside. I hate eating out and being dive-bombed every two minutes."

They found an agreeable spot by the window overlooking the river. The waitress sidled over to take their order, hair pulled back in a ponytail, a fixed smile masking her agitation at serving too many tables.

Jaz pointed out Logan behind the bar. "Don't look now, but he's the guy with the toothpaste-commercial smile. Seems nice."

Logan was talking to a tall man wearing a huge girth of Sumo proportions, a white apron, and chef's hat, black curls protruding from it. Brian, Jaz presumed. She told Dan about the previous evening with Trish. They'd gone to Dan's, shared a takeaway, and a bottle of wine. Dan had made his excuses to watch television around 9pm. He wasn't a big TV fan but adored cricket and had promised himself an hour's indulgence, savouring the highlights of an England Australia Test match. He'd left Jaz and Trish in the kitchen, chatting over a cup of coffee. For the first half hour, they'd mulled over what they knew about the body in the river, reviewing conversations with Victor and Joe, piecing together everything they'd learned from the police.

"And what did you come up with?" said Dan.

"Trish reckons the prime suspect must be somebody the dead man knows well."

"Suicides usually are people the dead know well."

Jaz ignored him, but lowered her voice. She reasoned there was something disrespectful about discussing the details of a man who, a week ago, was alive, well, and chatting happily, perhaps at this table. A whisper of restraint seemed appropriate.

"I don't think it was suicide."

"The police do."

"Well, I think they're wrong."

"Why?"

"He had two young children, with their whole lives in front of them. Even if his marriage was breaking up, surely he had reasons to carry on. According to the police, he'd planned to take his daughter out for a birthday treat. I just can't get my head around how he could walk out of this room after serving lunches on a hot Sunday afternoon and blow himself to kingdom come. It makes no sense. And there's another thing."

Dan laughed. "You even sound like one of those TV detectives."

"Oh, never mind."

"Sorry, Jaz. Go on, what is it?"

Jaz told Dan about her conversation with Joe and Victor, and their recollections of Roger sustaining his old cricketing injury. The deteriorating frozen shoulder down the years, so painful he could no longer haul beer crates. One stiff arm stuck permanently at his side, limp, lifeless, like a bird's broken wing.

"What relevance has that?"

"I've been looking up the length of a twelve-bore shotgun barrel."

"Really?"

"Between thirty and thirty-four inches. Sometimes twenty-eight inches for ladies, but not shorter."

"Unless sawn off. I've done scores of stories about bank raids and gang shootings when sawn-off shotguns are used. In parts of the criminal fraternity, it's the weapon of choice. Looks menacing, and the short barrel is easy to control and conceal."

Jaz looked deflated. She hadn't thought of that.

The waitress arrived with a pint of beer for Dan and an orange juice for Jaz, setting the drinks down, laying cutlery and napkins on the table. Jaz had pictured Roger Mansell shooting rabbits or foxes out in the fields, not holding up a High Street bank Bonnie and Clyde style.

The night before, while Dan was watching cricket, Jaz had given Trish a retractable metal tape measure, asking her to hold one end 30 inches away from her body while the other end touched her chest. Impossible. Trish couldn't get close. Arms too short, and even if they'd been long enough, the stretch involved would need considerable effort and elasticity of movement.

"Roger was a big bloke. His arms would be much longer and stronger than Trish's," said Dan.

"It's not about strength. It's about being able to stretch and pull a trigger."

Dan drummed his fingers on the table. He was thinking. "Was Roger right-handed or left-handed and which shoulder was it?"

"I don't know."

"Think you need to know both if your theory is to have legs."

Dan watched the waitress negotiate the swing door out of the kitchen. She walked towards them with two roast meals and all the trimmings, including huge Yorkshire puddings overlapping the plates. She'd reached the end of the main bar when two men staggered from the snug, grappling with each other, volleying profanities back and forth. The waitress tried to avoid them and almost succeeded, raising one hand and pirouetting to her left. A beautifully improvised fluid movement, and lightning fast. As she brought the plate down, one man threw a long, swinging punch. It missed the jaw of his intended target and smashed into the plate. Vegetables flew across the bar, gravy splattered the wall, brown streaks chasing down white paintwork. A Yorkshire pudding splatted at Dan's feet and the plate smashed to pieces in the middle of the dining area.

Oblivious to the carnage, the men rolled on the wooden floor, clawing and punching.

"Scumbag. Lying scumbag!" screamed the smaller man.

Dan jumped to his feet. Neither big, muscular, nor a fighter by temperament, he was lithe and had wide shoulders. He moved with a power and intensity only seen in those who take care of themselves, courtesy of the early morning cycling regime that saw him burning up country lanes. Having covered wars in Afghanistan, Iraq, and Syria, where spontaneous skirmishes required instant decision-making and a clear mind free from emotion, conflict situations didn't faze him.

"Stop, right now. There are kids in here."

Dan's bark carried instant authority. He grabbed the smaller man by the shoulder, dragging him along the floor. His T-shirt ripped in Dan's grasp and Jaz glimpsed a distinctive swan tattoo on his upper arm. The ginger beard, spiky hair, and big teeth were unmistakable. *Crime.*

The commotion alerted Logan, who emerged from the kitchen with Brian, showing a dainty turn of foot for such a bulky figure. Each grabbed an arm of the bigger man and wrenched him backwards. Still seething, spittle running down his chin, blood oozing from his nose, the man fixed Jaz squarely in the eye. No one heard her gasp as Crime aimed a barrage of oaths at his assailant.

My God, it's Trish's ex. Jaz had seen Terry only once, entering the pub a couple of days ago, but there was no doubt. Black curly hair flecked with grey, distinctive round shoulders.

Logan and Brian frogmarched Terry out of the pub. He still snarled and cursed.

"What on earth did Trish see in him?" Jaz mumbled to herself.

Logan and Brian returned, and the waitress scraped Dan's lunch off the floor and walls, rounding up stray peas with a brush and pan. Families resumed eating. An air of unease lingered, furtive glances cast towards the exits. Crime was nowhere to be seen. Jaz presumed he'd slipped out the back door while Logan and Brian escorted Terry out the front. Logan approached Jaz and Dan.

"Terribly sorry about that. I don't know what it was all about, but it's out of order for two grown men to behave like that at Sunday lunchtime with lots of people around."

Jaz detected a flicker of recognition.

"Didn't I see you the other day? You're the reporter from the *Journal,* aren't you? You were talking to Victor and Joe."

"That's right."

Logan turned to Dan. "Please, have two lunches on the house and a bottle of wine. It's the least I can do. If you hadn't acted to break up the fight, it could have been a lot worse."

Dan glanced at Jaz, catching the merest glint of reservation. Conveying messages without speaking was one of Jaz's many gifts. Dan had a phrase for it. *Eloquent eyes.*

"That's very kind of you, but I think we'll give it a miss. The fight's rather spoiled our appetites. I think we'll go for a walk down the river instead."

"Okay, no problem, but whenever you pop in again, drinks are on the house. If there's anything I can do, just let me know."

Dan turned to leave. Jaz slung her handbag over her shoulder. Logan picked up a couple of dirty plates, but before he headed to the kitchen, Jaz spun around as if she'd forgotten something.

"There is one thing, Logan," Jaz said.

"Yes?"

"I believe Roger Mansell had a bad shoulder that stopped him from lifting heavy things. Do you know which one it was?"

Logan looked puzzled, grimacing as if in serious thought. He then reverted to one of his trademark smiles. "Why would you want to know that?"

"No reason. Just curious."

"It was the right, I think. Yes, definitely, the right, which was a shame because he was right-handed. That's why he took me on."

"What do you mean?"

"To be his right-hand man."

Jaz thought the play on words inappropriate in the circumstances. Smiling anyway, she strode out of the pub. Her theory had grown legs.

10

Loud, urgent, fearful. Caught in that bleary void of confusion between sleep and consciousness, Jaz didn't know whether the scream was real.

She lay in dark silence, wondering if she'd imagined it. Hoping she had. *What dreadful incident had occurred in the vicinity? Or could it be the skirl of a cat?* Nothing quite like a screeching catfight in the early hours to generate paroxysms of fright. *Yes. That's what it was.*

The alarm clock's fluorescent hands signalled ten past three. Turning over, Jaz closed her eyes, drifting away once more when another scream penetrated her subconscious. This time closer. In the room. In the bed. *Dan.* The bed creaked and his arms flailed, trying to fend off an invisible force, skull banging against the headboard with a continual thud. A shaft of moonlight streaming through a narrow gap in the curtains captured beads of perspiration on his brow.

Jaz heard him breathing. Heavy, laced with whimpers. Reaching across, she laid her right hand on his chest, felt his heart palpitating through sweat-sodden pyjamas. "Dan. Dan. It's all right. I'm here. Jaz's here. It's only another nightmare." She snuggled up to him.

Hyperventilating, he opened his eyes.

"No, Dan. Calm down. Breathe easy. Everything's okay. I'm here. It's Jaz. Don't worry." Her soft voice reassured as she stroked his cheek.

After a while, his breathing became measured. A deep sigh. "Sorry, Jaz. Sorry, I woke you."

"Don't be silly. I'm always awake at ten past three. That's when I do my best thinking, you know that."

Dan chuckled. It wasn't the first time his nightmares had disturbed Jaz's sleep at an unearthly hour. Since she'd sold her house and moved in with him, every two or three months, visions and memories from Dan's eventful past surfaced. Post-traumatic stress disorder was the diagnosis. Quite a mouthful. PTSD for short. Dan had another name for the unnerving occasions when his heart pumped for England and his mind raged with anxiety. Please Take Some Dan. And he did, popping the odd pill or two.

Few people knew about the condition that sneaked out to shake his hand, arms, and head under the cover of darkness. *The coward in me* was Dan's harsh description. For too long, Dan being Dan had convinced himself he didn't need help. Strong and private, he dealt with personal problems on his own terms. Help groups and arty-farty organisations weren't for Dan. They were for soft, vulnerable types. And Dan, most definitely, wasn't one of them.

Even when friend and colleague Lance recommended a specialist, Dan refused, despite Lance sharing many of the same terrors in far-off lands. Jaz had reasoned with Dan. At first, gentle cajoling followed by strident appeals. *Come on, Dan. You're sane, logical, and letting a horrible, tiny part of your past ruin your present and future.*

Eventually, Jaz's persuasive overtures succeeded. Dan joined Lance's self-help group in north London and hadn't missed a single session in 10 months. With tender, measured steps, he reached the stage where he could talk through his time in Iraq, when he'd witnessed the death of Farez Osman, his interpreter and best friend.

"No, let's get it straight. I *caused* the death of my best friend." He'd insisted on the correction.

He could have kept himself, Lance, and Faz safe by sneaking away from the battle they were observing. Instead, he chased the first big exclusive of the invasion of Iraq, and ended up seeing an American missile vaporising Faz. Killed by friendly fire. Killed by the stubborn, reckless ambition of his best friend.

It had taken Dan years of soul-searching to admit as much publicly but, when he did, he felt a heavy cloud lift. The nightmares didn't cease, nor the occasional panic attacks, but they'd become fewer, less severe. Dan propped himself up on a pillow and put an arm around Jaz, pulling her close. "It wasn't about Faz this time."

"What was it then?"

"It was strange. Horrible, actually."

"Why?" Jaz was concerned.

"I was at work and had to call all the staff into my office one by one."

"What's strange about that?"

"Because I was reclining behind my desk wearing a Nazi uniform with my jackboots up on the desktop and every time one of the staff came in, I demanded to know how many stories they'd written for the paper over the past month. Pete Rainford was first. He said, 'Fifteen,' I said, 'Not enough,' and told him to stand against the wall."

Jaz's eyebrows knitted. This sounded disturbing. "What happened then?"

"Two of the security guys, Jim and George, entered the room with rifles and shot him in the head."

"Oh, Dan, that's terrifying."

"It got worse. I called in Alison from features. The same happened to her, then Jack Ashton. He pleaded with me. Said he'd only been there a short time, was young and still learning the job. He'd get better, work harder. It sounded like rain on a tin roof when he broke down in tears and fell onto my desk. He begged me, Jaz, but I snapped my fingers and Jim and George came in like a ruthless firing squad and blew his head off."

Jaz hugged him tighter. "Oh, Dan. Where has all that come from?"

Dan reached for a glass of water on the bedside table. He took two long, noisy slugs, feeling the cool liquid trickling down his throat. Comforting. Refreshing. He considered popping a couple of pills, decided against it, and replaced the glass. "If there's one thing I've learned this past year, a combination of events triggers nightmares. That fight in the pub at lunchtime could be one of them. A conflict situation. I felt adrenalin kick in, my heart racing."

"What was the other event?"

Dan swallowed, breathed deep, and even then remained unsure whether he should say anything. But he and Jaz harboured no secrets. When they got engaged, he told her everything. About Annie, his former wife, and the drugged-up joyrider who knocked down and killed her on her way home from work. She was pregnant. He told Jaz about his life on the road and the time in Afghanistan when a bomb exploded, peppering him with shrapnel. She knew he'd won Journalist of the Year for his *Daily News* dispatches from Syria. He picked up his prize in London, then suffered what he described as a *funny turn*, in reality a panic attack, leading to the Master of Ceremonies escorting him from the stage. Dan no longer did secrets. Not with Jaz. He raised a fist to his mouth, cleared his throat.

"Remember when Thomas Henry was in the office yesterday?" he said.

"Yes."

"Well, he wasn't there to tell us what a good job we're all doing. He wants me to get rid of three or four members of staff. Let them go. Fire them. Make them redundant. Call it what you want. He says there's no way around it and, what's worse, I think he's probably right."

Jaz hugged him tighter. "But he didn't tell you to blow their heads off."

"No, I thought that up all by myself."

11

Dan rose early and jumped on his bike, yearning for an exercise blood rush to purge the effects of the nightmare. He needed a tough session to restore his confidence and tend his wounded pride, and was spinning up a moderate incline at a decent clip when he sensed a presence on his right shoulder.

"Morning, lovely day again." A woman's cheery voice. The cyclist was wearing a long hi-vis yellow coat, pedalling smoothly, gripping the handlebars with her left hand while in her right she held a circular sign on a long pole. Like a lollipop. The sort elderly ladies used to help children cross the road, STOP emblazoned in bold black letters.

Many things can bruise a mid-life man's ego. Point out his beer paunch, denigrate his job, ridicule his salary. Few beat being overtaken by a lollipop lady on a bicycle.

Dan gasped. "What the—" He stood on his pedals and accelerated, but the more muscles he burned, the farther the stop sign stretched away.

Glimpsing the battery mount on the down frame in the middle of her bike, at last the penny tumbled. No wonder she was doing a good lick. Probably on her way to work. Relieved, Dan sat back in his saddle, breathing easier.

Later, he related the story to Jaz as his car waited to negotiate the bend by the Three Tuns pub. The tapered point of Lexford High Street made it difficult for two vehicles to pass in either direction without wing mirrors folding and drivers offering a prayer to the patron saint of tight spaces. A dustbin wagon in front of Dan was making a mess of the manoeuvre.

"See, things aren't always what they seem," said Jaz. "Your lollipop lady wasn't an Olympic cyclist, just like the case of Roger Mansell might not be as straightforward as the police think."

"Bit of a stretch that comparison, Jaz."

"Maybe, maybe not."

A few minutes later, Dan swung into his reserved parking space in the work's cramped car park. Editor-in-Chief boasted the spot's nameplate, alongside another sign bearing Thomas Henry's name.

Jaz rarely worked on Mondays. Tuesdays, Wednesdays, and Thursdays formed her usual rota, but little about last week could be considered normal. Dan picked up a bundle of national newspapers from reception before climbing the stairs to the editorial floor. Jaz headed to the staff kitchen. The priority. However calamitous the news or pressing the deadlines, few mornings in Jaz's life began without strong coffee.

She handed Dan a coffee as he skimmed through the papers and opened a pile of mail. "Think I'll catch up on admin today. Fell behind last week with all the excitement."

"Okay."

Dan didn't look up from his desk. Instead, he tossed two empty brown parcel packets into the wastebin and sliced into three more envelopes with the letter opener staff had gifted as a welcome the year before. Jaz considered the gesture warm, kind. Dan thought it a clever way of telling him his job description included the mundane role of dealing with the daily post. He didn't disagree, believing local newspaper editors must view the big picture while tracking trivia if they were to trace the pulse of a community. Although most readers contacted the *Journal* via email, Dan maintained that newsy nuggets still arrived by Royal Mail.

He smiled, reading the first letter. From a Mr Derek Thompson, in the first sentence proudly revealing that he was 84, but conceded his eyesight no longer served him as it once had. Apparently, for the past two years, Mr Thompson had deposited his letters in a red post box fixed to a metal stalk at the end of his lane. One problem. Last week, he discovered the 'post box' was for dog poo.

'I wonder if you would be so kind to warn everyone in the village, so they don't make the same mistake,' his letter concluded.

The next letter criticised the Lexford bus service. A familiar refrain. The *paper* received at least one complaint a week on the subject, mostly from pensioners left stranded by the bus company's inability to stick to its timetable. Most letters contained the same sentiment: Never mind running a bus service. They couldn't run a bath.

Dan nurtured a sneaky suspicion that the letters came from the same person using bogus addresses. He scribbled a reminder to ask Pete to visit Mr Thompson. A photograph of the pensioner posting a letter into the poo box could make an entertaining snippet, and the picture would serve as a warning to others. He also made a mental note to raise the bus issue again in his comment column. Opening the third letter, his attention immediately sprang to the name written in bold capitals at the top of the page.

ROGER MANSELL

Addressed to 'The Editor' and postmarked Saturday, the letter, written in uppercase, was in a scruffy, sloping hand, verging on italics. Two brief sentences.

NO WAY ROGER TOOK HIS OWN LIFE. THERE WERE TOO MANY QUEUING UP TO DO IT FOR HIM.

No signature. Dan's instinct told him the letter was a hoax. Written by an attention-seeking teenager, a disgruntled drinker, one of Lexford's nutty fraternity, or a sad individual craving an anonymous bit-part in one of the newsiest local stories of the year. He thought of screwing the letter up, intending to consign it to the recycling pile. Instead, he dropped it on Jaz's desk.

She picked it up casually while sipping coffee, then put the cup down. Grabbing the letter with both hands, she read it again. And again. Dan sensed excited determination in her eyes. "I knew it, Dan. Someone else thinks the same as me."

"Not exactly. You think he had too much to live for. Whoever wrote this letter obviously thinks there were reasons for him to die. That's if it isn't just a nutter on the number sixty-four bus to Lexford Junction."

"I'm going to speak to his wife. She'll know if he had enemies."

"Do you think she'll see you?"

"Don't know, but Pete has her number. I'll ring, try to set up a face-to-face. You can't build trust on a telephone."

"I agree, but take Trish with you."

Nodding, Jaz grabbed her handbag, begged the phone number from Pete, and skipped down the office stairs two at a time. From the front seat of her car, she rang Mrs Mansell's mobile, surprised at how quickly she agreed to a meeting at 11 that morning in Cambridge. It took a few minutes to brief Trish, who was more than happy to interrupt the dreary task of washing bed linen, then they were on their way, winding through flat south-east countryside, with its enormous crop fields and long hedgerows.

No one would ever contend Lexfordshire was the prettiest county in England. It didn't boast the dramatic elevations of the Chilterns in neighbouring counties, nor have a reputation for film-making, motor racing, impressive castles, or National Trust elegance. A poor cousin of Cambridgeshire, whose charming sights, university heritage, and biomedical campus were envied around the world.

Still, Jaz had grown to love the county. She adored the history. That Lexford once formed a subdivision of the kingdom of Mercia in 585. The county's Celtic and Roman origins and Anglo-Saxon influence fascinated her, as did the notion that Henry VIII once meddled in local politics, and soldiers fought many battles during the English Civil War on its turf.

The county's history provided intrigue, but Jaz also appreciated the thatched roofs, country pubs and meandering rivers, as well as the attraction of being close to London, yet distant in terms of temperament. No one rushed in Lexfordshire.

"Watch out, Jaz, there's a speed camera."

A flash jolted Jaz from her musing.

Busy applying mascara, Trish's warning came a fraction too late. She went nowhere without full make-up. She'd listened to those who would cheerfully burn every tube of face primer, blusher, and bronzer in existence. Studied their arguments, weighed them up. Yes, she had, and after much deliberation, arrived in typical Trish fashion at her considered verdict. "Bollocks."

Trish owned fine features, high cheekbones and looked younger than her 40-something years. She didn't wear make-up to impress men or look more beautiful. She enjoyed wearing it. To Trish, it was an art that rendered satisfaction. *Why would a girl not want to look her best?*

"Oh, Trish, you should have warned me earlier about that camera."

"I was busy, Jaz."

"Your mascara's cost me a hundred quid."

"No. Your driving's cost you a hundred quid. Slow down. There's no rush. We'll be there well before eleven."

Jaz eased back on the accelerator. "Sorry. You're right."

They sat in silence, Jaz scolding herself for becoming distracted, Trish putting the finishing touches to her make-up. Eventually, she clicked the mascara brush into its tube.

"Wasn't this the route Dan used to take us to the Barrett Bailey?" said Trish.

Jaz pointed out three huge telescope dishes in the distance. "Think so. I always wondered what those dishes were for. What they were looking at. That month we had radiotherapy went by so fast. We were rushing past every day talking nonsense, while someone was watching stars and planets that are billions of miles away. Looking thousands of years into the past. Isn't that fascinating, Trish?"

"To be honest, I've always been more concerned about the present, Jaz. The past has gone. The present you can do something about."

"Talking about the present, I saw your ex again yesterday."

"Surely that's the past, Jaz."

Jaz rolled her eyes, posting an exasperated look in the direction of the passenger seat. Trish was oblivious.

"He was fighting with one of those men we met at The Anchor. You know, the one called Crime. Quite a dust-up. They were rolling around, punching each other. Plates went flying. Dan helped break them up, and the chef weighed in. It was scary. Put us off our lunch."

Normally, Trish would have responded with a ready quip. She enjoyed a burst of action. Instead, she tightened her grip around the crushed tissue in her fist and looked down. Jaz thought she seemed sad.

"Was Lynn there?" Trish's voice was low.

"Your daughter? No, I don't think so. Terry was alone, although no one had a clue what the altercation was about. Something and nothing, probably. In the end, no real harm was done."

Jaz could sense Trish smouldering. Heavy breathing, eyes glinting with anger. Trish had endured a bellyful of Terry's behaviour and Jaz's apparent willingness to make light of his recent altercation triggered pent-up force deep inside. The mention of his name by her loyal, caring best friend in a new life jarred on Trish's subconscious, tectonic plates of her old existence colliding with the new. Grating and grinding, spewing out all sorts of vicious mental debris.

"He doesn't need a reason to be a grade one wanker. He just needs to get up in the morning. Some people are evil because life deals them an unfair hand and I get that. Some people are just born evil. Terry's one of them."

"Wow! Sorry, Trish, I didn't realise. Did he ever hit you?"

"What sort of question's that?"

"The obvious one."

Trish shrugged. "No, he never laid a hand on me, but you don't have to punch someone to be violent."

"What do you mean?"

Trish wiped her nose with the end of the tissue. She wasn't crying, but the emotion aggravated the lining of her sinus, provoking a trickle of moisture.

"Control, Jaz, that's what I mean."

"Oh."

"Where are you going? Why did you buy that? Who was that man you spoke to at the bar? And I'd say, the barman, you pillock, and he'd sulk for a week."

Jaz stifled a chuckle, but Trish wouldn't have noticed. She was in the zone, the domestic war zone that had been her life for the two years she lived with Terry.

"When will you be home? That dress doesn't suit you. Why have you done your hair that way? Jaz, I swear, whatever I did was wrong. You know me. I'll give as good as I get, but it wears you down after a while. I didn't need another battle because I'd bought skimmed milk instead of semi-skimmed. Didn't need every domestic chore to turn into a chapter from *War and Peace*. I couldn't hoover properly, was useless at ironing and apparently, I'd ruined his shirts in the wash, though when I pointed out that he could always wash his own sweaty, stinking shirts, he'd stomp off in a strop. Life's too short."

With her free hand, Jaz squeezed Trish's right hand. They said nothing for a time. A gesture of sisterly solidarity. *Thelma and Louise*. Jaz wasn't leaving it there. She didn't want to prolong Trish's discomfort but was intrigued to know what drew such a dysfunctional relationship to a head.

"I presume it ended badly then."

Trish laughed. Not an angry or maniacal laugh. A sad laugh. The sort that starts at the back of the throat, rises to a crescendo, then culminates in a sob and shaking shoulders. Except Trish didn't sob, nor did her shoulders shake. She stayed still and focused, as if the memory of Terry's steady, critical thumps had exorcised emotion from her body, a desperate emptiness all that remained. *How sad.*

"Badly? That's one word for it. You're probably wondering how I hooked up with him in the first place?"

"Yes. I am."

"At an open mic pub night. I'd sunk a few drinks. I thought he was funny, a bit brash maybe, but he could sing a bit, wasn't bad on guitar, and was a laugh. We had a brilliant evening and when he called to ask me out again a few days later, I thought, why not? What's the worst that could happen?

"For a few weeks, months even, we were good together. If only I could have fast-forwarded two years. Sometimes I wonder how I could have been so blind. I knew things weren't right. Living with him was like a scene from one of those films, inching down a stairway towards a dark basement, unsure what you'll find. Knowing there's no happy ending, getting scarier with each step, yet somehow drawn to the horror. The week we finished was the week from Hell. No. Worse than Hell."

Jaz squeezed Trish's hand again. Trish took a tissue from her bag and dabbed her nose.

"One Wednesday night, we went to the pub. As usual, I was driving to let Terry have a few drinks, even though it was one of my mates from work who'd invited us. Terry started having a go at me before we left the driveway. 'Watch those gears tonight. Don't rev too much. First gear for starting, not cruising.'

"The pick, pick, picking continued in the pub. It was embarrassing and I could tell everybody else thought the same. My mate's husband even had a go at him. I remember he said, 'How does your missus put up with you? Leave her alone for a minute, will you?' I thought Terry was going to lamp him, but he didn't. He smiled and said, 'She knows what's good for her and so should you if you want to go home with any teeth.' Thankfully, my mate squeezed her husband's knee as if to say, 'Suck it up.' He did."

Jaz coughed. An uncomfortable sound, as if she'd arrived at a place she wished she'd never visited. "So you did. Go home, I mean?"

"Eventually. Of a fashion. We got in the car and straight away he was in my ear again. 'Put your beam on. It's quicker turning right. Why have you gone down here?' It was eleven o'clock, and we were on the motorway in the outside lane. I'd just overtaken a truck when he said, 'Come on, put your foot down,' and I did, but not in the way he intended. I slammed on the brakes, stopped dead in the outside lane, jumped out of the car and screamed something like, 'If you're such a good driver, you fucking drive.'

"There was panic and disbelief on his face and for a moment the feeling was absolutely wonderful. Fortunately, there was nothing behind us. It felt so liberating. He leapt out of the car and staggered around to the driver's side, calling me a mad cow and all sorts of things. I suppose it was dangerous but, do you know what, I didn't care. At that moment, I didn't care. In fact, I secretly hoped he would get pulled over on the way home because he'd drunk four pints and a whisky chaser in the pub."

Jaz pulled up at a set of traffic lights and looked at Trish. "I'd no idea it was so bad. Poor you."

"No, don't pity me, Jaz. It was my fault for staying with that lump of shit for so long. Terry didn't need a partner. All he needed was someone to blame. Those men are like bad weather. You can do sod all to change either of them."

"So, that's when you chucked him out?"

"Not exactly. The next day, I got back from work and there was a note on the table in the hallway. It said he'd gone and taken Lynn with him. She was nineteen, Jaz. I'd no idea they were up to anything, although when I look back on it, they'd probably been carrying on for a few months. To be honest, Terry had always got on with her and taken her side when we argued. Then, I thought he did it to have a go at me. Now I know different. I haven't seen her since, not until the other day outside The Anchor."

Jaz shook her head. "Trish, that's truly awful. The sort of story I hear on those trashy morning TV shows."

"You watch trashy TV?"

An embarrassed smirk played on Jaz's lips.

"Holy shit! And I thought we had nothing in common."

12

Jaz drove into Cambridge after toying with the idea to catch the bus. Parking in the busy centre always proved troublesome. Few chores were more fraught than searching out a free space in the city's assault course. Rising bollards, kamikaze cyclists, unfamiliar road signs, and an army of parking wardens. Fortunately, Trish spotted an estate car leaving its spot. Jaz steered her car in and paid four quid for her ticket. Two hours. More than enough time.

"We have time to spare. Let's soak up a bit of the atmosphere. Could do with a chill." Jaz secretly hoped to raise Trish's mood following their revealing journey.

They passed the gates to Clare College, regimented chimneys rising to a deep blue sky, marvelled at the majestic vista afforded by King's College Chapel, then turned into Garret Hostel Lane, its bridge spanning the River Cam. Pausing on the arched crossing, they enjoyed the gathering heat of a sparkling morning, watching punts slide by. A punter guided a vessel overladen with passengers, the pole sticking as it sailed under the bridge. His inexperience prompted squeals of laughter, amplified by the curved chamber as he attempted to free the pole. All he did was incite more giggles when the pole released in an unexpected rush and his trousered leg dipped mid-thigh in the water.

"Story of my life, that. One cock-up after another," chuckled Trish, wondering how many tourists and students the river's bridges had trapped in similar fashion down the centuries. What oaths they must have witnessed, and in how many languages? Bet those bridges could tell a few stories.

Apart from the perils of parking, Jaz loved the city. "You know, Trish, Charles Darwin and Isaac Newton walked these streets. Probably stood close to where we are now. Isn't that fantastic? Don't you get a sense of communing with the greats? I do. Maybe Newton's famous apple fell near here."

"Cor! Makes you think, doesn't it?"

"Brilliant, Trish. I saw what you did there."

"What?" Trish looked puzzled.

"Cor. Apple. Never mind."

Jaz dodged an omnipresent bicycle, and the pair turned into Senate House Passage, tall buildings on either side of the cobbled lane consigning it to a near permanent shadow. Jaz stopped and twirled. "I imagine spies plying their trade down here."

"Or prostitutes."

Jaz glanced at her watch: 10:50. Time to listen to the busker in front of St Mary's Church. A hairy individual with shaggy brown beard and flyaway locks in tattered blue jeans and white tee, strumming his guitar, singing Ed Sheeran's *Castle on the Hill*.

"Sheeran's everywhere these days. You can't move for hip-hop, looped music, and relationship lyrics," said Jaz.

"This guy's good, though. Sounds just like him."

Jaz pushed through the crowd, dropping a pound coin in the busker's guitar case as they moved onto King's Parade. She'd arranged to meet Mrs Mansell at a café-cum-bistro overlooking King's College porter's lodge to the right and a wall-mounted statue of King Henry VIII to the left. A busy spot, but Jaz reasoned a handy place to remain unnoticed. Lost in the hurly-burly of one of England's most famous and appealing university cities, even if most students were enjoying summer vacation.

Jaz and Trish arrived at exactly 11am. Under an awning, offering welcome protection from the sun, Mrs Mansell sat at a table for four wearing a striking red-rose patterned yellow summer dress, the outfit she'd agreed with Jaz for easy identification. Jaz's first impression gauged the woman prettier and younger than expected. Around 37, auburn hair tied in a loose bun highlighting delicate features. The shape of her mouth matched rosebuds on her dress, and mascara applied with an expert hand enhanced exquisite big eyes. She sat cross-legged, the hitched up hem of her dress revealing tanned, toned limbs ending in stylish red sandals on pretty feet. Manicured painted toenails completed the look. A sophisticated woman who looks after herself, Jaz thought.

"Mrs Mansell?"

The woman stood to shake hands. "Please, call me Cheryl."

The accent defeated Jaz. Soft and correct, it could have been north London, possibly a hint of Dublin.

"This is Trish. She works with me at the Journal."

Trish offered her hand, then ordered lattes for herself and Jaz. Cheryl poured fine Earl Grey from a pot. Jaz had wondered how to start the conversation. She needn't have worried. For all her elegance, Cheryl didn't seem interested in niceties or small talk.

"Let me get one thing straight from the start. I'm not here to tell you Roger was an angel. He wasn't. And I don't want sympathy. All I wish is that I'd been there for him when he reached his darkest moment, but I wasn't, and for the rest of my life, I'll wonder if I could have prevented what happened. I keep picturing him in that murky river …" Cheryl's voice trailed off. She bit her lip and blinked.

Jaz thought Cheryl was going to cry, but no tears came. "I'm sorry. We don't want to upset you. We're trying to build a picture of Roger and—"

"I'm okay. Don't worry about me. I came today because Roger deserves the truth. Deep down, he was a good man. It's good to talk it through. It helps, really it does. I don't think it's sunk in yet that he's gone."

"How are the children coping?" said Jaz.

Cheryl shivered at the mention of children, then dug inside her handbag and pulled out a tissue. She wiped away a tear.

"Roger loved Jennifer and Tobias. He would do anything for his kids. He saw them every week, never missed, and we were even talking of getting back together once he'd left that pub."

"Really? He was leaving The Anchor?"

"Well, no, he hadn't told the brewery or anyone else, but we'd been getting on so much better recently. He'd asked if there was a chance of us getting back together and I hadn't said no."

"But you hadn't said yes?"

"No, but he knew I would never go back to the pub."

"Why?"

"Have you ever worked in a pub?"

Jaz and Trish shook heads.

"Well, it's not work. Not these days. It's a prison sentence. You can't make money from serving beer, however many regulars you have. Taxes are high. Margins tight. You need to serve food, which means paying for a decent chef, even then doing most of the kitchen work yourself.

"I was chained to that kitchen six days a week when I should have been devoting time to Jennifer and Tobias, while Roger was racking his brains to put different entertainment on seven nights a week in order to earn a meagre living. We did three quiz nights, an open mic night, a race night, a themed night. You name it, we tried it. We did boat trips down the river with breakfast or lunch thrown in, always worked weekends and bank holidays. It reached the stage when I was in the kitchen and he was in the bar or on the boat and we wouldn't talk to each other from one day to the next. One week to the next sometimes.

"We were together, surrounded by people enjoying themselves every day, but I felt miserable and alone. I think we both did. All the time. In our own house."

A waiter and two frothy lattes paused the conversation. Trish heaped demerara sugar into her cup. Jaz mixed the froth with a thin wooden stirrer. A beggar wandered past, hand outstretched, one of Cambridge's homeless fraternity. Unwashed, matted, unkempt hair, a vacant look suggesting food and water weren't priorities.

Trish waved him away. Looking apologetic, Jaz shook her head. Cheryl searched for her purse and handed him a £5 note. His eyes lit up, and he muttered thanks as the waiter ushered him away.

"That was kind of you," said Jaz.

"Don't judge people. That's the first thing I learned in the pub. He looked like he was going through a bad time. If I was down, I'd hope someone passing would lend me a hand, wouldn't you?"

Jaz strained to work Cheryl out. Albeit separated, a shotgun killed her husband five days ago, yet no sign of grief clouded her demeanour. A hint of anger, a spark of injustice, a determination to do right by him, but no sense of grief. Still, everyone deals with death differently. Maybe Cheryl blamed herself for the split. If she'd tried harder and kept the family together, perhaps Roger wouldn't be lying in a Lexford mortuary. Ifs and maybes were not the stock-in-trade of journalists. Jaz preferred to concentrate on facts. She told Cheryl about the anonymous letter sent to the *Journal*.

"Are you trying to say it wasn't suicide?" said Cheryl.

"I don't know. Maybe the police have been a little hasty in their conclusions, that's all. Tell me, Cheryl. Did Roger have enemies?"

The question was direct; the answer fired back with speed, surprising Jaz.

"Definitely. You can't run a pub without making enemies. Always someone spoiling for a fight when they've sunk a few pints. Always someone who thinks they've been short-changed, complaining about the beer. Too warm, too cold, or suggesting you've watered the spirits down. If things became nasty or got out of hand, Roger would bar the odd customer. That comes with the territory. There's not a landlord in the country who hasn't had cause to bar someone. But Roger left a suicide note, explaining everything. I verified his signature. It was definitely Roger's."

"What makes you certain the note was genuine?"

"I knew Roger. In the note, he referred to Tobias as Tobes, and he was the only person who did that. I hated the kids' names being shortened, especially Tobias. I'd chosen that name as a tribute to my grandfather, who was Greek. It's a proud, noble name. I knew people might shorten it to Toby, but not Tobes. Roger did, even though he knew it infuriated me, as did each swirly *r* in his spidery signature. He always signed his name that way. Thought it was artistic."

Cheryl sipped tea. With a tinge of envy, Jaz noted the elegance Cheryl brought to the routine task of raising cup and saucer to her lips. Little pinkie standing to attention, as though she'd attended finishing school. When she put the cup down, fire burned in Cheryl's eyes and her shoulders trembled.

Jaz looked concerned. "What's the matter?"

Cheryl spat out words. "It's Jennifer's birthday this Thursday. She'll be eight years old. Roger adored her. He asked me what she'd like for a present, and I told him she loved lions, tigers, and monkeys. I'd been reading *The Jungle Book* to her, and she was fascinated and frightened at the same time. Frightened in a good way, like kids often are at that age. She said she wanted to see a real Shere Khan, so I suggested Roger take her to Woburn Safari Park for her birthday. He wasn't intending to tell her. It was a surprise. How could he do this and disappoint her?"

Trish had been quiet, taking notes, observing Cheryl's demeanour. Struggling to determine how a seemingly serene lady ended up skivvying to help run a pub in Lexford. She sensed the conversation needed a switch of direction. "Cheryl, what was the Roger you fell in love with really like?"

Cheryl composed herself, hands making fists so her knuckles turned white. "Not a saint. He loved his cricket, a bet, and a pint. The Mansell family's short fuse had seen him get into a few fights in his youth. Apparently, he threw a parking cone through one of the department store windows on the High Street, but it was typical teenage stuff. He was ashamed of that. Too much drink and youthful testosterone.

"I never saw that side of him. Yes, he could be sharp and occasionally swear at customers who were out of order, but he could also quote Shakespeare as a party trick. Whenever anything went wrong, something simple like changing a beer barrel, he'd quote from Macbeth or Julius Caesar as he marched off. He did a fine Mark Antony, 'Cry havoc! And let slip the dogs of war.' Or when one of the kids woke up at night after a scary dream and he went to them. I would hear him quoting Henry the Fourth in a soothing voice. I can still remember the first few lines."

Cheryl paused, recollecting precious thoughts and happier times. She glanced up at the stone-faced Henry VIII, then slid into a rendition from one of his predecessors. She didn't ham it up. Too classy for ham, thought Jaz. Instead, the precise amount of theatrical tone to suit the occasion.

When she finished, her bottom lip trembled, a frown clouding her delicate features. For the first time, Jaz and Trish detected depth of emotion. They thought Cheryl was about to cry. She didn't.

"Wow!" said Trish.

Shakespeare was the last person Trish imagined appearing in her notes that morning, but piece by detailed piece, investigations drew back the curtain on Roger Mansell. Though a flawed husband, a rounded, intriguing personality emerged.

Cheryl went on. "He knew scores of sayings. When I left college, I trained as an actress for a year and studied drama. I appreciated his little performances. He could pull one out for every occasion. That was Roger. Quite a thespian. A hard worker, too, but also a bit of a dreamer. He was sure one day he'd hit the big time. One day, he'd make enough money to pack in the pub and that would solve all our problems and we would all live happily ever after. Or so he thought."

"How would he do that?" Trish said.

"Don't know. Winning the National Lottery maybe. He played every week, never missed, but over the last few months, he'd been certain something good was going to happen. 'Just wait and see. We'll have all the time and money we need,' he kept saying. Well, I'm still waiting."

Draining her latte, Jaz caught sight of a man and woman dressed in white aprons and chef hats, wearing sunny smiles and carrying trays. She presumed they were students earning holiday cash by handing out free samples from The Fudge Kitchen nearby. Some passers-by regarded them suspiciously. Not Trish. She grabbed a couple of creamy chunks, offering one to Cheryl and Jaz. Both declined. Trish shrugged, popping one into her mouth.

"I'm sorry, Cheryl. It does look as if the letter we received was from a sick prankster and I'm sure you've told the police everything you've told us," Jaz said.

Cheryl nodded. "The police asked me many questions. Wanted to know where I was on the night he died."

Jaz fashioned one of her most comforting expressions. "They have to do that, Cheryl. They always question the nearest and dearest when there's an unexplained death. It's routine. But not everything can be explained. People who take their life do things out of character. They're not themselves. By definition, they're not acting rationally. Some regulars at the pub said Roger seemed preoccupied and down. Depressed even. Maybe he was one type of person in the pub, then tried to hide it from you and the kids. I must admit, would be interesting to see the note he left."

Cheryl picked up a red leather handbag from underneath her feet and rummaged inside. She pulled out a mobile phone. Shielding the screen from the sun's glare, she scrolled down, turning the image towards Jaz. There it was. A letter printed on official notepaper, The Anchor logo, in the top right-hand corner.

Jaz's eyes flicked to the signature at the bottom. Christian name only, handwritten, bold and expressive, distinctive swirls in blue biro. Heat surged through her veins. *Here lay evidence that held the key to Roger Mansell's death.* The suicide note. Knowing the police were fastidious in preventing such evidence reaching the public domain, until they'd completed investigations and handed the matter to the coroner, Jaz never considered being able to cast eyes over the note. Yet there it was, in its entirety, lit up on Cheryl's phone screen.

"How did you come across the note?" said Jaz.

Cheryl looked puzzled.

"I mean, the police usually keep such evidence under lock and key."

Cheryl explained a police family liaison officer visited her in Cambridge on the afternoon the three schoolboys discovered her husband's body, and drove her to Lexford. "I was in shock. The police told me immediately they were pretty sure it was Roger, and I felt numb. I phoned Mum, and she came over to look after the children. I sat in the back seat of the police car on the way to Lexford, watching the fields go by, like it was happening to someone else.

"We went to the mortuary first, and I identified Roger's body. He looked peaceful, as if in a deep sleep. Hardly a scratch on his face, although with his beard it was difficult to tell. His long hair was tied back, and he looked neat and groomed. Kind of distinguished, like a well-to-do character from a Dickens novel. I don't remember feeling sad or anything. I was numb."

"Who showed you the note?" said Jaz.

Cheryl paused for a moment, as if straining to piece together the chronology of events. Only five days had passed, but so much had happened. A pendulum of emotions. One moment she described her mind as an empty void, the next as being inhabited by a flock of migrating starlings, tweeting and twittering all manner of chaotic thoughts.

"That's right. I remember. The police took me to Lexford police station, and I went into one of those interview rooms and the liaison officer brought me a cup of coffee. Minutes later, she returned with a folder and took out one of those see-through wallets. The note was inside. She said I couldn't take it out of the wallet but asked if I could verify Roger's signature."

"How did you get it on your phone?" Trish asked.

"She said she'd give me a minute to read the note and then someone knocked on the door and asked to have a word with her. She was only out of the room for a few seconds, but I whipped out my phone and took the picture. They were Roger's last words to me. I didn't think there was any harm. After all, it's my letter, isn't it?"

Jaz nodded. "Of course it is. Do you mind if we read it?"

Cheryl handed over her phone. Jaz didn't consider it appropriate to read the note out loud, even in a whisper, so she looked at Trish, putting forefinger and thumb together in a scribbling action. Trish accepted the cue, peering over her shoulder with pen poised to make a copy.

The note was short and easy to read, mainly because it had been composed on a computer and then printed, apart from the handwritten signature. Turning the phone to landscape mode, Jaz pinched out the image with her fingers. As she read, she couldn't help wondering whether these were the words of Roger or the words of his killer.

I don't want to lie anymore and I write this with a heavy heart, not because of what I am about to do, but what I've become.

I can't go on. I've done many bad things. I'm not a good husband, not a good father, and I don't have any real friends. I'm not even a good landlord. All I have is worry and stress. I can't run this pub anymore. I just can't.

I want to say sorry to many people, especially my beautiful children, Jennifer and Tobes. And my wife Cheryl. What I want to say is, I owe all the happiness of my life to you. You have been entirely patient with me and incredibly good. I want to say that—everybody knows it. If anybody could have saved me, it would have been you. I can't go on spoiling your life any longer.

I know everybody will be okay and continue without me. I can't live like this anymore.

Goodbye.

Roger

Jaz looked at Cheryl, her natural empathy for a moment overwhelming her suspicion. She'd convinced herself the body in the river wasn't a suicide victim, but now was uncertain. The words were simple, yet wonderful. They seemed honest. Heartfelt. She reached across to clasp one of Cheryl's hands, squeezing tight. "Oh, Cheryl. The words are beautiful."

Cheryl looked away, staring vacantly at a crowd of sightseers milling around the porter's lodge, attempting to gain entry to King's College. When she composed herself, in a tone of excruciating melancholy, she said, "Yeah, the words are lovely, and I know people don't die from suicide. They die from sadness. Even so, in his darkest hour, Roger couldn't bring himself to call his son by his proper name."

Jaz squeezed Cheryl's hand again.

"*Tobes.*" Cheryl muttered the name with unbearable sorrow. "Like a weed in that beautiful garden of words."

13

Jaz and Trish navigated the same picturesque route back to Lexford. The windy one with its bumpy road, so uneven that sections were like turbulence Trish experienced on a recent trip to Ibiza. She spent too long describing the ups and downs of that journey while Jaz revealed her last holiday was to the Welsh village with the famously long, unpronounceable name.

"Llanfairpwllgwyngyllgogerychwyrndrobwilliantysil iogogogoch, you mean," said Trish, syllables tripping off her tongue as if she'd spoken Welsh all her life. She was full of surprises.

Jaz shrieked. "God, that's brilliant. You even sound Welsh. How do you know that?"

"I remember Bill talking about it once on the way to hospital. Think the name's shortened to Llanfairpwll or Llanfair PG to set it apart from other places called Llanfair. The way Bill said it was hilarious, but I never know when he's joking."

"If his lips are moving, he probably is. Why did he mention that village?"

"He said he and Jean were on a driving holiday to North Wales and they stopped off at Llanfair PG for a coffee. He asked the waitress to speak slowly and say where they were."

"What did she say?"

"Burrh Gurrgh Kiing."

Jaz chuckled, the warmth of Bill's humour swaddling her in a comforting glow. "I'm pretty sure that was a joke, Trish."

"Probably, but you can never be sure with Bill."

Jaz drove carefully. She had no intention of speeding again and returned to mulling over the meeting with Cheryl. She didn't know what to think. Cheryl seemed intelligent, rational, and appeared convinced about the authenticity of the suicide note, but anyone could forge a signature, especially one with distinctive swirls. Was the shortening of Tobias's name sufficient evidence of the note's legitimacy? Jaz thought not. Until she reached 30, her parents had called her Jasmine unfailingly, but as the years wore on, and everyone else called her Jaz, occasionally they conformed to the norm, using the shortened version too. Jaz wondered if the same was true for Trish, who she assumed had been christened Patricia. The County Radio news jingle trilled in the background, interrupting the thought. Habit prompted Jaz to reach for the volume button to soak in the headlines.

One presenter and a newsreader, who sounded around 15 but was probably 10 years older, had one of those obligatory, meaningless local radio chats. This one, about the endless heatwave.

"It ain't half hot again, Meghan. Any tips for getting to sleep at night?"

"Tell me about it, Nick. Every night, I'm running my wrists under cold water before going to bed."

"Does it work?"

"No, but I've never had cleaner hands."

They laughed before the newsreader switched to serious mode, assuming a perfectly modulated accent. "Police have ruled out foul play in the case of Roger Mansell, the Lexford landlord whose body was found in the River Lex last week."

Trish detected a measure of disappointment on Jaz's face. They listened to the rest of the report, which revealed that following a post-mortem, police believed no one else was involved. Fingerprints and DNA on the shotgun retrieved from the river proved inconclusive.

"That's that then," said Trish.

Jaz shrugged. "Suppose so."

When they arrived at Trish's house, Jaz asked Trish for her notebook.

"Why?"

"I want another look at that suicide note."

Jaz flicked through the pages to where Trish had copied the note in neat black biro. She took a picture, then handed the book back. "Thanks, Trish."

"What on Earth do you need the suicide note on your phone for? You can't print it."

"I know. I don't know. Just want to … I don't know, maybe this isn't the end of the story."

Trish shook her head in resignation. "I know now why Dan calls you a tenacious terrier."

"Does he?"

Jaz rewound to the conversation in the churchyard with Dan the day before when he'd likened her to the Jack Russell he owned when he was a boy. A chance but intimate revelation, she thought. The fact Trish already knew annoyed her. She knew that was trivial, and she was being silly. Even so, the annoyance persisted. Not that she let it show.

"Okay, Trish, thanks for coming. I'll call you."

Trish swung her legs out of the car, grabbed her handbag and waved before pushing open the iron swing gate leading to her path. Jaz waved back, sensing Trish freeze. Her handbag dropped to the ground, and she staggered, spreading her arms to steady herself. Something had caught Trish's attention at the doorway, shaded by a wooden arch bedecked with striking purple clematis.

Jaz strained to see. In the shadow, a young, dark-haired woman wearing black, wraparound sunglasses. Jaz had seen her once before, clinging to Trish's ex. Behind the shades, Lynn, Trish's runaway daughter.

Jaz covered the brake of her car and considered stopping to offer Trish support. Her natural empathy yearned to take a front-row seat. To hear the real story, understand the rift between mother and daughter, offer help. Jaz decided against it. *She'd only be interfering, and that could make things worse.* She pulled away, storing a reminder to ring Trish that evening.

14

With her usual jaunty stride and natural optimism, Jaz wandered into the office. She loved being a cog in the newspaper world, particularly when stories were breaking. Still marvelled at the buzz a big story generated, how it took on a life of its own. Building in colour and detail, snippets spearing in from all directions. The skilled editorial team weaving together facts until the finished product was ready to read and enjoy on what had been a sterile piece of paper or a clinical computer screen.

She treasured the newspaper containing her first byline. Not much of a story. An old lady's dog had gone missing and when everyone presumed it dead or dognapped, it turned up on the doorstep six weeks later. Barking, skinny, but otherwise no worse for wear.

Jaz interviewed the old lady, took photographs, and the story appeared under the headline, 'Mystery of the Rover's Return' even though the dog was called Rex, thus complying with the old newspaper maxim. *Never let the story spoil a good headline.* The paper's email account almost crashed the next day under the weight of goodwill messages for Rex and his owner. Ever since, Jaz had appreciated the power of the written word to spawn a multitude of varied emotions. Anger. Joy. Sadness. Thoughtfulness.

One of her previous jobs at the Foreign Office, supplying British nationals with travel advice to overcome difficulties occurred overseas, was a source of immense enjoyment. She'd travelled to Malaysia, Bangladesh, the Philippines, and might have remained a civil servant for life if her father hadn't developed an aggressive form of dementia needing daily care. Jaz, being Jaz, offered to help her mother, taking a part-time job closer to home. She delighted in being useful.

Nothing compared with the satisfaction she now experienced at the *Journal*, even if the job officially only amounted to three paid days each week. "I'd do it for nothing," she told Dan after sinking a couple of glasses of wine one night.

"I may hold you to that one day."

Today, Jaz detected a strange atmosphere as she headed to her desk. No usual hum of conversation. Pete sat at his computer terminal, trawling through pictures taken that lunchtime of the poo-box pensioner pretending to post letters into the red box. Normally, Pete would have gift-wrapped a cheery smile for Jaz, accompanied by an awkward quip. Pete lacked experience with women, although Dan reckoned he had a crush on Jaz. This time, Pete didn't notice her.

Jack had also fallen under Jaz's charming spell, although he too sat quietly in the corner, head in a computer screen, polishing the latest online story about the body in the river, complete with full police statement. On the features desk, Alison sat cross-legged, arms folded, her suspicious eyes and sullen expression leaving Jaz in no doubt something was amiss.

As Jaz slid into her chair, she glimpsed Dan in his glass-panelled office in earnest conversation with Thomas Henry. She couldn't hear the words, but the body language—arms flailing, fingers pointing—appeared more confrontational than convivial.

She caught the eye of Angela Frayne sitting at the desk opposite. "What's going on?"

"I thought *you'd* know."

"Why?"

"Pillow talk and all that. You sleep with Dan, don't you?"

Jaz's cheeks burned. She thought Angela had spat out the question with unnecessary aggression. Everyone knew she and Dan were an item. Hell, she'd been flashing her engagement ring around long enough. *Why was Angela being so mean?*

"Pardon?"

"You must know about the redundancies. Don't suppose they'll affect you."

"What are you talking about? I only knew they were a possibility. Honest to God, I don't know what's going on."

Jaz didn't mention the *Journal's* firing squad blowing Pete, Jack, and Alison's brains out in Dan's dream, although any further spiky comments from Angela could tempt her.

"Oh, yeah," said Angela, her tone disbelieving. "Mr Henry called us together on the editorial floor and spelled it out. Two of us are for the chop right away. Maybe more later, and he's asking for volunteers. As if there are lots of jobs for reporters and sub-editors in Lexford. All everyone's done here is work hard for this firm for not much in return, and now we're being shafted."

Dan's office door opened and Thomas Henry marched down the office towards the rear stairs, expression stern, back ramrod straight. Much the same as on the Sandhurst parade ground in days past.

"Privileged prick," Angela muttered, still seething at the news and spoiling to strike out at someone.

Thomas's gait momentarily faltered, but his countenance betrayed no sign that he'd heard. Anyway, he'd been called worse.

Jaz summoned all her Foreign Office diplomatic training and chewed her tongue. She wanted to inform Angela that Thomas Henry was one of the good guys. He'd offered a challenging job and a change of career when Dan needed it most. Championed Dan's hard news agenda when the rest of the local newspaper world churned out diary items and space fillers in a battle to cut costs. Salvaged the print edition even though it haemorrhaged money at an alarming rate. He'd even underwritten staff expenses with his own personal cash. Damn it. Thomas wasn't the bad guy. More a knight in shining armour, whose sword was less mighty right now than the pens of faceless bean counters.

"The pen is mightier than the sword. Who wrote that?" Jaz muttered. "Come on. *Think.* That's it. Edward Bulwer-Lytton's Richelieu."

In her final exam at Durham, metonymy—the name of one thing used for another—presented itself. In *Richelieu*, Bulwer-Lytton used *pen* for the written word, *sword* for military force. Try telling that to someone like Angela with a mortgage, two children and their job on the line.

Jaz kept quiet.

15

"Oh, Mum, I'm sorry. I wouldn't blame you if you never talked to me again as long as you live. What I did was unforgivable. Thoughtless. Mindless. Selfish, too. Damned selfish."

Trish didn't contradict.

Tears streamed down Lynn's cheeks, drops dripping off the end of her nose. Her shoulders shook and staccato whimpers caught in her throat as she tried to speak. Panda's eyes formed. "Can you ever forgive me? Please say yes."

Trish didn't speak. She'd recovered from the initial shock of finding her errant daughter on the doorstep. First instinct had been to slap her face. Oh, how she'd rehearsed that moment. More times than she cared to admit. Call her a selfish bitch, resort to violence for the first time in their mother/daughter relationship. That's what she'd thought she'd do. Instead, she surprised herself by brushing roughly past Lynn, unlocking the door and holding it open. Curt nod, stony expression, eye roll, then eventually motioning her daughter to enter.

Trish's mind fought with a tangle of thoughts. She needed a cup of tea. Craved something stronger, but it was a while since she'd touched alcohol. Not good for the brain. She switched on the kettle and busied herself making two teas, black for herself, the other with milk. On the fridge door, she noted a treasure that had hidden in plain sight for years. A fridge magnet holding a picture of her and four-year-old Lynn tending flowers in the garden.

There was a time that joy filled Trish's heart whenever she glimpsed that picture. No longer. Two years since Lynn ran away with Trish's ex-partner. Two years in which Trish had undergone chemotherapy and radiotherapy for a brain tumour, left her job in an insurance call centre, and climbed a mountain, ticking off a bucket-list wish with that yomp to the summit of Mount Snowdon.

In all that time, no phone call from Lynn. Not one text, nor card explaining where she was. Not a single word, even on Lynn's twenty-first birthday. Trish sat at the kitchen table. Lynn joined her, wiping her face with a paper tissue, blowing her nose, removing mascara from stinging eyes.

"You've missed a bit," said Trish.

Lynn dabbed again.

"Can I forgive you? Good question. Actually, that's a question I've been asking myself for two years and guess what? I still don't have an answer."

Trish's tone remained cold and detached. She swallowed hard, clenching her teeth, but as she gazed across the table at Lynn, she sensed cold detachment crumble. Fighting to contain emotion, Trish involuntarily hyperventilated, shallow, rapid wheezes whistling through her nose, thoughts of betrayal straining their way to the surface. Her voice rose in pitch. "You're my daughter, my only child, and I'm supposed to love you unconditionally, but when you walked off with that lump of, lump of …"

Trish was no stranger to foul language. Quite the opposite. She viewed F-words, C-words, B-words, any words causing shock and outrage, as old friends to be visited regularly and appreciated for the colour and honesty they brought to conversations. But though her mind trawled her extensive repertoire, she couldn't muster a description to do Terry justice. Her body tensed, lungs aching with pent-up rage, demanding exorcism. If she didn't release the fury, she may have collapsed there and then on her kitchen table. When the moment came, an emotional dam burst.

"Aargh!" Over and over Trish screamed until her throat was raw.

All the bitterness and hate building long before Lynn and Terry ran off together, spewed forth. In sheer frustration, Trish raised her arms, beating the surface of the plastic table so hard with both fists, the teacups had no option but to obey Newton's law of equal and opposite forces. They leapt into the air, spilling steaming liquid all over the table.

Trish burst into tears and sobbed, hands to her head. On the other side of the table, Lynn sobbed too. For what seemed an age, mother and daughter reunited in a sea of tea and tears.

Eventually, Trish looked up. She yearned to reach over to hug Lynn, the hurt still too raw. Instead, her mind revisited those years with Terry when a constant quest for control replaced his initial charm. She remembered his quick temper, the way he manipulated conversations and circumstances to seize every opportunity to belittle her. Recalled the incident on the motorway when she might've killed them both because of his incessant sniping.

If he could drive a mature, resilient Essex woman of sharp tongue and feisty personality to such lengths, then what chance did a naïve teenager have under his spell?

"Did he hit you?" Trish was back in control, her voice again steely. She'd concentrated on deep breathing, packing the emotion of the past few minutes into a mental safe and turning the key.

Lynn shook her head.

"Are you still together?"

"No."

Trish didn't reveal that she'd seen them at The Anchor pub. "Sure?"

Lynn nodded. Trish stood up. Tea had pooled on the uneven table and a meandering brown stream channelled a route to the edge of the surface. A steady drip splattered onto the ceramic floor tiles. Trish grabbed a cloth and tore off half a dozen sheets of paper towel. She soaked up the liquid, observing Lynn at the same time. Despite the thermometer on the kitchen wall, closing in on thirty degrees Celsius, Lynn shivered.

Maybe nerves or, more likely, the emotion of their meeting, thought Trish. "Are you cold?"

"Mum, I'm scared."

"Of what?"

"Terry's been acting strange. Ever since we returned to Lexford. We'd gone to Cromer at first and he worked as a taxi driver."

"Cromer? Why Cromer?"

"Terry knows a group of old school friends there. Some dropouts, others, small business owners. One ran a taxi firm. He wouldn't let me get in touch, Mum. Honestly. I wanted to call or text, just to let you know I was alive, where I was living, even though I knew you'd hate me by then, but he said it was best to make a clean break. I tried to phone you once on your mobile, but he snatched the phone out of my hand and threatened to smash it if he found me trying again. After that, he'd go through my texts and calls every day to make sure.

"He worked strange hours, and I wanted to get a job in a pub or a nail parlour, anywhere really, but he wouldn't let me. Said we'd be rich, seriously rich soon enough with all the work he was doing and I wouldn't have to. I was in the flat he'd rented for hours and hours, going out of my mind. It was boring."

Lynn dabbed her eyes again and Trish reached over to pluck a fresh tissue from a box on the kitchen worktop. She handed it across the table.

"Thanks, Mum."

"So, why come back to Lexford?"

"I don't know. Not really. About a month ago, he came home late one night and announced we were moving. I was happy and worried at the same time. Happy to get out of that depressing flat. Worried about what you'd think. You were bound to find out because some mutual friend would clock us soon enough. Lexford's not that big a place. I told him we might bump into you on the High Street, but he didn't care. Said we were going, and that was that."

Trish walked over to the worktop and flicked the kettle switch. Everything Lynn said rang true. Terry, the control freak who'd trapped her for so long, had worked the same Machiavellian trick on her daughter. Lynn hadn't betrayed her. Terry had kidnapped her. On her watch, under her roof. It wasn't obvious at the time, but it was now. *How had she let it happen? Was it her fault, after all? Had she failed her daughter?*

Trish hadn't expected to feel sympathy when Lynn returned, but now waves of pity flooded through her veins. And what goes with sympathy?

"Let's have more tea, and this time I'll try not to send it into orbit."

A smile lit up Lynn's face at Trish's sense of humour, immediately replaced by a frown.

"Mum, how are you feeling? I mean, since the treatment."

Trish spun around. "How do you know about that?"

Lynn explained that Maria, her best friend from school, stayed in contact. "She works as a nurse and spotted you in the Honeycomb cancer centre. Remember Maria? She gets where water can't. Knows everyone.

Never lets anything go. She asked around and found out you had four weeks of radiotherapy at the Barrett Bailey hospital."

Trish gave a dismissive wave. "It's fine, all sorted now, nothing more to worry about. Anyway, never mind that. When and why did you and Terry split up?"

"Yesterday. He came home in the afternoon in a filthy mood with blood on his face, but he was spitting blood too. I mean, he was furious. Not with me this time. He'd had a barney in the pub and was ready to tear someone's head off. He's always had a short fuse. We both know that, but I'd never seen him so angry. I was frightened. He went upstairs rummaging around and came downstairs with …" Lynn paused, looking up with wide eyes bruised from crying and rubbing.

For a fleeting moment, Trish saw her daughter as the little girl once more, playing with flowers in the garden. But this time, she was in danger. This time, she required comfort and security.

"With what?" said Trish.

"A gun. A handgun. I've never seen a gun in real life before. I freaked. It was black and shiny, and he held it as if he knew exactly what he was doing."

"What was he doing?"

"He didn't say, but I assumed he was on his way to put the frighteners, or worse, on whoever had bloodied his face."

"So what happened?"

"I blocked his way to the front door, told him he was being stupid. I pleaded with him not to go out, but he ordered me to get out of the way and when I wouldn't, he grabbed my arm and twisted it."

Lynn rolled up a sleeve of her cotton top and pointed to a bright, explosive bruise above her left elbow. The colour of petrol in a puddle.

"The bastard," said Trish.

"I still wouldn't move. Then he raised the gun and, honestly, I thought he was going to cave my skull in. I put my hands over my head and slumped to the floor, back to the door, half-screaming, half-crying. He laughed. I told him if he went out of that door with a gun, I wouldn't be there when he got back."

"What did he say?"

"Fuck off and good riddance."

The kettle reached the boil, whistling and bubbling, but Trish didn't hear. Again, her eyes overflowed with tears as she stumbled around the table and threw her arms around Lynn.

They hugged and cried, neither of them saying anything until Trish growled, "I'm glad you're home and hope that bastard's gun has a bullet with his name on it."

16

Dan had a knife, blood on his hands, and a decision to make. Would the bolognese recipe work better with a shot of chilli sauce?

Oh, go on. Live dangerously. Dan squirted two dollops into a frying pan, threw in an assortment of ingredients, turned up the heat, and enjoyed the satisfying sizzle while sipping punchy Rioja. Glass in one hand, spatula in the other, he jabbed playfully at the concoction. "Gordon Ramsay, eat your heart out."

Wearing a white dressing gown, Jaz walked in barefoot, drying her hair with a fluffy white towel. "Mmm. Something smells nice."

Dan pulled her close, burying his nose in her wet hair. "You're not wrong there."

A hug, a kiss. Then Jaz pointed at Dan's glass. "I'll have one of those. It's been one shitty day."

Dan poured another glass. Jaz leaned against the kitchen worktop, savouring the wine's aroma before taking a glug, then detailing the meeting with Cheryl Mansell. As one may, when certain of something but struggling to convince others, Jaz considered stressing her suspicions about the suicide note, but didn't. Instead, she paraphrased the meeting with meticulous accuracy before showing Dan the note on her phone.

With a studious expression, Dan read the note while stirring the bolognese and waited for Jaz to finish recounting the meeting.

"What did Trish think?" he said.

"Done and dusted. Case solved."

"What about you?"

"I still think something stinks."

Dan pursed his lips, head rocking forward as if in deep thought. "You can see why the police believe it's an open and shut case, Jaz. That suicide note is fairly conclusive. It's difficult to see what else can be done. I've informed Inspector Cross about the anonymous note we received, but I didn't impress him. Says it happens a lot when nutters attach themselves to cases for all sorts of reasons."

"I could root around a bit more. Take a couple of days and see what I can find out. Talk to some more of Roger's friends. One of them may have sent that note."

"Jaz, chances are you'd find out he was a good cricketer back in the day. Some people liked him as a landlord, some didn't. I'm not sure it's worth ..." Dan paused.

There was a weary edge to his tone, one stoking fire in Jaz's belly.

"Go on, say it. Not worth the Journal's time and money."

Jaw set firm, Jaz put her wineglass down, folded her arms and looked away. Dan knew that pose. It didn't happen often. Jaz wasn't a sulk, but when she dug in, he knew only a rocket would shift her. He put an arm around her shoulder. She shrugged him away.

"Jaz, it's not a good time right now."

"Okay then, I'll resign. Take redundancy. I'll be one cut. Then you'll only need to get rid of one more journalist. I'm one of the last in. Only fair, I should be one of the first to go."

Dan took a stride forward, planting his hands on her shoulders. Her hair fell forward, damp ringlets brushing against him. "Whoa! What's this all about? Where's all that come from?" His tone was tender, caring.

She looked up at him, shaking her head. "Nothing. Never mind."

"Come on, we know each other better than that. Who's upset you? Has someone said something?"

Jaz confessed she'd witnessed his confrontation with Thomas Henry in the office that afternoon, relaying the poisonous atmosphere in the newsroom, although she was careful not to mention names.

"I love my job, Dan, you know that, but many people have been there longer than me. They have kids, mortgages, bills to pay, and don't deserve to be sacked for no reason. I can always get my job back at the petrol station."

"It doesn't work like that, Jaz."

"What do you mean?"

"Think about it. You work three days a week. Or at least you get paid for three days, although you're often in the office four or five. As far as the accountants are concerned, you're part time and earn secretarial wages. That was the case when we hired you. You're as cheap as chips, Jaz. Sack you and the savings are negligible. They're looking for bigger savings. Quickly. They want, need, to get rid of some of the big earners."

Jaz raised her eyebrows. "Cheap as chips? Thanks."

"Sorry. I know it sounds harsh, but that's the way bean counters think. No emotion, no allowance for long service, no loyalty, no thought of mortgages or kids. No reflection of competence. Their calculations come down to plain numbers. Simple as that."

"What a horrible job. I'm glad we work with words and grammar."

"Yeah, so am I. Grammar's the difference between knowing your shit and knowing you're shit."

Jaz looked perplexed. "What?"

"Never mind. Think that's a joke you need to see in writing."

Jaz put her arms around Dan's waist, rested her damp head against his chest and squeezed him close.

"What I'm trying to say is you're stuck with us, Jaz."

"I'm not the only thing that's stuck."

"What do you mean?"

Jaz pointed behind Dan to the bolognese, no longer sizzling in the pan but contracting into a dried-up, congealed mound. A giant, overcooked cowpat.

"Bollocks!" Dan brushed past Jaz and grabbed the spatula. He snatched the pan off the heat, at the same time trying to stir the bolognese. It didn't budge. Stuck solid. "It's supposed to be a non-bloody-stick pan. Says so on the handle. There. Look. Even says guaranteed." He growled, pointing out the manufacturer's warranty. "Does anybody tell the truth these days? I mean, come on. I expect to walk away from a non-stick pan for ten seconds and not return to find it soldered to the food I'm cooking. Ridiculous. I've a good mind to take it back and ask for a refund."

Dan held up the pan. Jaz chuckled.

"What's so funny?" Dan threw an exasperated look.

"I was thinking what a difference an *m* makes."

"What?"

"Well, a minute ago, your bolognese was a wonderful creation. Now it's a cremation."

Dan threw back his head and gave a long, throaty laugh, then scraped the charred mess into the bin. He flung the blackened pan into the sink full of dishwater, grabbed Jaz around the waist and lifted her up. Winding her legs around his hips, she gripped him tight, and they exchanged a long, passionate kiss. After breaking the clinch, Dan put Jaz down.

"That's why I love you, Jasmine Sharkey."

"Why?"

"Because you make me laugh. You see what other people don't see. Goodness. Honour. Light in darkness. Fun in failure. Humour. Ems in creation. All that mushy stuff. And your journalist instincts are usually bang on."

Jaz's heart leapt. "What do you mean?"

"You can have another week looking into Roger Mansell's death. If nothing turns up, then do a feature on why male suicides are on the increase, complete with all those stats Inspector Cross told us about. Any more days like today and I may bump up the numbers."

Jaz jumped into Dan's arms, wrapping her legs around him once more. She kissed him full on the lips. "Thanks," she squealed, drawing back her head and fixing him with an inquisitive expression. "You're sure it's not just because I'm sleeping with the boss?"

Dan carried her off towards the bedroom. "Of course, it's not."

"Liar." She gave him a playful slap on the head as her phone rang.

"Never mind that."

Jaz wriggled from Dan's grasp. "I'd better answer."

It was Trish. Jaz disappeared into the bedroom by herself, traipsing back into the kitchen an hour later, wearing dry hair and a dazed look. She found Dan serving up his second attempt at bolognese. He handed her another glass of wine.

"You won't believe it," said Jaz.

"If it's Trish, I probably will."

"No. Even for Trish, this is pretty full on."

They sat down and Jaz chased pasta around her plate with a fork while telling the story of Lynn's unexpected return. The tearful reunion. Terry's abuse. The fight. The hand gun. The fact Lynn was now terrified of Terry, and hiding out at Maria's, her old school chum. Dan listened as he ate. When Jaz finished, he whistled through his teeth as his journalistic instincts set his heart and mind in pursuit of a potentially intriguing potboiler.

First a shotgun. Now a handgun. Two guns in one week. Lexford's sounding like Dodge City.

"I wonder if they're linked?" Dan said.

"What?"

"The guns. The one that killed Roger Mansell and the one Lynn says she saw Terry with."

Jaz's mouth opened wide in concern. "Should we tell the police?"

"Not yet. We've no proof Terry's gun is real. Sounds like Lynn was upset. She could be mistaken and I've no desire to let Inspector Cross laugh us out of his office if it turns out to be a plastic pea-shooter."

"Me neither. So what should we do now?"

"Turn off our phones."

"Why?"

Dan put an arm around Jaz's waist and pulled her close. "No more interruptions."

17

Jaz and Dan stood outside Bill's front door. They'd knocked twice and heard movement, but it was taking Bill an age to answer. When he did, it became clear why. Bill was behind a Zimmer frame and the simple act of opening the door required a four-point turn.

"Congratulations! You've won the Nobel prize. What's wrong with my bell? Only policemen knock on doors."

"Sorry, Bill. I hope you didn't think we were the police," said Dan.

"No. I know a policeman's rap when I hear it. They came to my door once, and I didn't let them in. One shouted through the door, 'We want to talk'."

"Really?"

"I asked how many there were and he said, 'two.' So I said, 'You can talk to each other, then.'"

Dan chuckled. Bill's sense of humour and flat delivery were infectious.

"We can't stop long, Bill."

"You haven't come in yet."

Bill completed his manoeuvre and shuffled down the hallway into the lounge. Dan and Jaz followed.

When Bill slumped into his armchair, Jaz handed over the crossword books. "Sorry, it's taken so long, but we've been busy."

"The dead landlord?"

Jaz nodded. "The story's caused a stir in Lexford and we've been chasing all the angles."

"How's Trish?"

"Why?"

"She didn't look herself the last time I saw her. Sort of worried. Not like her."

Jaz told him about Terry and Lynn turning up in Lexford while Dan filled in details about the fight in the pub and Lynn spying Terry with what she thought was a handgun.

"Have you told the police?"

"Not yet. We want to be sure."

"Better safe than sorry, though."

"Yes, Bill, don't worry. We're on top of it." Dan cast an anxious look at Jaz, who shrugged.

"You two get all the fun. Highlight of my day is meals on wheels."

"I thought a carer made lunch for you."

"Not now. It's cheaper to get meals on wheels. The van should be here any minute. What time is it? Can you pass my watch, Jaz? Behind me, on the sideboard."

Jaz looked. There was a silver-framed photo of Bill and Jean holding champagne flutes, laughing into the camera on the deck of a cruise liner, a biography of Morecambe and Wise and one of those snow globes children enjoy at Christmas. No sign of a watch.

"Are you sure, Bill? It's not here."

"I'm sure that's where I left it. Not worn it for a day or so. It's got a gold strap and a brown face."

"It's not here."

"Maybe I left it in the bedroom."

"Do you want me to look?"

"No, you get off. You must have lots to do. I've probably had another senior moment."

The confusion wasn't like Bill. In Jaz and Dan's experience, his mind had always been pin-sharp. But then

Jaz remembered the £10 note that wasn't where he'd thought it was a few days before. Maybe a coincidence, but two episodes of confusion so close together were worrying.

"Are you sure you're okay, Bill? You haven't been forgetting other things as well."

Bill put a forefinger to his head and lowered his eyes as if in deep thought. "I can't remember."

"Okay, you win," said Dan. "You're sharper than either of us."

"I'm not losing my marbles, not yet anyway." An exasperated edge to Bill's tone.

The doorbell rang.

"That's the way to do it." Bill cast a smug expression in Dan's direction.

"Don't worry, stay where you are. I'll get it." Dan went to the door and reappeared with Bill's meals on wheels. He read the label. "Shepherd's pie."

"I won't crack the obvious joke," said Bill.

"There's a first time for everything."

"Oh, go on, Bill. You know you want to. What is it?" said Jaz.

"I had a shepherd's pie yesterday. He wasn't happy."

Dan groaned, and Jaz shook her head. "On that note, we're definitely going," said Jaz. "Have fun with the crosswords and we'll drop in later this week."

"Great. You can tell me all about the man with the gun."

As Dan and Jaz walked down the path, a woman with a sweet smile craned her head around the doorway of the neighbour's house. "Hi, I'm Pat. How's Bill?"

"He's good, unless you mean his jokes. They're awful," said Jaz.

The woman chuckled. "Tell me about it."

When Dan and Jaz reached the car, they voiced their concerns about Bill's apparent confusion. Dan argued that most men approaching 80 had senior lapses. The *Journal's* letters page was full of such stories. The dog-poo pensioner of recent times. The husband who wrote in asking why he often found furniture polish in his fridge. Or Dan's favourite story. The man who turned his car around halfway to the supermarket because he thought he'd forgotten his car keys.

Jaz smiled, but then her tone became more serious. "I'm worried about Bill."

"I'm sure he's fine."

"You're right. I think he's fine, too. But if his memory isn't failing, then there's another possibility."

"Think I know where you're going with this."

"Dan, we've done enough stories on vulnerable pensioners. When things to go missing, there's usually a good, or should I say, bad, explanation."

"Well, I don't think it's the meals-on-wheels man. He was on his way back to his van when I opened the door. Looks like he drops lunch off on the doorstep, rings the bell and goes. Probably the only way he can get around to everyone in time."

"That leaves the carers."

"It's difficult. We can't start accusing people he relies on. By the sound of it, he has two carers a day now, not always the same ones. There could be ten or more people traipsing through his house every week. We can't accuse them all. And, anyway, his watch may turn up safe and sound."

"His money didn't. That's still a mystery, and he's so trusting, Dan. Telling his jokes, making people laugh."

"Sounds like you've made your mind up."

"If it looks like a duck ..."

"Don't start that again. I'm on board. I have an idea."

18

While waiting at traffic lights, a two-man chat in the back seat of the ambulance car spiked Dan's attention.

"Did you read about the guy in the river, Neil? Nasty business. Half his chest blown away, I heard."

"I used to drink in The Anchor, John. Didn't know the landlord, but things must have been bad to top himself like that."

It was Dan's day to transport cancer patients to the Barrett Bailey hospital. Two years ago, he'd become a full-time driver for the Honeycomb Voluntary Car Service while taking a sabbatical from reporting duties on the *Daily News*. That's how he'd met Jaz and Trish. He'd bonded with the service so well that when he landed the editor's job at the *Journal,* he persuaded Thomas Henry to let him continue driving every Tuesday.

"Good for the soul, even better for contacts," Dan told Thomas.

That morning, after dropping Jaz at work, Dan walked to the hospital to pick up an ambulance car. He collected three patients—Neil and John in the back, Rachel in the front. She had a kind smile and jolly expression, but avoided conversation. Difficult to talk with throat cancer.

The lights turned green. Dan gunned the accelerator. As the car crossed the bridge, they all peered over the low brick wall into the swirling, murky water, forming a skim of scum and foam around the bridge supports.

"Not nice" said Neil.

"No place to end it all," said John.

"No," agreed Dan, omitting to reveal Roger Mansell's final floating place was under a bridge at least a mile upstream.

Neil pointed to a distant figure on the towpath riding a bicycle with distinctive sit-up-and-beg handlebars. "Isn't that Charlie Brook? You know old Charlie, don't you?" He nudged John, but by the time John looked up, Dan had reached the far end of the bridge and accelerated behind one of the endless hedgerows defining the Lexfordshire countryside.

"Who's Charlie?" said Dan.

Neil's tone mocked. "*Who's Charlie!* I thought everyone knew Charlie in Lexford."

"I know one man who doesn't."

Neil chuckled at Dan's sarcasm. "Charlie's a legend. Went to the same school as me, although he was a few years older. Made a million quid by the time he was thirty, trading jukeboxes and amusement arcades when they were all the rage. Back then, a million quid took some earning. By forty, he'd lost it all. Went bust overnight. House gone, boat gone, wife gone."

During his time with Honeycomb, Dan had met a cross-section of Lexford's pensioner community. Many feeble, struggling with mild forms of dementia and cancer. Some were forgetful. Others remained pin-sharp. Dan decided Neil and John fell into the latter category.

"What does he do now?" Dan said.

"Lives down by the river in one of those static caravans. Has done for years, probably since he went bust. Rides up and down that towpath all day, every day, wavering from side to side as if he might go for a swim at any moment. You can't miss him. Always a couple of white carrier bags dangling from his handlebars. God knows what's in them."

"His every possession by the sound of it," said Dan.

John elbowed Neil in the ribs, then with a little chuckle said, "Funny, he didn't hear the shot."

Dan stiffened in the driving seat. His mind whirred, busily computing the topography of the riverbank. "Tell me, Neil. Where does Charlie live?"

"That's a story in itself."

Dan, anticipating another convoluted answer, steered Neil in an informative direction. "Just the spot will do, Neil. Is it upstream from the bridge we crossed?"

"Yep."

"How far?"

"Past the next bridge, you know, the small wooden one, then a short walk from there."

Dan calculated Charlie's home could be within a few hundred yards from the mooring of *The Artful Roger*. He made a mental note to tell Jaz. Charlie may have heard something. Any gun discharge would almost certainly be in earshot of the caravan. Unfortunately for Dan, Neil was also still in earshot.

"His caravan's on a ridge surrounded by willow trees on a bend in the river. It's a lovely spot. Only one problem, he's let his place go to rack and ruin. Broken fences, dirty van, chickens running loose everywhere. There are some big properties to the back of him and the neighbours are complaining. Forty years ago, he might have been living in one of his neighbours' properties. I'm sure he wouldn't have liked to put up with a run-down gypsy site at the bottom of his garden. Don't see why the local council stands for it ..."

What seemed like an hour, but was only 10 minutes later, Dan turned into the Barrett Bailey entrance. Neil's monotone drone of local council planning regulations on riverside properties and, bizarrely, the merits of combination boilers, had the car's occupants traumatised. Neil and John shuffled to their treatment rooms, while Dan's firm arm helped an unsteady Rachel to oncology reception. When she'd settled in the waiting area, he made his way to the drivers' lodge via the coffee shop.

In a quiet corner, Dan savoured a full fat latte, until Martin, another Honeycomb driver, sauntered over. Martin usually worked Mondays, and the pair hadn't seen each other for months. Dan jumped up to shake hands.

"Good to see you, Martin. I was hoping to run something past you."

"Sounds ominous."

"Just your opinion as a former copper, that's all."

Martin's laugh trailed off into a nervous titter. "Don't tell me you're mixed up with an international crime syndicate again."

Dan lifted his coffee cup as if raising a toast. "Good one, Martin, but as far as I know, Jimmy Collins and his henchmen are in Belmarsh prison and won't be getting out anytime soon."

Dan recalled two years ago when he'd stumbled upon the Lexford arm of a crime syndicate after witnessing shady activity and a savage beating at a local car wash. Curiosity led him to investigate. The car wash acted as a cover for a cannabis farm and people-trafficking hub. While nosing around the site, one of the gang bosses captured him. If Jaz and Trish hadn't alerted police, Dan may now be keeping shoals of fish company at the bottom of the River Lex. Instead, the publicity surrounding the case landed him a top job at the *Lexford Journal* and cemented his relationship with Jaz. Collins and his crew got between 10 and 15 years and ever since, Lexford folk regarded Dan as something of a local celebrity.

"No, Martin. I was wondering how much credence the police might give to a case with a dead body and a suicide note."

"You mean the landlord in the river?" The story was still the talk of Lexford.

"Yes."

"Well, the police investigate every case with meticulous intensity."

Dan raised his eyebrows. "I'm not looking for the party line, Martin. You sound like a public relations executive. Next, you'll be telling me all those speed traps are for our own good and not to make money."

"Look, Dan, I haven't been a copper for five years. They do their best, honest, they do, but even when I was coming up to retirement, police forces were under pressure. Cuts here, cuts there. No spare capacity. The problem is the public want to see cops on the beat. Lots of them. People want a police presence. It makes them feel safe, but they don't want to pay for it. Five years ago, we had a local referendum asking the people of Lexfordshire whether they'd pay a fifteen per cent rather than two per cent levy on their council tax to fund fifty extra police officers. Do you remember the result?"

Dan shook his head. He had a good excuse. At the time, he worked in Syria, where people tended not to have a vote on paying for policing. Or a vote on anything.

"Ninety-two per cent said no, Dan. Ninety-two per cent said two per cent was all they'd pay."

"What are you saying?"

"The police have had to cut their cloth. They don't turn out for every theft. Won't send a car to pick up every shoplifter. They don't even attend all burglaries. If no one's been hurt and not much taken, then your chances of seeing a police officer anytime soon are probably the square root of diddly squat."

"But if someone has died?"

"Investigated with meticulous care. As long as it's suspicious."

"And if there's a suicide note?"

"Come on, Dan. They're not looking for work. If there's a note and everything fits, they'll close things down pretty fast. That makes sense, doesn't it?"

Dan drained his coffee and lobbed the cup into the recycling bin. "Thanks, Martin. Pretty much what I thought."

19

Treatment complete, Dan and his passengers wound down country lanes, taking the scenic route back to Lexford.

Rachel sat up front again, silent, sipping juice through a straw. In the back, Neil and John discussed wartime heroes. Extolling the virtues of the Second World War's Spitfire crews, when the average life expectancy of an RAF pilot stretched to a mere four weeks, was Neil's passion.

"Did you know, John, when the Battle of Britain started in nineteen forty, the Luftwaffe had two thousand five hundred planes ready for action and the British just six hundred and sixty?"

John shook his head. Dan contemplated tuning into the radio's classical music channel.

Neil continued. "Yeah, those airmen were real heroes. Most of them were boys, barely out of their teens. Younger than my grandkids. Doesn't bear thinking about."

"Douglas Bader was one of those pilots, wasn't he?" said Dan.

"Spot on. Dogsbody, they called him. But he wasn't a kid in the Battle of Britain. Lost his legs ten years earlier in a crash, while performing acrobatics. Silly sod. Still, he signed up with two artificial legs when war broke out, destroying a pile of enemy aircraft before being shot down and ending up a prisoner of war in Colditz."

"You know your stuff, Neil."

"Well, you have to have an interest." Neil chuckled, deep and throaty.

"What's so funny?" asked Dan.

"I remember the story about Bader addressing the pupils at a posh girls' school after the war." Proud of his knowledge and expecting to lure an appreciative audience, Neil paused.

"Go on, you can't leave it there," said Dan.

"No, no, there are ladies present."

Dan glanced across at Rachel, whose eyes had shut, the draining effects of daily radiotherapy having kicked in. He motioned to Neil. "Think you can risk it."

Neil needed no further push. "There were about four hundred girls in the hall and Bader was relating the tale of one of his aerial dogfights." Neil cleared his throat to assume the posh vowels of an officer. "So there were two of the fuckers behind me, three fuckers to my right and another fucker on the left."

In his natural voice, Neil went on. "The headmistress went pale and interrupted in a stern tone. 'Ladies. I think it's important for you to know that the Fokker was a German aircraft.'"

Neil paused, intent on milking the punchline, again assuming Bader's voice. "That's as may be, madam, but these fuckers were flying Messerschmitts."

Dan laughed, John guffawed, even Rachel opened her eyes and smiled.

"Good one. I'll have to remember to tell, what the f—"

Dan restrained himself from completing the expletive, but his body tensed, crushing the steering wheel in his hands as a high-powered red car with a growling engine screamed past. It narrowly avoided a vehicle travelling in the opposite direction, churning up a dust cloud as it fishtailed back onto its own side of the road. Dan was doing 50mph. He calculated the red car's speed on the topside of 90. Seconds later, a black 4x4 with tinted windows overtook in similar fashion.

"Bloody idiots," shouted Neil.

"Boy racers," said John.

Rachel's squeaky, hoarse voice uttered the first complete sentence she'd said that morning. "Lock 'em up in Colditz, that's what I say."

Dan settled back, studying the two cars tearing up a twisted hill in the distance, weaving in and out of traffic. He cursed himself for failing to note registration plates, but the incident had passed in a blur. A few miles on, at a spot where sprawling fields merged with the outer reaches of Lexford town, Dan turned a corner and hit the brakes. A queue of vehicles. He eased the car to a halt, craning his neck out of the window to determine the cause of the hold-up.

This time, he couldn't restrain the expletive. "Shit! Sorry, Rachel."

Up ahead sat the wreckage of a red car, crumpled bonnet pointing to the sky. Radiator steaming, shattered lights, engine hissing. Metal casing hugged a telegraph pole leaning at a crazy angle, severed phone lines swinging in the breeze. Several residents from a nearby hamlet milled around. Two men tugged at the mangled passenger door. Stuck fast. A woman shouted into a mobile phone, face contorted in a concerned grimace. Dan presumed she was alerting the emergency services.

Pulling the ambulance car into the verge, Dan killed the engine, acting on instinct. "Stay put guys. I'm off to see if I can help."

Without waiting for a reply, Dan jogged up the road. By the time he reached the red car, the two helpers were frantic in their efforts to open the door. The reason was clear. Petrol fumes filled the air. Dan spotted a blue and yellow puddle forming on the road. Not yet noon, and another cloudless day in Lexford's heatwave had pushed the temperature to 34 degrees Celsius. Dangerous heat. The front airbag had deployed, and Dan saw a motionless man slumped in the driver's seat.

Panic rising, one helper screeched, "The door won't budge!"

The car lay wedged tight, propped against the telegraph pole with the driver's side halfway across a ditch. No way to reach the driver from that side. Dan looked around for a brick or branch. Anything to smash the window. No luck. Turning, he sprinted to the nearest queuing car and yanked open the driver's door.

"Do you have a wrench in the boot?"

"Think so," said the driver, a man in his sixties. His languid demeanour suggested he didn't appreciate the desperate predicament.

"Let's have it then. Now!" ordered Dan.

The driver hit the boot release. Dan grabbed the wrench, at the same time clutching an old gardening jacket stuffed in a corner of the boot, and raced back to the wrecked car.

"Get out of the way!" The two helpers staggered back, releasing their grip on the door handle.

Using his left hand to protect his eyes, Dan swung the wrench as if wielding an axe. The window shattered. A shard clinging to the side gashed his wrist, but he ignored the blood trickling down his palm. Clearing a few remaining shards from the edges, he placed the gardening coat over the door rim. The stench of fumes stung Dan's nostrils and eyes, but he wriggled his torso inside the car, stomach resting on the gardening coat. He reached over to release the seat belt. It clicked out first time. *Thank God.*

The stocky, short driver was unconscious. Judging from purple bruising and grotesque, misshapen forehead, he appeared to be seriously injured, probably after striking the side strut or window on impact. Blood stained his face and beard. Dan realised the danger of moving such victims, the risk of paralysis commonplace in car accidents, but being burned alive was the likely alternative. *Not much of a choice.* He stretched across to grab the man's shoulders, his stomach and arm muscles straining, wrist dripping blood. Using all his power, Dan disengaged the driver from the air bag. The man's body lolled sideways and Dan grasped him under the armpits, wrestling him to the passenger side.

Men half Dan's 50 years would have struggled with his next manoeuvre as he took the man's weight on his forearms, easing him upwards until his head poked half-out of the window. Lungs bursting, sweat streaming down his back, lactic acid degraded Dan's muscles. Coughing and choking on petrol fumes, he heard sirens in the distance and felt two helpers reach past him to pull the driver clear of the car.

Staggering back, blood soaking his hands, Dan fell to the floor, sucking in oxygen. Strong arms linked on either side and frogmarched him across the road. All the while, he anticipated the heat and blast from the expected explosion. It never came. Dan slumped on the opposite grass verge, allowing his heart rate to subside, his breathing to ease. He tugged a wedge of tissues from his pocket and wrapped them around his bloodied wrist. Two fire engines pulled up, approaching ambulance and police sirens wailing in the distance.

Dan the reporter kicked in. Three bystanders attended to the car driver. One, an off-duty nurse, pumped his chest with a violent rhythm, regularly locking mouths to administer lifesaving breaths. Dan stood and walked to the casualty scene. Someone had placed the driver's wallet, keys, and mobile phone in a pile on the grass verge. He picked up the wallet, rifling through three or four compartments, finding a handful of credit and debit cards, plus a driving licence, all assigned to Mr George Campbell.

Three firemen jumped from an engine, dousing the red car in foam to coat the escaping fuel. Paramedics relieved the off-duty nurse and police swarmed around, organising a one-way system to clear the traffic.

Dan replaced the wallet and jogged back to the ambulance car, stopping several times to photograph the scene from different angles on his mobile phone. When he arrived at the vehicle, Rachel snoozed in the front seat.

Neil was the first to speak. "What's going on? Blood all over your shirt. You look awful and stink to high heaven."

"Thanks, Neil. Love you too."

"Smells like petrol. Better not light a match in here. We'll go up like a Roman candle."

"I've no intention of lighting, ah, never mind," said Dan wearily.

He reached inside the glove box for a rag to wrap around his wrist, explained the bare bones of the crash scene to his passengers, and punched Pete Rainford's number on his phone. For the next few minutes, he relayed the details to Pete, omitting mention of his own involvement.

"Call the cops and hospital in an hour, Pete. They'll be able to update you by then. The story should make a good newsy lead for the online edition."

Dan turned to see Neil and John holding their noses. He wound the windows down. "Right, let's get you all home."

It took an hour to drop off all three patients following the police's protracted detour through Lexford's outskirts. After helping Rachel to her front door, Dan's phone rang.

"Dan, you won't believe this," Jaz said.

"What?"

"George Campbell, the guy in the crash."

"Yes."

"We've just researched him for Pete's story and no one calls him George Campbell."

"What do they call him?"

"Crime."

20

"Nice of you to come. Would you like a cup of tea?"

"No," Inspector Cross grunted.

Dan waved Cross into his office and made the introductions. "I think you know Jaz."

The inspector nodded, mouthing 'the duck lady.' Jaz glowered.

"And Pete," Dan said.

The chief reporter stood, offering a handshake that was left hanging.

"This is Trish Parker and her daughter, Lynn."

Inspector Cross acknowledged both with a pout and a raise of bushy eyebrows. "Quite a little gathering, Mr Armitage. To what do I owe the pleasure?"

George Campbell fighting for his life in the intensive care unit at Lexford Royal Infirmary was a routine item for the *Journal*. That he was Crime from The Anchor, of goatee beard and swan tattoo fame, raised the news value a significant notch.

Until receiving Jaz's phone call, Dan perceived no need to speak to the police after assisting at the crash scene. He'd done his bit. Saved a fellow motorist. Filed a story. Ruined a shirt. Donated blood. Left without fuss to take his patients home, showered, then bandaged his wrist, all the while believing the speeding red car driver deserved everything he reaped for his recklessness. Now, connections and coincidences couldn't be ignored.

"First things first, inspector. I presume you heard about the crash outside town this lunchtime?"

Cross sneered. "It's all over your website."

Dan shrugged. "Well, we are a newspaper." He almost added, *The clue's in the title*, but decided against it. No point provoking the police. "I have to admit, I was at the scene of the crash. I saw the red car speed past me, doing close to a ton a few miles before crashing."

"Hardly surprising it came off the road then." Cross's tone was matter-of-fact. He didn't seem overly concerned.

"That's right, but when it went past me, there was another car chasing it."

"A black four by four?"

"Yes."

"Don't worry, Mr Armitage, some folk are more public spirited than you. We received several reports of an idiot in a black car on the same road. Looks like they were in a stupid race. Doing it for a dare, or more likely, a bet. Boy racers, some call them. Irresponsible bloody idiots in my book. Unfortunately, no one noted the registration."

The public spirited comment set Dan's blood simmering. He gritted his teeth and stroked his bandaged wrist. "Looked more like a chase than a race to me, and now *we* know who was in the red car, there's something else I think *you* should know."

"Go on."

"Jaz and I saw a fight between George Campbell, the driver of the red car, and another man. Sunday lunchtime in The Anchor. They were going at it, knocking seven bells out of each other. Fists flying, tables turned over, wrestling around on the floor. Pretty heavy stuff. Could have been worse if the barman and chef hadn't broken it up."

"Who was the other man?"

Dan looked across at Trish.

"That would be a low-life I used to live with." Trish spat.

"Does this low-life have a name?"

"Terry scumbag Marsh."

"A double-barrelled individual. Very posh. And for what reason would Terry scumbag Marsh and George Campbell be fighting?"

"I don't know, but Terry's got a gun." Trish blurted.

For the first time, the meeting gained Inspector Cross's undivided attention. He sat up in his chair, elbows resting on the desk. Clasping his hands as if in prayer, he stroked his chin. "How do you know? Have you seen it?"

"No, but Lynn has."

Trish turned to Lynn and flashed her eyes, encouraging her to speak up.

Lynn's voice trembled. "Well, I think it was a real gun. He'd kill me if he thought I was telling you. I've never seen a gun up close, but he was mad as cheese after the fight in the pub and stormed out of the house with it."

"Whose house?"

"Mine and his."

Inspector Cross turned to Trish. "But I thought he lived with you."

"He did, but then he lived with her and now neither of us live with him. It's complicated. I told you, he's a scumbag."

"And this fight was on Sunday?"

Dan and the others nodded in unison.

Cross's tone scolded. "And none of you thought to tell the police? So, let me recap. The editor of the local newspaper fails to report vital information in what may turn out to be a murder case, probably because he's too busy taking pictures at the crash scene for his precious newspaper, and his staff and family members fail to report a suspected firearm in the possession of a man with clear intent to use it. And you have the cheek to criticise the police." Cross fixed Dan with an icy glare.

Dan's blood raised a notch. From simmer to boil. *God, this man knows how to press every button.* The strain in Dan's voice told Jaz the fight to remain civil was touch-and-go, but he clung to his temper. "I think that's unfair. The reason I asked you here today was to tell you all we know. No one's failing to report anything. As Lynn told you, she's not sure it's a real gun, but if it is, then this Terry Marsh is a dangerous individual. Obviously."

Inspector Cross rose to his feet and pointed at Lynn. "You need to come down to the station to give a statement and the address of this Marsh chap. In the next hour."

Lynn nodded, although she looked terrified.

"By the way, does he drive a black four by four?" Cross said.

"I don't think so, but he's a taxi driver. He drives lots of cars."

Inspector Cross shuffled out of Dan's office and made his way down the corridor, muttering to himself. As Dan and the others debated the merits of the meeting, Jack Ashton knocked on the door. Dan waved him in.

"Thought you'd like to know, guys. Just heard from my contact at the hospital. George Campbell's dead."

21

The sky grumbled and heavy rain fell for the first time in forever when Jaz and Trish crossed the wooden bridge over the River Lex on their way to Charlie Brook's caravan. Dan had given Jaz directions the night before, after relating his conversation with Neil in the ambulance car. Like the terrier Dan compared her to, Jaz pounced on the information.

"He may have heard the shot. May have seen something," she said.

"Or he may have been snoring the night away after polishing off a bottle of whisky. Best not get too excited."

Jaz hardly slept after that, her mind churning through a multitude of fanciful permutations. At 8am, she rang Trish, and the pair set off an hour later for the wooden bridge where Roger Mansell's body turned up. From Neil's description, Dan reckoned Charlie's caravan must be a quarter of a mile upstream. Huddling together at the top of the arched bridge, Jaz and Trish sheltered under a small umbrella, trousers soaked to the knees after tramping through long grass in the car park.

"Trust the bloody heatwave to crack today," said Trish, rainwater dribbling from the umbrella and running down her neck. She bent over to brush down her designer jeans.

"Good job you changed out of those heels, though." Jaz peered down the riverbank in search of the caravan. No sign. Too many willow trees blocking the view.

The pair linked arms, walked down to the towpath and set off upstream, passing the sprawling gardens of five properties backed onto the river, all set in many acres protected by high fences or razor wire.

Upstream, they rounded a bend, spotting a caravan sitting on concrete blocks perched atop a mound. A shabby cabin looking tired and sorry for itself, flaking green and white paint. Fashioned in the mound, half a dozen steps gave access and decking timber provided a makeshift veranda. At ground level on one side, chickens, heads jerking and bobbing, scurried around a wire mesh run. In a small allotment on the other side, grateful beetroot and onions sucked up the downpour. Abandoning the shelter of Trish's umbrella, Jaz climbed the steps and saw a faded wooden plaque screwed to the door:

Be afraid. The good Lord and a gun protect this house.

Religious nut. Cult member. Gun fanatic. A myriad of possibilities crossed Jaz's mind, none of them healthy. Then again, she reasoned, hard core nutters rarely advertise their nuttiness. He could be an old man with an odd sense of humour. Simple as that.

Jaz knocked three times. No answer. Scanning the surroundings from her elevated vantage point about 100 yards upstream, she spied a boat tied to moorings, blue and white tape fluttering around it. The type routinely used by police to cordon off areas for forensic examination. Jaz's heart leapt. *The Artful Roger.* She pointed it out to Trish.

"You could hear a shout from where we're standing, never mind a gunshot," said Jaz.

She knocked again. Nothing. Rain lashed in on a swirling breeze and Jaz's frustration mounted. She joined Trish at the bottom of the steps, grateful for the umbrella.

"Oh, let's get out of here. This is miserable," Trish said.

"Not so fast. Let's see what's around the back. It'll only take a minute."

They skirted the allotment plot, pushed through a small, wooden swing gate and followed a short path into a fenced area resembling a breaker's yard. Strewn cans of oil and boat fixings, lawnmowers in various states of disrepair cluttering one side, and a wood-burning stove, its steel chimney leaning at a weird angle. Two bikes, one with sit-up-and-beg handlebars, lounged against the fence. Queueing along another wall, a dozen plastic dustbins holding scores of hessian sacks.

Jaz lifted dustbin lids. "Who stores this many sacks? What on Earth would you need all these for?"

"Potatoes?"

"Not from that weedy allotment, Trish. Far too small."

"Can I help you?"

The girls jumped at the menacing rasp from behind. The greeting sounded more of a threat than a question. Spinning around, Jaz dropped a lid, sending it clattering to the ground.

Before them stood a heavy-set man looking like he'd escaped a rock tribute band, long whiter than white hair tied in a ponytail. His brown leather jacket had seen better days, as had blue jeans. He held a shotgun, its barrel broken over his forearm. Jaz gauged his age to be mid-to-late seventies, perhaps older, judging by the deep furrows in his brow and limitless lines on his suntanned face.

"I'm sorry. I knocked on your door. Are you Charlie?" Jaz said.

"Who wants to know?"

Jaz explained that she and Trish were local reporters trying to tie up loose ends in the case of the body in the river.

"What loose ends? Police've been crawling around here for best part of a week. Thought they'd decided he committed suicide. Blew himself away, I heard."

"Did the police speak to you, Charlie?"

"Someone in uniform knocked on my door. Looked as if he should have been on school holidays. If it's right that you're getting old when policemen look young, then I must be pushing ninety."

Trish laughed. She thought he was. "I'm having that problem, too."

"Do you mind if we ask a few questions inside out of the rain? It won't take long," said Jaz.

Charlie grunted, turned, and motioned them to follow. He offered a cup of tea. Trish declined. Jaz accepted. Her stomach had no desire to drink after spying the curdling milk on Charlie's draining board, but reasoned there was no better way to foster trust in a relationship than the age-old custom of taking tea. Soothing. Therapeutic. Give her and Trish a chance to snoop around the cabin.

Charlie snapped the shotgun barrel shut and placed it in a metal cabinet bolted to the wall, secured by a padlock. He filled the kettle.

"Do you enjoy shooting, Charlie?" said Trish. An edgy opening question, but Trish didn't believe in softening up her interviewees.

"That depends," said Charlie, studying her with suspicious eyes.

"On what?"

"On whether I'm holding the gun or looking at it." He let the words sink in before laughing. "Don't shoot much these days. The odd rabbit, that's all."

"Did you see anything the night the landlord died? I believe you can see his boat from your front veranda," Jaz said.

"The police asked me that."

"What did you tell them?"

Charlie wasn't the sort to elaborate. "I told them I keep myself to myself. I'd been downstream on my bike that night. Called in the pub for a pint—just one—then rode back before ten. Nothing out of the ordinary. Nothing to report."

"Did you tell the police if you heard anything?" said Jaz.

"No."

"No, you didn't tell them, or no, you heard nothing?"

"No, I didn't tell them."

"Why not?"

"Because they never asked."

"Did you hear something?"

"Yup."

Pulling teeth. Blood from a stone. The clichés swirled through Jaz's mind. She wanted to scream. *Just tell me the story, you fucking idiot.* But that wasn't Jaz.

"What did you hear?"

"A shot."

"From a shotgun?"

"Yup."

"What time?"

"About ten."

"Wasn't that unusual?"

"Nope. Could've been someone taking a pot at a fox. Cause havoc around here in hen houses. They're always having a snap at my chickens when the light's faded and there's no moon. I've popped a few down the years."

"Didn't you go to look?"

"I put my nose out the door. Heard flocks of ducks and geese, quacking, honking. Couldn't hear myself think."

"So you didn't see anyone fall in the river?"

"No."

"Could you see The Artful Roger?"

"No, but there were a couple of lights on the river."

"A boat was moving?"

"One boat was. One wasn't."

"There were two boats?"

"Not much gets past you two, does it?" The tone was sarcastic, but he chuckled. Charlie didn't get many visitors; he was having fun. He passed a mug of steaming tea to Jaz.

"Did you tell the police?"

"No. Told them I didn't see anything."

"Why?"

"Because I didn't. Saw two lights, that's all. One looked to be a lot further away than the other, but at night it's hard to gauge distances on the river. All I know is, the ducks were making a din, and later, the geese were screeching and screaming. Sounded like my ex-wife when I got home from the pub. Something was going on, but this time of year there's always boats on the river. Ten. Midnight. Two in the morning. You name it. People having a drink on board. Anyway, the cops and me are like foxes and my chickens. We don't get on."

"Why not?"

"Long story."

"We're all ears."

"Another time maybe."

Jaz sipped her tea and looked around the van. Despite the curdled milk and scruffy exterior, Charlie kept his home clean and tidy. Spartan almost. A small table, two chairs, a folding settee swinging down from the wall that doubled as a bed, and a small kitchenette. A few copies of the *Times,* folded at the crossword page, overflowed a magazine rack. The only extravagance was a shiny metal cabinet in the corner, an arm protruding from its right side.

"Haven't seen a one-arm bandit for a long time," said Jaz.

Charlie went to the cabinet and flicked a switch on the wall. The machine burst into life, orange, yellow, and red lights glowing. Charlie's face lit up. He pulled the arm, and a bell dinged, a central drum sending pictures of spinning fruit. The drum halted. Three cherries in a row.

"Reminds me of Vegas. I spent time on the fruit machines there. Won a fortune, well, three or four hundred dollars, then piled it all back. A mug's game, but fun while it lasted." Trish said.

Charlie agreed. "Tell me about it. I made a fortune once and have been trying to win it back ever since."

"Sounds interesting," said Jaz, hoping to coax Charlie to elaborate on what Dan had told her. Her prompting produced the opposite effect.

"If you don't mind, I've things to be doing," he said.

The girls thanked Charlie for the tea and information and trudged back through puddles on the towpath towards the wooden bridge.

Jaz turned to Trish. "Find whoever was on that other boat and we may have our killer."

22

Back at home, Trish kicked off her shoes. She'd bought a magazine, grabbed some shopping, and was looking forward to a strong coffee and leisurely flick through the celebrity gossip.

First, a long soak in a hot bath to purge that riverside yomp from the system. Trish glided through the lounge, bare feet enjoying the feel of a lacquered oak floor. Balancing the magazine in one hand, she scoured the contents page while unbuckling her damp trousers. She let them slide down her legs, stepped out, and unbuttoned her blouse, poised to cross the inner hallway to the bathroom when her nose twitched and sniffed. A stale scent, like an old woollen jumper pulled from a dusty drawer. An odd, yet familiar smell. *Was that cigarette smoke too?*

A jolt of fear sent hairs rising on the back of Trish's neck. Her heart thumped against the wall of her chest. *Had someone broken into the apartment?* Only the week before, the *Journal* reported a spate of burglaries in the exclusive Lexford Park area, prompting police to warn residents to beef up security. Trish had scribbled a note on her memo board to invest in a burglar alarm, but it languished on her to-do list.

She sucked in a breath, fumbling to fasten the buttons on her blouse. Her eyes darted around the hallway as she weighed up two thoughts. Open the front door and run like hell or scream a warning. She did neither. Grabbing a heavy silver letter opener with an ornamental pistol grip handle, Trish pushed her bedroom door open. Nothing untoward.

Trish moved to the kitchen, the smell stronger as the door swung back. Trish throttled the impromptu weapon, raising the blade above her head as if ready to stab. Her knuckles turned white. Tiptoeing through the entrance, she turned right, casting an eye down the work surface on the main wall. Everything in order. Utensils in place, pots and pans hanging in chaos from hooks, gold watch laid out where she'd left it, acting as a paperweight atop two twenty-pound notes. Her grip relaxed on the letter opener.

A sideways movement flickering in the glass-fronted kitchen dresser caught her attention. Trish froze, expelling a startled gasp followed by a high-pitched squeak. A wave of prickly heat surged through her.

Reflected in the glass and oozing menace, a man clad in black leaned against the refrigerator. An unlit cigarette dangled from his lips, the shining blade of a carving knife tapping against his palm to a slow, sinister beat.

●

23

Thunder greeted Jaz as she pulled into the car park at The Anchor. The weather signalled board games, not pints, and picnics by the river. Jaz stepped out, turned up the collar of her raincoat, and hunched her shoulders against the squall. She'd dropped Trish at home and headed to the pub on a whim.

Dashing to the entrance, Jaz spied two men talking, one of them aboard a narrowboat, the other on the grassy bank. The boatman flicked his cigarette butt into the river, then disappeared below deck. The other man turned towards the pub. A baseball cap hid his blond locks, but the permanent smile gave him away. Logan.

"Hiya." His shout was friendly, the wave welcoming.

Jaz waited under the waterproof awning at the pub's entrance. Logan bounded down the bank and up the pub steps, letting Jaz admire his athletic gait and easy physical strength. Sweat and rain stained the front of his blue denim shirt underneath his open anorak, but he was oblivious.

Logan dragged off his cap and shook away the raindrops. "Jaz, isn't it? You're quite a regular these days. To what do we owe this pleasure?"

Jaz had already determined Logan was a charmer, a people person, the sort who remembered everyone's name. Perfect as a front-of-house barman, and she felt flattered by his attention, even though the feeling annoyed her. Not that she let it show. "Well remembered, although I suppose the last time we spoke was memorable considering two guys smashed up your bar and one's now dead. Thought I'd see if any of your regulars wanted to pay tribute."

"Oh, George Campbell, you mean. Poor old Crime. I heard he was in a car accident. Nasty business. Some of the snug drinkers said he was a bit of a boy racer. Hardly said a word in the pub. Just sat in a corner sipping his pint, listening to everyone around him. Quiet as a mouse, but once behind the wheel he turned into a wild boy, apparently."

"What was the fight about?"

"No idea. Honest. Haven't seen Crime or the other guy since we threw them out."

Jaz raised a hand to shield her head as the awning swung and another thunderclap sounded.

"Let's get inside." Logan put his arm around Jaz's shoulders and ushered her into the lounge bar.

Two couples sat at tables in adjoining alcoves. One man chomped on meat pie, gravy running down his chin, while his girlfriend munched through a bag of crisps. In the snug, two young lads threw darts. That was it. The Anchor's lunchtime clientele served by one barmaid-cum-waitress.

"The lull during the storm." Logan chuckled at his little joke and offered Jaz a drink. "On the house, of course. I did promise."

"Okay, make it lemonade. I'm driving."

Logan ducked behind the bar to search the drinks chiller. Rising with languid grace, it dawned on Jaz why he was so familiar. *Oh, God. He's the image of David. Same blond hair and dazzling blue eyes. Same suave manner.*

In her twenties, Jaz shared a London flat for nine years with David. A charmer, like Logan, David loved surfing, playing guitar, busking through life, avoiding hard work and responsibility. Lazy, vain, but Jaz adored him for his sharp wit and measured intelligence. Only when she met Dan did the scars of their broken relationship heal.

Shivering at the memory of emotional times, Jaz raised her glass to Logan, who'd pulled himself a half pint of beer. They clinked glasses from either side of the bar.

"Actually, I wanted to talk about Roger," said Jaz.

"Why? I thought the police had finished their investigation."

"Yes, but I'm doing a feature on what drives men to suicide, especially in Lexford, and it may help our readers if I could identify some of the danger signals. You probably knew him as well as anyone this past year, and seem the sort of solid, sensible guy capable of fitting the pieces together."

Logan raised his eyebrows, pursed his lips, and nodded. Stroking his ego, as Jaz did with David, made the pet poodle in Logan come running.

"It was obvious Roger was going through a tough time. Marriage break-up didn't help, although from what I've seen of Cheryl Mansell, he was well out of it."

"Why do you say that?"

"No reason. I didn't know her well. She'd practically left the pub by the time I arrived. She just came across as stuck up. Seemed she was always looking down on him. I think she did. Thought she was too good to muck in serving riff-raff in a riverside pub. Can't be easy to live with that attitude day after day.

"Expect it became too much for Roger. This pub's not the easiest to run, even when everyone's on the same page. Each season has varied demands. Buy in the wrong food or a beer that doesn't sell, and it knocks you back. Roger worried about it all too much. I would tell him to lighten up and have a drink, but he couldn't relax. Some people are like that. Born worriers."

"Not like you."

"No. My mates used to call me Bob Marley."

"Why?"

"Don't worry about a thing." Logan spoke in a passable Jamaican accent, at the same time swaying his hips in a reggae groove.

Jaz smiled. Logan had an engaging confidence she warmed to. "What's your story? What brought you to Lexford?"

"Oh, I won't bore you with all that. Suffice to say, after leaving university, I was a big disappointment to my parents. They thought I'd use my English degree to become a journalist like you, or a teacher or professor. I ended up ducking and diving, scratching around in bars and supermarkets."

"I have an English degree too."

"Ah, great minds. I knew we'd have lots in common."

For the first time, Jaz detected a hint of flirtation in Logan's demeanour. "I was into Jane Austen, the Brontës, all the English classics. What books did you study?"

"I'll show you."

"Pardon?"

"Come on." Logan motioned to Jaz to walk around the bar.

He took her into a narrow passageway leading to the pub's kitchen and living quarters. There were four doors leading off. Logan pushed the first on the left and held it open.

"Wow!" Jaz considered the full weight of the wall of books, sitting snugly on shelves, stretching from floor to ceiling, scanning the bespoke library from left to right. With meticulous precision, someone had catalogued them by author in alphabetical order.

Jaz spotted half a dozen novels by Isaac Asimov, including *The End of* Eternity, and *I, Robot,* kicking off the collection in pole position on the highest shelf.

Wherever her eye turned, there was a classic novel from a multitude of genres. *Anna Karenina. Catcher in the Rye. To Kill a Mockingbird.*

For a minute, Jaz bathed in the warm glow she always experienced when surrounded by sublime literature. She sidled along the collection, running her fingertips across the covers, soaking in the texture, as if touching the jackets of literary greatness may infuse inspiration. She turned to see Logan leaning against the wall of the study, watching her with the devoted expression a father wears while showing off his newborn child.

"This is fantastic. An A to Z of the world's greatest fiction, but how did you come across all these books and have you read them all?"

"Unfortunately, the answer to the second part of that question is no, although I've read a few. I wrote a dissertation on D H Lawrence at uni and my course majored on the romantic poets. I read lots of Byron, Blake, and Coleridge, but wasn't a big novel reader. Pick one up now and then, but they remind me of how inadequate I am with creative stuff."

"Did you want to be a writer?"

"Hmm, one time, maybe, but I didn't have a feel for fiction. I think you need to live the story inside your mind, bond with the characters, hear their voices, speak their language. Writing is such a lonely business. Too much introspection and rejection. I can't handle rejection." In marked contrast to his easy-going demeanour, Logan spat out the last sentence with venom.

The trademark smile returned as he explained how he'd compiled his collection. "It's not what you think. It was no great love affair for literature. When I finished uni, I didn't know what I'd do. I owned quite a collection of books, most begged, borrowed, or stolen. That's a lie. I didn't actually steal any.

"At night, I earned a living as a barman in a pub and during the day helped care for my grandmother after her stroke. On weekends, I sold books from a stall on Cambridge market. Helped pay the rent for a few years. I'd buy used books for pennies, buff them up and sell them on for a tidy profit, but whenever I came across a classic, I'd keep it. The idea was to amass a stock of the world's greatest books and open a shop."

"What would you call it?"

"Logan's Novel World. I thought that had a ring to it, but then along came eBooks and electronic reading devices and many independent book shops died a death. I kept the classics and when I came to The Anchor, Roger allowed me to store them in his study. He'd moved out and was living on his boat by then, although he still used this study as his pub office. He even gave me a few books that were lying around the pub. Ones his wife left behind."

Jaz glanced around the rest of the room and wondered how chaos and disorder could exist in proximity to the pristine, regimented bookcase. Paint-spattered stepladders slouched haphazardly against a wall. An old-fashioned computer, printer attached, sat on a table in one corner, and a wastepaper basket overflowed with shredded cardboard and old invoices. The carpet was dusty, stained in places, and an assortment of papers, pens, and pencils cluttered the desktop under a window looking out onto the garden. Resting against the wall, a framed picture of two children. A boy and girl.

"Was Roger still working from here?" said Jaz.

"Yep, right until the end. He used to do all his ordering and planning from that desk. Roger wasn't the tidiest. He would say no one ever died wishing they'd done more housework. He wasn't wrong there, but recently the office had passed untidy. Maybe that has something to do with his depression. Perhaps a confused mind leads to disorganisation in all aspects of life. Sometimes, he sat in that chair, put his head in his hands and complained about what he called the merciless scream of time. I didn't know what he meant, but maybe it was a portent."

Jaz reached inside her handbag and fished out her mobile phone. "Logan, do you mind if I take a photo of your wonderful book collection? It would be a treat to look at my leisure. I'm hoping to find a Jane Austen in there at some point."

"You'll find two, Jaz. Northanger Abbey and Persuasion, both published posthumously, as I'm sure you know. I always thought that was the saddest thing about Austen. People can't get enough of her these days, but she never realised tangible success or real fame during her lifetime."

"Same with Emily Brontë," said Jaz.

"Funny you should say that." Logan reached up to the top shelf and tapped a copy of *Wuthering Heights*. "I always thought she was saddest of all. Died at thirty without knowing how famous her only novel would become. Made me a pretty penny, though."

"How come?"

"One day, someone brought a box of old books from a house clearance to my stall. Fifteen books, most of them tatty and dog-eared. I paid twenty quid for the lot, thinking I was being generous."

"Sounds like a good deal."

"It was. When I got home, I found a copy of Wuthering Heights, in good nick, with what looked like the original cloth covers. An American edition. That's unusual, I thought, so I did some research and discovered it was a first edition. Sold it to a bookseller in London who deals in rare editions. Seven thousand pounds."

Jaz's mouth dropped open, eyes widening. "That's what I call a good day's work."

A satisfied, smug look played on Logan's lips. "I dare say the bookseller turned a tidy profit too, but hey-ho. Anyhow, if pictures of books float your boat, fire away."

The barmaid shouted through to Logan and he stepped out of the office to answer the query. After snapping the bookcase, Jaz took a few extra shots of the study and desk, reasoning they may help build a picture of Roger's last days. She slipped the phone inside her handbag as Logan returned.

"All done?" he said.

"Sure. Thanks for the tour. You've reminded me, I must read Northanger Abbey again. When I was at uni, I tried to identify with the heroine, Catherine Morland. Young and naïve, discovering the world, revering happiness and virtue above wealth and social position."

Logan flicked a book from the top shelf of the bookcase. "Read and return." He handed the book to Jaz, holding onto it a fraction longer than necessary, so she looked into his eyes. His smile was more radiant than usual.

"Are you sure?"

"Of course. All it's doing here is collecting dust. Anyway, it means you'll have to return for another literary chat."

"Okay."

Jaz smiled graciously. She hadn't expected this, but realised she'd underestimated Logan. An hour ago, her mind perceived a happy-go-lucky drifter pulling pints for a living, who indulged in frivolous conversations with vacuous girls in the bar. Not a man who knew his Tolstoy from his Steinbeck, used words such as *portent*, and conversed with confidence and sensitivity about most things literary.

For a delightful interlude, Jaz's bookish passion had deflected her mission at The Anchor. Now she cast a critical eye over the study. "I have to admit it feels strange and a bit sad to be standing here wondering what thoughts were going through Roger's head when he was sitting at that desk."

Logan pointed through the window at the river, running fast and fuller than it had for months. The squall billowed the willows. "You wouldn't think so looking at that view, but Roger must have been in a dark place to top himself like that. Such a waste."

"Is there any chance he didn't kill himself?" Jaz paused, bit her lip and an awkward silence ensued.

"What do you mean?"

"A possibility Roger was mixed up in something sinister, or made enemies, or maybe an altercation got out of hand? With a drinker in the pub, a boater on the river, or one of the farmers. Is there any chance this was a murder and not a suicide?"

Jaz hadn't planned on divulging her suspicions to Logan, but they'd been stirring in the depths of her mind for days. Bubbling, fermenting. She tried to snatch them back. Revealing innermost thoughts to a comparative stranger hardly amounted to professional behaviour, but the pressure proved too intense. They'd gushed to the surface, spilling forth in a sudden, uncontrollable surge.

"Where's all that come from? I thought you were doing a feature on suicide. Anyway, thought the police had evidence."

"Yeah, they do, and I am doing a feature on suicide, but I keep replaying in my mind what might have happened that night on Roger's boat and suicide makes no sense."

Logan shrugged. "Well, if you want any help or need to look through his stuff, you're very welcome. You know where to find me. In fact, give me your mobile number and I'll ring if I think of anything useful."

"Okay."

Jaz handed Logan a business card, and they returned to the bar. As she walked around to the public side, she spotted two familiar figures strolling through the door, one wearing a cowboy hat, both displaying the lumbering gait of a farmer. The twins from the snug. Joe and Victor.

Joe doffed his hat, nodding politely, although he didn't seem to remember her. The twins would have walked past, but Jaz stepped away from the bar. "Sorry about your friend George."

"Huh, bloody idiot. We told him that car would be the death of him."

Considering George Campbell had been a regular drinking companion and a former cricket teammate, Joe didn't seem overly sympathetic. *Maybe that was the way with country folk.*

A flicker of recognition crossed Joe's face, and he fixed Jaz with a granite expression. "You're that reporter, aren't you?"

Jaz nodded. "I wondered if you wanted to say something about your friend for a piece in the Journal. Tribute to one of The Anchor's regulars, that sort of thing."

"No," said the twins in unison.

"Oh." Jaz couldn't mask her surprise.

"Maybe you should consider not coming here anymore. Every time we see you, someone ends up dead," Joe said.

The men lumbered into the snug. The doors swung shut behind them.

Logan shook his head. "Don't mind them. They're more upset than they let on. The three of them were inseparable in that snug. Crime never said much, but they had some laughs together."

"How well did you know him?"

"Not that well. No one did, apart from Joe and Victor."

"Thanks again for the book." Jaz turned and headed for the exit, guessing Logan would watch the sway of her hips all the way to the door. She was right.

24

Frantic, Trish screamed. "Get out. Get out of my house now, or I swear I'll kill you."

"With a letter opener?" Terry's tone carried bewildered derision.

Trish lunged, swiping the improvised weapon at his head. She missed, lunging again. This time, Terry dodged inside her attack, grabbing her wrist.

"I'm going to kill you," Trish shrieked, writhing in Terry's grasp, then thrusting a knee at his groin.

Terry anticipated the move, sliding sideways to deflect the blow with his thigh. Trish screamed again. The letter opener clattered to the floor, and she clawed at Terry's face. The contest was far from even. Seven inches taller, four stones heavier, he drove her backwards, pinning her against the fridge.

"Shut up and calm down, you mad bitch. Can't you see I'm the one with the knife?"

"It's my knife."

"No, it isn't. I bought the cutlery. Carved the Christmas turkey with this knife."

Terry held the blade in front of Trish's face, pressing his body against her so close she could smell his sour breath, taste the salt of his sweat. For the first time in her life, Trish experienced a loathing towards another human being that turned her stomach. A plug of bile stung her throat. She thought she would vomit. Fighting to free herself from Terry's grasp, her muscles burned, strength ebbing as he delighted once more in controlling her. Exhausted, Trish ceased struggling, tears of anger and frustration in her eyes. Terry held her a while to ensure the fight had subsided before relaxing his grip and throwing the knife onto the work surface.

Trish slumped to the floor, back against the fridge. Terry swung a wooden chair from under the kitchen table, straddled the seat, and rested his arms on the back. For a minute, no one spoke. She avoided looking at him, but her peripheral vision provided all she needed to know. He'd aged more than the two years he'd been gone, flecks of grey hair now wide streaks, stubble more salt than pepper. Cold, merciless eyes. *How could I have lived with someone like that?*

When Trish finally spoke, her voice was calm and steely. "You won't get away with this. You can't just break into someone's house brandishing a knife. I'm calling the police."

Terry fished inside his pocket and dangled a bunch of keys in front of her. "No, you're not. I haven't broken in. I may have left my keys behind two years ago, but Lynn kept hers. Where is she?"

"You go near her and I'll kill you."

"There you go again. More threats. You never knew when you were well off and neither does that girl of yours."

"The police are onto you, Terry. They'll put you away this time. They know all about the gun and your fight in the pub with that guy who died the day after."

"Where do you think I've just come from?"

"What do you mean?"

"I've spent the last couple of hours at Lexford police station answering questions because of that halfwit daughter of yours and her accusations. There is no gun, Trish. There never was a gun. It's a figment of her hysterical imagination. Why would I need a gun? She's got cotton wool for brains. It'll be all that pot she's smoked."

Trish rubbed her eyes, struggling to unscramble the mess of thoughts rushing through her brain. Lynn was no longer the beguiling picture of innocence on her fridge magnet. She'd fallen in with a dubious gang during her teenage years. The usual stuff. Shoplifting. Drugs. Some of her friends even lured into prostitution. But Trish diverted her from the worst of it. Lynn had a sharp brain and caring nature, at least she did before Terry groomed her, which is how Trish viewed their relationship. Lynn seemed certain about events the day she left Terry. Her description of the gun appeared a shade vague, but her recollection of Terry's rage and her own terror rung true. Trish could vouch for that temper.

"What about the fight in the pub? I suppose that never happened either," Trish spat.

"I've admitted that to the cops. I'd never seen the guy before. We were enjoying a pint, chatting about something and nothing on a quiet Sunday lunchtime. I knocked over a glass that was almost empty and he flew at me. Before I knew it, we were rolling on the floor punching each other. It was self-defence."

Trish's eyes burned with contempt. "The cops might believe that. I don't. Remember, I've lived with your temper. I know who you are, what you're capable of. You're a grade one shit and always will be. I wouldn't put it past you to have run that poor guy off the road the next day. Bit of a coincidence that he should snuff it in a high-speed smash, don't you think? And you being a driver with a reputation for driving fast."

"You should be careful throwing accusations around, Trish."

"If the cap fits."

They scowled at each other, faces set in a hostile oil painting. Terry stood up as if to leave but halted as he reached Trish sitting on the kitchen floor, chin resting on her knees. He sneered at her.

"Your problem is bearing grudges, Trish. You can't get over the fact that I left you, and your daughter preferred to be with me rather than you. Have you ever asked yourself why? Why she preferred a crummy bedsit rather than a fancy pad like this? Has it ever entered your brain that you could be the one in the wrong, that you're impossible to live with? No wonder you got a brain tumour with all the poison swirling around your mind."

The callous jibe about cancer triggered an emotion deep within Trish. She lashed out, aiming for his groin, but Terry was ready for her, deflecting her jab with his leg, at the same time grabbing a clump of Trish's hair. He yanked hard, twisting her onto her back. He raised his foot, ready to stamp on her stomach, when pummelling fists on the front door distracted him.

"Are you all right in there, Trish?" Alarmed by the commotion, Oscar, from the apartment above, decided to investigate.

As the banging continued, Terry bent over Trish, so close she could feel hot spittle as he seethed in her ear. "I was in Cromer when that guy was killed in his car. If you don't believe me, ask the cops. They've checked it all. Don't worry. I'll find out where Lynn is. You can be sure of that. Don't bother getting up. I'll see myself out."

He strode to the French windows leading to the back garden, turned the key, and was gone.

Violent shock waves shook Trish's body. Feeling sick, she tried to get up, but wobbly legs refused. The banging on the door ceased, but Oscar, a pensioner with sprightly frame, generous heart, and tenacious temperament, continued to call her name, the anxious tone suggesting he was about to call the police.

To calm herself, Trish sucked in a series of deep breaths before rising to her feet and staggering to the door. "Oscar, I'm sorry. I had an unexpected visitor and things became a little heated. Sorry about the noise."

"Never mind that. Are you all right? You don't look well."

Trish managed a weak smile. "Thanks. I'm fine. Just had a little shock, that's all."

Oscar looked dubious.

"Honest, I'm okay. Thanks for caring enough to check on me."

Trish shut the door and picked up her phone, contemplating ringing the police. *What would she say?* Terry hadn't broken in. He didn't threaten her with the knife and she'd started the fight, trying to stab him with a letter opener. She put the phone down.

25

Thursday. Print day at the *Lexford Journal*. Dan flicked through the dummy pages of the newspaper, a studious expression carving mini craters on his face.

Pete, Jack, Jeremy, and Jaz filed into his office. In the last few months, Dan had instituted a morning editorial conference to thrash out the best location for the newsy stories of the week. The lead items on pages one, three, and five were crucial, and while some editors played the great dictator, handing edicts down the chain of command, that wasn't Dan's style. He preferred listening, debating, making staff feel inclusive, with the proviso that his decision remained final.

"Okay, let's crack on. Everything's pretty straightforward. News in Lexford has certainly picked up, and thank heavens for that. Page five lead is a good fit for the piece on the bins. To save cash, the council has proposed that collections switch from weekly to three-weekly. Residents are worried about rats and disease and I don't blame them. It's not the first time we've covered stories like this. It won't be the last, but there's nothing like a council-knocking story to get readers involved."

"I think it's a rubbish story," said Jack.

Everyone groaned.

"All agreed?" said Dan.

Nods all around.

"Next, how about making two and three into a double-page spread using pictures I took of the car smash outside town?"

Dan's computer generated a set of images on a wall-mounted TV screen at the head of the conference table. One captured the red sports car leaning against the telegraph pole, a haze of rising steam visible from the bonnet pointing skywards. Pictures of police at the scene and fire crews smothering the car in foam also provided active, dramatic images.

"Ever thought of becoming a photographer?" said Pete, impressed with the balance and movement.

Dan was modest. "In the right place at the right time for once, that's all. I'll write the words to go with the pictures, weaving in what I saw and heard. Both cars were doing best part of a ton when they passed me on a dusty, winding road, forcing other cars to swerve to avoid them."

"What's the headline?" said Jack.

Dan paused for a moment. "Who killed crazy George? That should get our readers thinking."

"Can we say that?" said Pete.

Dan shrugged. "Why not? Both drivers were doing twice the speed limit, endangering other motorists and themselves. Pure madness. They may have been joyriding. It could have been an accident and George paid the ultimate price, but from what I witnessed, the driver in the black car was the aggressor. Didn't look like he was racing. Seemed to me he tried to run the red car off the road. Let's ask our readers for help in tracking down that car and driver."

Dan knew that wasn't Terry. He'd phoned Inspector Cross first, following a call from Trish the night before. Trish told Jaz and Dan about Terry's visit, skating over the frightening bits, but revealing Terry had an alibi, claiming to be in Cromer at the time of the crash. Inspector Cross refused to share details but confirmed

CCTV cameras caught Terry in Cromer and he no longer featured in their inquiry.

"A spread like that would go down well with the police. It could jog memories. Someone may have recognised the driver. The police might also see the irony," said Pete.

"What do you mean?" said Dan.

"Oh, nothing."

"Come on, don't be shy. Let's hear what you have to say."

"Well, you've been complaining in your column for months about the cops making money out of Lexford speed traps. The police may think it's rich you campaigning against speeding."

"Wasn't anything like that, Pete. This wasn't someone doing a couple of miles over the limit in an area with new signs, and cops with radar guns hiding under tarpaulins. This was someone deliberately trying to kill George Campbell."

"Okay, just saying."

Jaz spoke up for the first time. "That will make a powerful spread, Dan, but what about the splash on page one?"

Dan clicked on his computer. An image of The Anchor appeared on the screen.

"That's not active or colourful. It's positively dull," said Jack.

"I'll grant you, it won't win any prizes for creative photography, but I want to superimpose a red splash headline over it."

"What did you have in mind?"

"Something to make the locals sit up and take notice. How about House of Horror?"

"Bit strong, isn't it?" Jack's face questioned.

"Is it? A week ago, a group of schoolkids found the landlord of The Anchor face down in the River Lex with a shotgun wound in his chest. Police reckon he's another suicide statistic and we've no reason to disbelieve that." Dan took a sideways glance at Jaz and thought she gritted her teeth. He went on. "Now, a car smash has killed one of The Anchor's most loyal customers. That could be murder. It may be a coincidence, an accident, or something more sinister. We don't know. What we do know is, the pub links the two events. That makes for a cracking, local story. Everybody in Lexford will recognise the venue. They either drink there, have eaten there, or passed the pub on a trip down the river. Let's not underplay it. At the moment, The Anchor is Lexford's inn of mystery."

Like all good newsmen on the scent of a big story, Dan crackled with energy. He jabbed at Jaz with one forefinger and at Pete with the other.

"I want you both to get your heads together to write the front page lead. On the mystery line. You write the news story, Pete. Jaz, you supply Pete with information you have from the barman about George Campbell, with a few quotes thrown in. You're the only person here who met him. Apart from me, and by the time I got to meet him, he was halfway up a telegraph pole, wearing an airbag, with his head caved in. Mention all that cricket stuff you told me about, and how he and Roger were teammates years ago."

Pete and Jaz rose from their chairs, heading for the newsroom. Jack and Jeremy made to follow, but Dan signalled them to stay seated.

"I need a quick word with you both."

The youngest and oldest editorial staff members on the *Journal*'s payroll glanced at each other, anxiety clouding their features.

Dan didn't bother with pleasantries. He waited for the door to shut and pitched right in. "I'm afraid there's no way of dressing this up so, I'll come straight out with it.

Your names are up for compulsory redundancy to take effect at the end of the month. It's not my decision. Wish it was. As you know, the company's in dire financial circumstances, but I won't insult you by trotting out the party line that your jobs no longer exist. We've never needed bright, young journalists like you, Jack, more than now, nor experienced editors who can run sport as well as pitch in on news, Jeremy. Please, believe me, I've fought against these cuts, but faceless accountants have matched names to numbers, and other departments are also shedding staff."

Jeremy, a tall man of loping stride and craggy face etched with the stress of a thousand match reports, fixed Dan with a look close to contempt. "How long have you been in charge here?"

"Nearly two years."

"I've put in thirty-five, and in thirty seconds I'm gone. Just like that." He clicked his fingers, stood up, and headed for the door with a parting retort. "Bloody disgraceful!"

Ashen-faced, Jack remained seated.

"I don't want to patronise you by saying you'll immediately walk into another job, Jack, but you will. You're one of the brightest young reporters I've worked with. You're heading for the nationals. They'll snap you up."

Jack raised a weak smile. Half a lifetime toiling in the editorial trenches had jaundiced Jeremy, but Jack still embraced the optimism of youth. He was grateful for the compliment. "I saw an advert in the Press Gazette last month saying the Times was hiring news trainees. I wish I'd applied now."

Dan smiled, his brow knitting in deep thought. Jack had given him an idea.

26

Next morning, Jaz and Trish set off for Lexford Country Marina in search of a boat. Dan fielded a complaint from Inspector Cross. Nothing new. Dan took calls from readers whenever a fresh edition of the *Journal* hit the streets. Part of the job. Often they pointed out daft headlines.

One-armed man applauds Lexford Samaritan

Alison still claimed she didn't understand the problem with that phrase, but Dan's favourite call didn't involve a headline. Rather, a gesture of concern from an old lady asking why that week's paper failed to contain a photograph of the mayor of Lexford, renowned for elbowing his way into every edition. "I do hope he's all right," she said.

Inspector Cross's call wasn't polite.

"Mr Armitage, are you deliberately trying my patience? I've rarely seen such irresponsible, gratuitous reporting. Your coverage of the crash is inaccurate, sensationalist. And the front page is scandalous. Utterly scandalous. Are you trying to scare the population of Lexford?"

"Which question do you want me to answer first?"

The Inspector ignored Dan's sarcasm. "I'm all for freedom of the press."

"Are you?"

"Don't be so bolshie."

"I'm not being awkward, but it strikes me that every time we point out a line of enquiry, you want to shut it down without exploration."

"Such as."

"The fact that George Campbell wasn't a joyrider and could've been run off the road."

"There's no evidence of foul play regarding the accident on the outskirts of Lexford. The investigation remains open because we'd like to interview the other driver who was travelling at speed. As a courtesy to your newspaper, I shared information about exonerating a man you and your associates pointed at. The CCTV clearly shows Mr Marsh a hundred miles away when the accident happened."

Dan sucked in a breath. He'd backed Trish and Lynn's allegations against Terry because of Lynn's apparent sighting of a gun. That evidence now appeared flimsy. While it seemed Terry couldn't have killed George Campbell, didn't mean someone else hadn't.

"Okay, I agree. Mr Marsh's no longer in the frame, but I know what I saw, and that crash wasn't an accident."

"Just like Mr Mansell didn't commit suicide, I suppose."

"We never said that."

"But that's what your headline implied. House of Horror? Did you not consider the implications that may have for a family riverside pub? If it goes bust, it will be on your conscience. You've painted the place to be dangerous, where murder's as common as pulling a pint, as if it's all part of some lurid television series. The plain facts are that Mr Mansell didn't die there, and neither did Mr Campbell. And there's no evidence either of them was murdered."

A slight pause as Dan considered his response. "I suppose when you view it like that, our coverage may seem a touch eager. But turn that on its head. What if Mr Mansell did die because of his association with The Anchor and likewise with Mr Campbell? It could turn out the *Journal*, not the police, is pursuing justice."

Dan heard a strange noise resembling interference on the line. In reality, choking back anger and frustration, Inspector Cross nearly fell off his chair. The line went dead. Dan smiled, scribbling an exact note of the conversation on his pad. Jaz would demand to know every word.

A surprise, apprehensive shiver shook Dan. *What if Jaz was wrong about Roger and he was wrong about George?* He could find himself hauled in front of the Press Complaints Commission. Maybe even sacked alongside Jeremy and Jack.

27

Jaz loved boats. During an idyllic year in Australia following university, former partner David introduced her to them. She learned to surf, sail, and steer small speedboats. Everything about boats appealed, and while Lexford Country Marina hardly resembled Sydney Harbour Yacht Club, the basics weren't dissimilar. Water, a sense of freedom, ropes and rigging conversing, rapping and clinking against metal masts in the wind.

Jaz and Trish strolled along the decking, Trish spewing out details of Terry's visit, the fight, and her fears for Lynn.

"It was horrible, Jaz. He seems intent on ruining our lives. I'm having all the locks changed. He's not taking me by surprise again. I'm not bothered about myself. I'll give as good as I get, but it's scary knowing he's out there looking for Lynn."

"Is she somewhere safe?"

"She's staying with a friend and I'm pretty sure he doesn't know the address, but it's only a matter of time."

"Oh, Trish."

Jaz linked her arm with Trish's and they walked on, admiring the diversity of craft, not knowing exactly what they were looking for, but Trish's mood lifting at her interest in the exotic names. *Blue Moon. Our Destiny. Serendipity. Endless Summer.*

"You can almost feel sand between your toes and taste salt on your lips. Discovering hidden grottos. Swimming naked in isolated bays. Enjoying holiday adventures."

Jaz deflated Trish's romantic dreams. "Most of these boats never venture further than the River Lex, and I wouldn't recommend swimming naked in all that green gunge." She squinted into the sun, pointing to a line of craft about 50 yards away. "Let's go look at the narrowboats."

Walking along the jetty, protecting the fat-bottomed boats, it became apparent that the water harboured a class divide. *Hunky Dory. Northern Soul. Pie Eater.*

"The Slow Dredger? What sort of name's that for a boat?" said Trish.

"Probably does what it says on the tin. Narrowboats are workhorses of the water. In the old days, they carried coal, cotton, and flour. Varied cargo, like barges. Up to seventy tons some of them. The UK's criss-crossed with rivers and canals. Some boats still carry cargo, but these days, owners also turn their vessels into mini hotels. They want for nothing. Toilets, showers, luxury bedrooms and kitchens. Some owners live all year in them or rent out to people searching for a unique holiday adventure."

Trish's interest deepened. "This is a sentence I never thought I'd say, Jaz, but what's the difference between a narrowboat and a barge?"

"Narrowboats are, wait for it, narrower. Usually seven feet wide."

"I'd still prefer a yacht sailing off the Caribbean." Trish thrust her face at the sun, enjoying the cool breeze wafting across the marina.

"I thought you might. Hold on. What's that?" Jaz pointed to one of the sleeker narrowboats at the far edge of the pier, less protected from the elements than the others, but moored with easy access to the outlet for the River Lex.

They walked a few metres closer, the drawing on the cabin near the helm sparking an intake of breath from Jaz. A swan, wings outstretched, rising out of the water in a majestic pose. In a flowing font under the image, the boat's name. *Ride a White Swan.*

"What's special about that?" said Trish, perplexed at Jaz's obvious interest.

"Don't you remember? In The Anchor when we met those friends of Roger Mansell in the snug. The little one called Crime, him who died in the crash, had a tattoo. We couldn't see all of it, but we thought it was a swan rising. Like this one. Like the one Dad had. You don't see many poses more angelic or distinctive than that."

"Yeah, you could be right, although I suppose lots of boats have pictures of swans. Rivers, boats, swans, they sort of go together."

"Maybe, but I have a feeling about this. Let's see if we can find the dockmaster or whatever they call someone in charge of a marina."

"Marina man?"

They tracked back to the gravel road serving the marina, then onto a timber-framed building flanked by boats in dry dock. Some looked miserable, reclining at drunken angles on the gravel. Some sat on trailers, others on concrete ground, awaited repair or painting, standing to attention on raised supports. As Jaz and Trish reached the entrance, a suntanned man emerged holding a bunch of keys. He looked around 60. Kind eyes, bushy grey beard, slight paunch, furrowed features. Jaz expected a seafaring accent, a man who sang sea shanties. Instead, he spoke in soft, elegant, local tones, more akin to an accountant. She was a tad disappointed.

"Hello, ladies, can I help you? I'm about to lock up for lunch." He dangled the keys, expecting them to take the hint.

Jaz assumed a chirpy voice and sweet smile. "Oh, I hope you can. We've been admiring your boats. It's a beautiful marina, by the way. There's something romantic about boats on the water. The sleek shapes, bright colours, graceful rise and fall with the ebb and flow of the water. They remind me of ballroom dancers. Magical."

"Know exactly what you mean. Worked with them all my life. Boats, not dancers."

Jaz chuckled. "We wondered if you could tell us who owns a boat moored here?"

"Why?"

"A narrowboat. We've heard many are rented out in the summer and we're looking to take a holiday on the river. It's such a beautiful boat. It would be perfect."

"Sorry. I can't divulge details such as names, addresses, and phone numbers, I'm afraid. Data protection and all. We're very strict on that." He turned the key in the lock.

Trish had an idea. "Oh, that's a pity. We don't want to get you into any trouble. We think we know the guy who owns the boat. My sister says she may have rented it before. The one with a rising swan on the cabin. If it's the same one, the owner's name's George Campbell. If you could check for us, it would be very helpful."

The dockmaster sighed and pondered Trish's request. "Okay, I don't suppose that'd do any harm."

He slipped the key in the lock and motioned the girls in, then ushered them through a workshop into a small rear office. Feeling hopeful, Jaz and Trish glanced at each other as the man sat at a sturdy wooden desk, wrestling a cumbersome log sheet from the top drawer.

"Now, which boat are you looking for?"

"Ride a White Swan, with a rising swan motif on the cabin."

"I'm afraid we don't catalogue by the name of the boat. We do it by the number of the mooring."

"Ninety-six," said Trish.

"How do you know that?" Jaz mouthed at Trish.

The man flicked over a few pages, running a gnarled forefinger down the narrowboat listings, logged in small, meticulous handwriting. "Yep, here we are. Number ninety-six, Ride a White Swan. Owner Mr George Campbell. You were right."

Trish smiled. "Oh, lovely. Thank you so much. We'll get in touch with him. We might be sailing down the River Lex this summer, after all."

"No problem. Now, I must get some lunch. My stomach thinks my throat's cut."

When they stepped outside, Jaz and Trish squealed, hugging each other.

"I knew it. George, Crime, or whatever you want to call him, owned a narrowboat," said an excited Jaz.

"May not be the boat on the river the night Roger Mansell died, though." For once, Trish was the cautious one.

"That's true, but it could be, and do you remember the word Crime used when we were at The Anchor trying to collect tributes for Roger Mansell?"

"Remind me."

"Shithouse. That's what he called Roger. Under his breath, maybe, but that doesn't sound friendly, does it?"

"No, but why would George Campbell want to kill Roger?"

"That's what we need to find out. First, though, tell me how you knew the mooring for the boat was ninety-six."

Trish tapped her head. "Powers of deduction and observation, Jaz. You're not the only one who thinks like a detective."

"Written on the floor decking, wasn't it?"

"You got it."

28

"The clue's in the note. I'm sure of it."

Jaz paced the lounge, scanning the copy of Roger Mansell's suicide note on her phone. Dan sat at a table studying the *Times* crossword.

"From where I'm sitting, the clue's twenty down. Hastier where bacon's concerned," said Dan.

"Rasher," said Jaz.

"I haven't told you how many letters yet."

"Don't need to. It's rasher."

Dan wrote the answer, again marvelling at Jaz's intuitive grasp of the English language. Crackling with nervous energy on arriving home, she'd told Dan the news from the marina, relaying suspicions about George Campbell, although she'd appeared less than enthusiastic with Dan's measured response. He was reticent to leap to the conclusion that George was a murderer, having told Inspector Cross that morning he believed someone had murdered George. Both might be true, but Dan determined it was time for considered reflection.

Jaz favoured action. "We need to show the note to someone. Maybe online. An expert. Someone who'll give a second opinion. See if there are clues we can't detect."

"Like a specialist on suicide notes? Do such people exist?"

Jaz pondered the question. She was a recent convert to social media, where everyone appeared to be an expert in their imagination. The plume of opinions emanating from such platforms reminded her of steam rising from a kettle. Ephemeral and insubstantial. Jaz quickly disregarded the online option. Roger Mansell's note required an old-school expert, immersed in the subject.

"How about Murph? He was a psychiatrist. Studied people's minds for years. He seemed to know all about the psychology of death and dying. We can count on him to give us straight answers."

"He retired years ago, Jaz, and he's not in good health. We don't even know if he's still with us. We haven't seen him since we all met at the top of Snowdon. That was a year ago."

"Come on, Dan. Let's go now. We know where he lives, and he always said nothing ever happened at his care home. I'm sure he'd love to see us."

Dan knew better than to protest. Jaz was on a mission and he secretly relished the prospect of renewing an acquaintance with Bob Murphy, part of the gang of five who'd travelled to hospital for radiotherapy every weekday for a month. Murph was the quiet one, although that was a relative comparison in a car with both Trish and Bill Murdoch, with his witty one-liners. Regardless, whenever Murph squeezed in a sentence, the sentiment proved worthy of consideration. A psychiatrist by profession, although long retired, he suffered from prostate cancer doctors controlled with medication.

It was approaching seven o'clock when Dan and Jaz pulled up outside the imposing Victorian building.

"This takes me back, Dan. I half expect Murph to appear from behind that tree, as he did every morning when you picked him up."

"Yeah, and then say he was going back inside for a pee."

They smiled at the memory. The entrance porch housed an intercom with buttons for each of the 12 apartments, a brass wall plate informing visitors that the building was a refuge for vulnerable adults aged 60 and over.

To Dan's relief, Mr Bob Murphy still lived at number seven.

"Surprise!"

Jaz hadn't told Murph who she was when he answered the intercom, but he recognised her voice and pressed the door release. When he opened the door, there were handshakes all round. By nature, Murph favoured reserve and decorum. Not a hugger, but his wide grin conveyed obvious delight. He looked no different. White curly hair and beard, bleached complexion, serene expression. Multi-coloured braces suspending brown corduroy trousers, white shirt, brown tie. Murph's idea of casual amounted to not wearing a wide-brimmed hat indoors.

Jaz enquired about his health.

"Still chugging on. You'll have a cup of tea, won't you?"

"Of course. Actually, we wanted to ask your opinion about something. Your professional opinion."

"Been some time since anyone did that."

Murph was interested, but first Jaz and Dan related the details of Bill's wife's funeral. A bout of flu meant Murph had missed the ceremony, but he was eager to chat about old times travelling in the ambulance car. While brewing a pot of Earl Grey, Dan and Jaz brought Murph up to speed with Bill's broken arm and increased infirmity. Murph insisted on using his finest china. Even filled a plate with ginger nuts.

Jaz recounted the story of Roger Mansell's body in the river, the verified facts surrounding the discovery and her suspicion that all may not be as it seemed. She dug in her handbag for her phone and scrolled the archives for the suicide note. Murph fiddled with his tie, a sure sign to anyone who knew him he'd afford the matter his undivided attention.

"So, let me get this straight. You want me to tell you if the suicide note is genuine or fake?"

"Got it in one, Murph," said Jaz.

"I'm sorry to disappoint you, but that isn't possible. I did some research into this subject twenty years ago. A case where a professor had asked his wife to write a suicide note ostensibly as part of an academic thesis. Three months later, she turned up dead in suspicious circumstances. He tried to pass off her old note as a genuine suicide note, but didn't convince the police. Eventually, he admitted murder. Because it was a high-profile case, the letter was published, and I used it as a test case to compare fake notes with genuine ones."

"What did you find out?" Jaz eagerly offered her phone to Murph.

"That it's difficult to distinguish between the two in any definitive way, but there are telltale signs that make genuine or fake more likely."

Murph popped on spectacles that rested on his chest, secured to a lanyard around his neck, took Jaz's phone and read the suicide note. Dan and Jaz exchanged looks, varying from optimistic to *was this really a good idea?* Murph put the phone down and the timid character the couple remembered evaporated, replaced by a confident font of knowledge.

"On the surface, this appears to be a case academics call anomic suicide. That means the victim's usual norms and values become displaced. Here, the individual no longer sees himself to have value. As a friend, a landlord, a father, even a husband."

"So, the note sounds genuine?" Jaz sounded disappointed.

"Unbearable psychological pain causes all suicides, Jaz. We call it psychache and there are elements of perturbation here."

"What?" Dan and Jaz grimaced in unison.

Murph's eyes weren't focused on anything in the room. Instead, his mind sifted through the toolbox of his professional zone. Back in the days, when he worked as an esteemed psychiatrist. "Perturbation. Put simply, it means when a victim's trapped in an intolerable state of anxiety and depression. The first thing I noticed was the amount of negative material. 'I don't want to live anymore. 'I can't go on. 'I don't have any real friends.' These are all stereotypes, the sort of generic sentiments many people associate with suicide and may be tempted to include if asked to write a pretend suicide note.

"In most genuine suicide notes, the writers don't accept responsibility. They don't blame themselves as Roger does here, and there are no explanations. Sometimes instructions are given in authentic suicide notes, often to a spouse or partner, because the individual has accepted that he or she will not be around much longer. The fake writer rarely takes that jump into reality. Fake notes remain in the pretend world."

Murph took a sip of Earl Grey. Jaz's eyes and mouth opened wide. This was everything she wanted to hear. She didn't dare speak, anxious not to deflect the flow. Picking up the phone, Murph read the note once more, then handed the phone back to Jaz.

"It's a tricky balance. I don't want to guide you in the wrong direction, but brief notes full of apologies are the easiest to forge and a portion of this certainly sounds like one of them. But then …" Murph put his fist to his chin, wrestling with the prose, trying to weigh up Roger's state of mind from a handful of typed sentences.

Jaz couldn't contain herself. "What is it, Murph?"

"I don't know. Difficult to put into words."

"Try, and see where we end up," Dan said.

"While people who write genuine suicide notes rarely give explanations, they often praise loved ones. Their writing's often complicated and moving. Roger's message to his wife is a perfect example. You'd have a heart of stone if the phrases referring to his wife didn't touch you. They come across as genuine. Part of the prose is consistent with a fake note, at least the academic analysis I've read on fake notes, but the most compelling portion seems real."

Dan looked at Jaz. His demeanour didn't say Murph's final analysis was the conclusion he favoured, but that's what he was thinking. "That's called hedging your bets, but I suppose it explains why the police are convinced the note is real."

Jaz wore a puzzled expression. Nothing she'd heard so far changed anything. Much of Murph's analysis reinforced her own view, although she remembered being close to tears when first reading Roger's message to his wife. She'd told Cheryl as much at their meeting.

"Tell me this, Murph. Are people, and by that I guess I mean the police, more likely to believe fake notes or genuine notes?"

Murph chuckled. "I don't think they've done any studies on that, Jaz. I think the police would probably take the circumstances of each case into consideration. What I can say is, that although we often feel we live in a world full of scams, crime, and rogues trying to cheat us out of our valuables, people are still more likely to believe what they see, hear, and read."

Dan nodded. "In journalism, we call it dignified by print. People wouldn't give the codswallop some reporters spout any credence if you told them down the pub. But print it, and they believe it."

Murph chuckled once more, this time removing his spectacles and letting them fall to his chest. "Dan, I don't disagree. Professors have even given that a name. The truth bias. The fact is, people, and that includes detectives, are plain bad at detecting deception. Some fakers, as well as genuine suicide victims, even plagiarise passages from actual notes to make theirs seem more authentic. It's a murky subject."

Jaz drained her tea and stood up. "I'm glad we came, Murph. It's great seeing you again. You've been a big help. I know more about suicide now than probably I should, but knowledge is more powerful than ignorance."

"Amen to that. By the way, how's Trish? Those nails and heels any shorter?"

Jaz laughed. "She's the same as ever. Eagle's talons. She's loud, lovely, opinionated, full of beans. Working with me on and off. She's … well, she's Trish."

"Long may that continue. Be sure to give her my regards and tell her to come and visit me sometime."

Jaz threw her arms around Murph in a warm embrace, realising why he refrained from hugging when she almost crushed his dangling spectacles. "Sorry."

Dan shook Murph's hand.

As he and Jaz walked back to the car, Dan remarked the trip had been a good idea. At least now they knew where they stood. He was about to add that it looked as if the police had been correct when Jaz piped up.

"Yeah, looks like I was right. It was murder."

Dan shook his head. He was thinking the opposite.

29

"You'll never guess who we saw last night." Dan waited for Bill to answer.

"You're right, I won't. Because I don't need to guess. Jaz phoned me earlier to tell me you were popping round, and we had a chat. Good man, Murph. I must look him up. Haven't seen him in ages."

"He was very helpful. Knew lots about suicide notes. He's a deep thinker."

"What did you come up with?"

"Nothing definite."

"That does sound deep."

Dan ignored the sarcasm, and talk turned to the woeful state of English cricket. Bill animated as he cursed the batting collapse in the latest Test match. While chatting, Dan's eyes weighed up the layout of Bill's lounge. Television in an alcove, Bill's armchair facing it like a throne in the middle of the room. Large, Napoleon case clock sitting on a small ornate table. Sideboard where he kept personal items, bank books and financial papers.

"Anyway, I'm sure you haven't called round to talk about cricket, Dan. What can I do for you?"

Dan fidgeted with his car keys. He'd sorted through back copies of the *Journal* since last seeing Bill and found a spate of cases a couple of years ago where elderly people had been robbed in Lexford. Turned out to be a rogue carer who'd set up as a freelance, undercutting legitimate agencies. A victim's family caught her by setting up a hidden camera and filming her rifling through their mother's purse.

"Did your watch ever turn up, Bill?"

"No, haven't seen it. No idea where it's gone. Never kept good time. I have the clock, so it doesn't really matter."

"What sort was it?"

"A Rolex."

"Really?"

"On the face of it."

"What do you mean?"

"On the face it said Rolex, but I bought it in a bazaar in Istanbul a few years ago when I took Jean on a cruise."

"How much did it cost?"

"About twenty-five quid. Maybe less."

Dan relaxed. The good news? The watch was a fake. Worthless. The bad news? Chances were the famous name had lured a thief, who might be back for more easy pickings. Only one way to find out.

"Bill, ever fancied being a spy?"

"No, they never stop working. Even when they're asleep, they're undercover."

"Very good. Actually, I was being serious."

"So was I. When I was in hospital for my arm, they took me to the spy room."

"Where?"

"The ICU."

Dan tried not to laugh. Bill's fund of jokes and one-liners were endless. Tripped off his tongue. Sparking his passion could mean losing an hour or more to absurdity. Entertaining as it was, Dan didn't have the time. He fixed Bill with an earnest expression.

"Bill, I think someone may have stolen your watch. The same person could be stealing money from you. Remember that tenner that went missing?"

Bill nodded. "Who could it be?"

"Hard to say. You've had so many people in your house lately. Nurses, carers, delivery men."

"But they're all so nice and helpful."

"Unfortunately, conmen and women always seem nice and helpful. They suck you in, get you to trust them and then nick whatever they can."

"Thieving bastards."

In the two years Dan had known Bill, it was the first time he'd heard him swear in anger. Bill was a giver, not a taker, rarely a complainer. He lived to make people smile, even when he was full of medication to keep the pain of various ailments at bay.

"So, how do we catch them?"

Dan explained that he'd consulted the technical department at the *Journal* and one of the young techies had loaned him a micro surveillance camera new to the market. Dan pulled it from his pocket. About the size of a small matchbox.

"Looks like something out of James Bond."

"Yep, it's linked to an app on my phone and means we can record everything going on here, well, at least in this room."

Dan's eyes swept the lounge once more, resting on the Napoleon clock. "Do you mind?"

Bill shook his head. Dan tilted the clock, opened the back, and fiddled inside. Space was tight, but after easing the battery housing to one side, he could insert the camera. He checked the lens was free of obstruction, then went around to the front. Anyone searching for it may spot the lens, but it could easily be mistaken for one of the clock's workings, and Dan reasoned no one would hunt for a high-tech device among Bill's retro furniture. Dan positioned the clock to give a wide-angled view of the lounge, pointing towards the sideboard.

"Okay, let's see if it works." Dan fished his phone from his pocket, activated his app, and a few seconds later the live feed flickered on his screen. He handed the phone to Bill.

"Bit boring. Don't think Match of the Day has anything to worry about, but it does what it says on the tin. Only problem is, there's nothing worth nicking."

"I've thought of that." Dan fished in his trousers again, this time pulling out a small wrap-around leather wallet. Two twenty-pound notes poked out of the top pocket.

"Aha, the cheese in the trap," said Bill, voice animated. "This is all very exhilarating. Beats drawing the curtains. That's the most excitement I get these days."

"I thought we'd leave the wallet here and wait for the clock to throw up any evidence." Dan placed the wallet on the sideboard in the same spot the tenner disappeared.

"Time will tell, I suppose."

Dan braced himself for another round of one-liners, but Bill was more interested in who would be watching the camera footage. Dan said it would be recorded and recovered via his phone app to view on demand.

"Better not pick my nose then," said Bill.

"Just forget about it and act natural. That's all you need to do. If there's a thief about we'll catch him or her. Let's hope so, because if not, then maybe your memory's not as good as you think it is."

"What did you say that camera was for?"

Dan chuckled as he headed down the hallway. "You never clock off, do you?"

"Well, I might not be a deep thinker like Murph, but I have my moments."

As Dan shut the front door, he heard Bill's parting shot. "Okay then, here's something deep. What was the best thing before sliced bread?"

30

Cathy Wheeler skipped up three steps at the entrance to the restaurant off the Strand in London's Covent Garden. Dan watched her share a friendly word with the receptionist before throwing a smile and a wave in his direction.

He waved back. He thought she looked fabulous, a healthy glow to her fine features. A touch of make-up, red dress matching her purposeful stride. Dan loved catching up with Cathy. It happened infrequently, but whenever it did, he gave thanks for the 30 years they'd known each other.

The pair met at journalism college in Sheffield. Worked together at the *Daily News*, she as foreign news editor, he, covering wars in Afghanistan, Iraq, and Syria. Dan was forever in her debt, mainly because she'd helped Jaz and Trish save his life when summoning the police task force to pull him from the arms of Jimmy Collins's crime syndicate. She'd never let him forget that. Never would.

Cathy collected Journalist of the Year for her work, exposing the gang that preyed on young, vulnerable immigrants, the same trophy Dan lifted the year before. Dan had opted out of the big time to take over the *Lexford Journal*. Cathy became editor-in-chief at the *Times*, but their friendship transcended work status.

Dan rose from his chair as Cathy approached and they hugged in the manner of friends who've shared grave and intimate moments.

"Lovely to see you, Dan, and great to be back at Joe's Joint. How's Jaz?"

"She's good. Almost a fully fledged journalist these days. Following in your footsteps, I shouldn't wonder."

"Good for her. Pity she didn't take up the trade when we did. She'd be a real high-flyer by now. Such a quick brain and a natural nose for news."

Dan ordered sparkling water and a bottle of Puligny Montrachet. He wasn't a big wine drinker, but favoured the finest Chardonnay when he partook.

"You're pushing the boat out. I didn't realise expenses on local weekly papers stretched that far. What have I done to deserve this, apart from saving your life, of course?"

Dan chuckled. "It's what you might do in the future, Cathy. Consider it a down payment."

"Sounds ominous."

The walls of upmarket, American-style deli Joe's Joint housed hundreds of sepia images of famous film stars, providing the restaurant with a striking look and pleasing ambience. Both ordered the house hamburger speciality with extra fries, Cathy opting for the vegetarian version.

"Joe's always did a great burger. Do you remember those nights when we'd pop out of the office and sneak in a couple of beers and a burger followed by a gooey dessert, then go back to check the page proofs? Good times."

Dan nodded, the couple continuing to reminisce while eating. They were too young to have worked in Fleet Street itself—all the nationals had fled for cheaper rental premises long before their careers took off—but they'd frequented many of the famous old journalists' watering holes. *The Bell. The Cheshire Cheese. Ye Old Cock Inn.*

They had stories to tell. Jokes to recall. Positioned on the fringe of theatreland, Joe's Joint became a famous haunt for actors and journalists.

Cathy recalled the time she'd met Robert De Niro and Dustin Hoffman sitting at the next table. "They were perfect gentlemen, except I couldn't tell a word De Niro was saying. He mumbles so much. I kept nodding, smiling, hoping it was in the right places. Those were the days." She laughed, sipped wine, then fixed Dan with a serious face. "Tell me, Dan, why did you invite me here today?"

Dan gazed across the table, his eyes lingering on the images of Lauren Bacall and Humphrey Bogart, as if seeking their agreement that this meeting was a good idea. He almost filed his proposal for another day, then went for it.

"I'll level with you, Cathy. The Lexford Journal's a great little newspaper. Newsy area, murders, suicides, you name it. The management's honest, the staff, hard-working, some of the talent as impressive as anything I've seen, but we're going through a tough time. We're ramping up our digital side and advertising's showing steady growth, but we need a bit of help."

Cathy looked engrossed, but curious. "As do all newspapers. Where do I come in?"

"I've had an idea. Actually, it was one of my young lads who gave it to me after spotting an advert in the online trade paper seeking trainees for the Times."

"I know the one. We're looking to extend our programme to capture the cream before they're snatched up by our competitors. We're committed to take on a couple of trainees at least every year for the next five years. Concentrating on digital, but primed for print as well. It's called investing in the future."

"Perfect. That's where I can help."

"How?"

"I have two brilliant young reporters. One's Pete Rainford, our chief reporter. His dad was an old hack on the Express, so he hits the ground running. The other's Jack Ashton, probably one of the best teenage reporters I've ever come across. They'd be ideal for your scheme."

"Perfect. Tell them to apply."

"I was thinking of something a bit more left-field."

"Such as?"

"I'd like you to take them on, pay them your trainee rates and let them do a year's training under me at the Journal."

Dan heralded a few seconds of uncomfortable silence. He tried to assess the mood, struggling to decipher whether Cathy seemed intrigued, bemused, or about to laugh him out of the joint.

"Let me get this right. You want the Times to pay them, but they'll work for you?"

Dan's tone was serious, but also brimming with energy and persuasion. "That's right. For twelve months only, then they switch to the Times. I guarantee by then they'll be the best trained young reporters on your staff, couched in house style and the ways of the national press. The finished article. Prize winners in the making."

Cathy scratched her head, long strands of wavy brown hair tumbling forward. Dan could no longer see her expression.

"One more thing, Cathy."

"What's that?"

"At the moment, they're both being made redundant. Mad, I know, but I'm afraid the board has decided, although Pete doesn't know yet. We have to lose three reporters, including one on sport."

"So, this is the only way to save them?"

"Yes."

"Oh, Dan, I do love you, you know that. You're always trying to help people and you're full of ideas, but I don't

186

know. Sounds like it could work, but we have protocols and these are hard times. I'm not sure I could get this past the board."

"You're not saying no then."

"All I can promise is, I'll give the idea some thought."

"That's all I ask."

Dan raised his wineglass, and Cathy clinked it with her own. Two hours and another bottle of Montrachet later, Dan sprinted down the platform, squeezed through the closing doors of the 20:50 from King's Cross and headed back to Lexford. He called Jaz.

"Hiya, did you have a nice dinner?" Jaz sounded in good spirits.

"Excellent. Cathy sends her best wishes. She was in fine form. We had an interesting catch-up. What are you up to?"

"On my way to The Anchor with Trish and Pete." Jaz sensed a weary sigh on the other end of the line. "For a drink, Dan. That's all. Well, maybe a chat with the locals, too. Pete was keen to visit the house of horror."

"Be careful, Jaz. We don't want to upset the locals any more than we already have."

31

Pete turned his car into The Anchor car park. Dusk was falling, a warm glow of artificial light and hearty laughter enveloping the pub. The lounge buzzed with drinkers. Chef had shut the kitchen, but a waitress still fussed around tables, clearing plates and dishes. Jaz and Trish found an empty table by a window and Pete went for drinks.

Loud guffaws sprang from a bunch of men standing at the bar, prompting Trish to lean towards Jaz. "Dan's headline doesn't seem to have bothered the natives, does it?"

"No, thank goodness. I suppose we think everyone's as close to the stories as we are when headlines stare at us in black and white in the office. It's our job, but we forget that people have lives, other stuff going on. We're merely a sideshow. Fish and chip paper someone once said."

"By the way, how was Murph?"

"Hasn't changed a bit. He asked about you and your nails and told me to tell you to go and see him."

"I will. I'd love to visit him. Honest." The snug door swung open and Trish glimpsed one of the twins. "There's Joe, or is it Victor?"

"Did he have a hat on?"

"No."

"Think that's Victor, although I can never be sure. They're identical."

"Wonder if their wives ever get mixed up."

The girls chuckled at the thought, spotting Logan heading in their direction, carrying a tray of drinks for another table.

He stopped as he passed. "Nice to see you two again." He looked at Jaz, eyes dancing on top of his permanent smile. "How's Northanger Abbey coming on?"

"Loving it. I'm up to where Catherine finds out Isabella Thorpe's no longer engaged to James, but now engaged to Captain Tilney."

"Sounds complicated. Never read it. Bit slushy for my taste, but glad you're enjoying it. By the way, I didn't spot your feature on suicide in the paper."

"Next week. Not finished yet."

Logan moved on as Pete arrived with the drinks.

"You two are very cosy," Trish said.

"He showed me his book collection earlier this week. It's huge."

"What you do in private has nothing to do with me, Jaz." Pete spluttered into his beer.

Jaz threw Trish a coy smile. "I expect better from you, Trish. No, scrap that, I don't, but it was strange he never mentioned the front-page headline and the story linking the deaths of Roger and Crime, don't you think?"

"No. It's Saturday night. He's battling with a pub full of rowdy drinkers."

Pete had been listening in while waiting for drinks. "One of his barmaids hasn't turned in. The bar staff are under the cosh." Another hearty guffaw from the bunch at the bar. "I think that lot are from the boats moored outside. Something about a stag weekend on the water."

Jaz had told Pete about the discovery at the marina, and the possibility that George Campbell's boat may have been alongside Roger's the night he died.

"I'll have a nosy outside, Jaz. Check out the moorings and boats. This is the nearest landing spot to the opening for the marina. It'll be good to acquaint myself with the geography."

"Okay, but don't be long. We'll try to have a chat with Victor, or is it Joe?"

Pete took a slurp from his pint, then wandered outside. The night felt cooler, and he hunched his shoulders against the chill. Light from a half moon reflected in the river's ripples, while borrowed rays from the pub's spotlights illuminated the nearside bank. Pete lit a cigarette and sauntered over to the boats. Two enormous narrowboats pointed upstream, three small craft lined up behind like obedient children. He chuckled as he read the name on the first narrowboat, words scrawled on an improvised banner draped over the real name. *Sotally Tober*. No prizes for guessing where the stag crew would sleep that night.

He walked on. The second narrowboat, furthest from the pub and deep in shadow, looked lower in the water than the rest. Though he knew little about boats, Pete found that curious. After reaching the vessel, he clambered down the grass bank onto the mooring, nursing his pint. Pitch black, no sign of life, the only sound, faint quacking of distant ducks and gentle lapping of water against the hull.

The blow came without warning. Pete's glass spun from his hand and he slumped to the ground, struggling to compute what was happening, eyes refusing to focus. Everything appeared black, mushy. Pete experienced the sensation of stumbling down a long tunnel where he saw a light and the shadowy shape of a big man, reminding him of old sepia films he watched as a boy with his dad. Then darkness came.

32

Cold and aching, Pete stirred. He didn't know how long he'd lain there. A lump on his head thumped and blood trickled down his face. He fought to remember what had happened, but his brain hurt, confusion from amnesia that often accompanies a blow to the head. He staggered to his feet towards the light of the pub, where Jaz and Trish sat by the window talking to a man.

"Did you know George owned a narrowboat?" Jaz asked Victor.

"Of course, a posh one too. He lived on it until a couple of years ago. Had a toilet, shower, kitchen, the works. Even had a wood-burning stove."

"How did he afford that, as well as a fancy sports car?"

"Crime was an only child and his parents died within six months of each other. He moved into their old house and they left everything to him. He was worth a fortune, but it took a persuasive man to drag a round out of him. Tight as the lid on a pickle jar."

Jaz and Trish had waylaid Victor on his way from the snug to the toilets. At first, he proved defensive, but they were charming, female, fragrant. Victor and his stammer rarely met such a combination.

"Tell me, Victor, how did Crime and Roger Mansell get on? Mates, or did they have issues?" Jaz's questions were direct.

"Huh. They got on all right, I suppose. They weren't big mates. Crime wasn't big mates with anybody. He'd bottle things up, then blow his top over something and nothing. They had a few ding-dongs over the years. Usually about cricket, when they were younger."

Trish noticed Victor's stammer had eased. She gauged he'd warmed up enough. She could push the conversation. "Did Crime have a gun?"

"Not that I know of. He had a temper, a powerful sports car, and a habit of not getting on with people. The last thing he needed was a gun."

"Did he ever take his boat out on the River Lex at night? Maybe have a drink or a cooling sail in the hot weather?"

"I never knew him drink anywhere other than here. Don't know about his boat. He may have gone for a sail, but I don't do boats. Joe's the boatman in our family. Haven't seen Crime with that boat for a couple of years. Think he might have rented it out, I'm not sure. Why do you want to know?"

Sensing suspicion growing in Victor's tone, Jaz chipped in. "We're doing a tribute on Crime for next week's paper. You've been very helpful. Thanks so much."

Victor sloped off to the gents.

Jaz glanced at her watch. "Where on Earth's Pete?"

After draining their drinks, Jaz and Trish headed for the door. They scoured the car park. No sign of Pete. Jaz was about to ring his phone when she and Trish spotted a familiar, unsteady figure trudging towards them.

"What happened to you?" said Jaz.

A nasty gash on Pete's head oozed blood, and he wore a dazed expression. His voice slurred. "Don't know. Must have tripped and fallen. I really love you, Jaz."

Jaz flashed a concerned look at Trish, who tried not to giggle. As Jaz and Trish fussed around him, trying to stem the bleeding with a couple of grimy tissues, a big man wearing a Stetson lumbered by on his way into the pub.

"Evening ladies," he said, touching his hat.

Jaz looked up. "Oh. Hello, Joe."

33

All the way to Lexford Infirmary, Jaz thought about one thing. Not blood dripping from Pete's head onto the car's cream upholstery, but one sentence from Victor's chat exploding in her mind.

"Think he might have rented it out."

That changed everything. If George Campbell rented out his narrowboat, he may not have been sailing it the night Roger Mansell died. Jaz's prime suspect may not be a murderer, the two deaths unconnected. Her doubts demanded another visit to the marina. *Surely the dockmaster would keep records of rental agreements.*

Jaz dropped Pete and Trish at the hospital entrance, then parked the car. By the time she reached A&E, it was gone 11. While a doctor assessed Pete in the waiting room, Trish pumped Maria for news.

"How's Lynn? Is she safe? If Terry's in touch with her, promise you'll ring me. Promise me, Maria."

"Yes, I'll ring. Don't worry. She hasn't seen or heard from him since leaving their flat. I should be home with her now. I'm only here because I'm doing extra night shifts to make ends meet. She's scared, though. He must have put her through hell. She hasn't told me everything, but I don't think she could breathe without his say-so."

"I can't breathe thinking about what that man's capable of."

Maria broke off to triage another patient, and Jaz appraised Trish with her latest thoughts on Victor's revelation.

"My God, Jaz, you never let go, do you? Dan was wrong when he called you a terrier. You're more like a Rottweiler with its teeth around a favourite bone."

"But you'll come with me to the marina on Monday morning, won't you?"

"Of course. Someone has to take you for walkies."

Pete emerged looking perkier, a pristine white bandage covering his head wound. Jaz insisted on dropping him at his house before taking Trish home then heading to Dan's flat. She'd return the car tomorrow.

Next morning over coffee, Jaz relayed last night's news to Dan. He shook his head throughout.

"I thought I said be careful. Three members of staff ending up in casualty hardly amounts to being careful."

"And you sound like one of those red-top tabloids whose headlines are always over the top and don't match the story beneath."

Dan knew better than embroiling in a verbal firefight with Jaz. She had a pretty face and body, but Dan had run into many such women. He didn't find them unattractive, but in his world, physical attributes were not all that counted. Dan preferred women with nuanced conversation born of experience, garnished with subtle shifts of passion and spirit. Sharp tongues went with the territory.

He attempted to lighten the mood. "Did I ever tell you about the first headline I wrote?"

"Go on. Was it memorable?"

"Sort of, but not for the right reasons. It was about a man who fell off a ladder into a rose bush while cleaning windows. He became ill and two weeks later died from tetanus after doctors discovered a small thorn embedded inside his neck."

"What was your headline?" said Jaz.

To generate comic suspense, Dan paused. "Killed by a little prick."

Jaz laughed. "I'll have to tell the guys in the office. They'd love to hear how a journalist of the year kick-started his career."

"Don't you dare. I wasn't trying to be clever. I was young and naïve."

"And now you're old and crikey, is that the time? We'd better move."

They grabbed their coats and Jaz jumped into Pete's car. Dan followed, the plan being to drive Jaz to St Anne's church, where the vicar had arranged a service for Roger Mansell. The couple made the service on time, Reverend Ford heading to the altar as they entered the church. Slipping into one of the back pews, Jaz calculated the size of the congregation. Around 70. An impressive gathering.

Rev Ford gave a message from the pulpit. "I would like to welcome three special people today, who are no strangers to this church. I only wish the circumstances bringing them here were different.

"You will have heard about the tragic death of Roger Mansell, landlord of The Anchor pub, a fervent charity benefactor and helping hand to so many in the local area. Our hearts go out to Roger's wife, Cheryl, and his beautiful children, Jennifer and Tobias, who sit today in St Anne's in the same spots they did every Sunday for many years. This is not a funeral service, nor an official memorial service. The latter will come when the storm of the past fortnight has passed and there's calm once more. Instead, it's a simple celebration of Roger's life, instigated at short notice by those who knew him well. We remember the love and companionship he shared with

Cheryl, the devotion he had for his children, the light he brought into the life of his many friends."

Dan whispered to Jaz out of the side of his mouth. "Never speak ill of the dead. Or, put another way, truth is the first casualty of a church eulogy."

The vicar added detail and anecdotes to Roger's virtues, not once alluding to the manner of his death or the angst and depression he must have experienced. Jaz craned her neck, scanning the congregation. On the right, she spotted several drinkers from The Anchor and a sprinkling of familiar faces, although she didn't know why. She half-expected to see Logan, but reasoned he'd be busy preparing for the hectic Sunday lunchtime trade.

Half-hidden behind a marble pillar, Jaz spied Victor and Joe. Neither wore a hat, and their lumbering frames looked uncomfortable in the church environment. Not for the first time did their similarity prove a source of fascination.

Aware of Jaz's scrutiny, Dan whispered, "What are you doing?"

She leaned into him. "Criminals often return to the scene of the crime. Or to church services like this. Especially if they're devoid of emotion and get a kick out of reliving what they've done. They like to revel in other people's suffering. Anyone in this congregation could be a suspect."

"You've watched too many crime movies."

"It makes sense. Some criminals think they're smarter than the police."

"In this case, they might be right."

Jaz followed the track of Dan's finger, motioning across the aisle at a middle-aged man with a big nose and sunken eyes. Inspector George Cross. When the service ended, she and Dan spilled out of the church at the same time as Cross. They exchanged polite nods, and Dan couldn't let the opportunity pass.

"Hello, inspector. Don't often see you here."

"Only right to pay my respects. We do so routinely in these cases."

Dan nodded, although he detected a curt edge to Cross's manner. "That's nice. I'm sure Mrs Mansell will be grateful. By the way, can I ask if you've had any joy with the search for the other driver in the George Campbell case?"

"Yes, and no. Yes, we now know the black car was stolen—we retrieved it from a car park ten miles away—but no lead on the driver yet. It's consistent with the spate of joyriding we've experienced in the area in the past few months. Kids steal high-powered vehicles, enjoy a blast for an hour or two, then dump the vehicle. In my day, kids would get a kick out of knocking on front doors and running away. Tap latch, they called it. Times have changed. Now, if you'll excuse me."

Cross sighed and shuffled away. He hadn't mentioned the *Journal*'s House of Horror headline and had been civil and informative, yet still Dan sensed an awkwardness between them. He and Jaz waited in the sunshine, watching the rest of the congregation file out. Victor nodded to Jaz as he exited the church portal. Joe wasn't as friendly, donning his hat and leaving without a word. Several churchgoers chatted with Dan, who was well connected with local councillors and owners of Lexford's largest firms.

Cheryl and her children were last to exit. Reverend Ford fussed around, thanking them for coming, hoping in some small way the service had helped ease their pain. Cheryl reached inside her handbag and put on a pair of sunglasses. An elegant widow, she held herself with dignity and poise. No outward sign of grief. Jennifer and Tobias clung close, Cheryl shielding them with a protective arm.

The vicar broke away to speak to another parishioner, and Cheryl spotted Jaz. She strode over, flinging her arms around Jaz in an intimate embrace. They'd met only once and Jaz found the warmth of the greeting surprising. Theatrical even. Eventually, Cheryl relaxed her hug but clutched Jaz's hands in her own, holding her close, their bodies almost touching.

"Remember what we talked about in Cambridge?" Cheryl spoke in a soft tone so no one could hear.

Jaz nodded.

"Well, I've changed my mind. I'm not sure it was suicide. The police have been to see me twice and maybe everything is not as it seems."

"Why?"

"Promise you won't say anything to the police. In fact, promise you won't say anything to another soul."

"Cheryl?"

"Promise."

"Okay, I promise."

"The last two weeks I've been sifting through Roger's affairs and yesterday I discovered, for the past year, Roger deposited ten thousand pounds a month into the children's accounts. Five thousand in each. That's huge money, Jaz. Where did a landlord of a small country pub in Lexford find spare cash like that? Some months, especially in the winter, we wouldn't take five thousand pounds over the whole business. After tax, Roger's share would be hundreds, not thousands."

Jaz's heart thumped. She detected determination and resolve in Cheryl's demeanour. "Have you thought of telling the police, Cheryl?"

"No."

"I think you should."

"They'll probably say he was a doting dad, and he was. He set up the children's accounts. For their education, their future, but the most we put in was a couple of hundred pounds each Christmas."

"Could Roger have funded the cash from another account, one that you didn't know about?"

"I don't know. I'm glad I've found out. It proves how much Roger loved his children and in years to come, they'll appreciate that."

An old lady had taken a shine to the children, asking them about their schoolwork. Dan patiently waited a few metres away. Jaz sensed he found the conspiratorial nature of her conversation intriguing. Instinct told her to continue.

"Cheryl, in Cambridge, you told me Roger was certain something good was going to happen. That he was going to hit the big time, be able to give up the pub and you could get back together. To my mind, there are only three explanations for the cash. He'd won the lottery and not told you. He had a secret bank account, maybe come into an inheritance, and not told you. Or, you really don't want to know."

"Go on."

Jaz hesitated. The time and place were hardly appropriate. Cheryl had trawled through a mire of emotions these past two weeks. The church service for her late husband helped, but it was also a trial.

"I need to know," Cheryl said.

"Okay, and don't tell me you haven't considered this. He earned cash from activity more lucrative, not to say dodgier, than pulling pints and organising quiz nights. Which do you think is most likely?"

Jaz couldn't see Cheryl's reaction behind the dark sunglasses. *Was that a catch of despair in her voice? Maybe, but it remained hidden behind a timely cough.*

After a long pause, Cheryl replied. "He was up to no good, wasn't he?"

34

Breaking a promise is like shattering a mirror. It changes the way you look at yourself.

The words clattered around Jaz's mind all the way home. Sage advice from the distant reaches of time, while sitting on her mother's lap as a 10-year-old following a schoolgirl spat with her best friend.

"Never break promises. It's the surest way to lose friends."

Jaz never had. Whenever temptation surfaced, even when breaking a promise seemed the right thing to do, her mother's words intervened. A family law seared into her moral code, yet rarely causing this level of mental turmoil.

Jaz hardly spoke on the drive home. Dan sensed her angst, asking about her intimate chat with Cheryl and receiving uncharacteristic grunts or monosyllabic platitudes for his trouble. He pulled up in his parking spot and took Jaz's arm when she opened the passenger door and placed one foot on the ground.

"What is it, Jaz? What's wrong?"

"Nothing. Just tired after that late night."

Dan's caring tone questioned. "Jaz? Come on, we both know that's not true."

She eased back inside, closing the door. "Dan, have you ever broken a promise?"

"Yes, lots of times."

"Really?"

"I worked as a war correspondent for twenty years, in places where life changes by the minute. A promise made one moment can risk the lives of friends and colleagues an hour down the line. If breaking a promise keeps people safe, then in my book, it's the right thing to do. Could mean some people would never trust you again, but I'd never forgive myself if harm came to someone just because I didn't want to break a promise."

Jaz toyed with her handbag strap, twisting it one way, then the other, trying to unravel knots Cheryl's information had tied in her mind. Slowly, she decided. "Cheryl told me something. Made me promise not to tell a living soul, especially the police."

"Will it hurt or save people if you break that promise?"

"I don't know. It's not that simple. Maybe hurt. Maybe save. I'm not sure."

"Can I help?"

"If I tell you, will you swear not to tell the police?"

"Only if no one'll get hurt. Put it this way, if I made you promise not to tell anyone something and it turned out that I was going to rob the post office with a gun and knife, would you break that promise?"

"Okay, I get it. Cheryl's news has nothing to do with guns and knives, I don't think."

For the first time since childhood, Jaz blew away one pillar, shoring up her family code of morals, relaying her chat with Cheryl to Dan, who listened without interruption. When she finished, her eyes fixed on Dan, seeking a solution. A light bulb moment. None came.

"I don't know what to say, Jaz, except the same as you. If she has suspicions, she should go to the police to track the source of the cash. May be dodgy, may not. There could be a bona fide explanation. I presume Cheryl wants to know the truth about her husband."

"I don't know anymore. I think she wants peace and quiet. She sounded pleased that Roger had provided for the kids and was looking forward to getting on with her life, but what about Roger? What about justice for him? The cash makes it more likely it wasn't suicide, doesn't it? I mean, who plans their death twelve months in advance? And if he was embroiled in something dodgy …" Jaz trailed off and got out of the car.

Dan did the same, took Jaz in his arms and hugged her close. "The promise on the police is your call. I'll support whatever you decide. That's a promise I will keep."

She smiled and squeezed him tighter.

Next morning, Jaz called for Trish, and they headed to Lexford Country Marina. It should have been one of Jaz's days off, but rotas were irrelevant this past fortnight. They skirted around the marina perimeter, a picture-postcard scene, early sunshine glinting on rippling water, before swinging towards the dockmaster's cabin. In contrast to the solitude of their last visit, the surrounds verged on boatyard bedlam.

Sailing sorts busied themselves attaching and detaching boats to and from trailers, the clink of chains and rap of ropes on metal masts forming a chaotic soundtrack to the working day. Workmen checked rigging, others milled around for no apparent reason, while the heady smell of paint and cleaning fluid hung in the warm air.

By contrast, the cabin was cool and quiet, the dockmaster at his desk running an eye over preparations for next weekend's Lexford regatta.

He recognised Jaz and Trish. "You two again. Any luck with the boat you wanted to hire?"

Jaz glanced at Trish. An awkward pause. The man looked perplexed.

"Actually, we have a confession to make. We weren't telling the truth before. We didn't want to hire the boat."

He fixed Trish with a disapproving eye. "Suppose you'll be telling me next that your sister never hired it."

Trish shook her head.

"Two lies and not yet ten o'clock. That means whatever you say now, I can't trust."

Jaz spoke. "We're sorry, truly we are, but George Campbell, the man who owns the boat, died last week. You can check that in the local paper. A terrible road crash. We are sort of investigating. We're from the Lexford Journal."

"Reporters?"

"Yes. Since we saw you, we've discovered that he rented out his boat, Ride a White Swan. We wondered if you kept a log of rentals."

"Depends."

"On what?"

"On how long the rental period might be. If it's someone renting out the boat for a week, or a fortnight's holiday, the owners wouldn't routinely inform us. A long lease, six months, a year or more, then we'd have it logged. The hirer would take on responsibility for marina fees such as trailer and repair costs. That sort of thing."

"Please, could you check who hired the boat?"

"As I told you before, we don't give out that kind of information. You'll have to ask the owners."

Trish was about to make a crack about Ouija boards and seances, but stopped herself in time.

The door opened. A small wiry man in grubby white overalls holding a paint pot and brush popped his head in. "Remind me, Jim. Which boat's next?"

"Number nineteen, Ricky, on the stand next to the Range Rover. One coat only," the dockmaster said.

Ricky grunted as he reversed through the doorway.

"Hey, didn't you do that paint job on the boat with the swan motif a few months back?"

Ricky scratched his head. "Yeah, I did. What was it called? Ride a White Swan. Yeah, that's it. Not a big job. Needed touching up a bit."

Jim winked at Jaz and Trish. "Two ladies here want to know who's sailing it."

"Some company, I think. If I remember right, the invoice went to LSE Limited, or something like that. I'm not sure exactly."

Trish seized her chance. "Ricky, did you see anyone on board?"

"Not when I was working on it, but I watched it go out a few days later. Admiring my handiwork, actually. A big, beefy chap on deck. Looked like he could handle himself. Bit surly, I thought. Never returned my wave."

"Was he wearing a hat?"

"Think he was, but that's not unusual. Most sailors wear a hat of some description. He wore sunshades too, so I didn't get a good look."

"Thanks, Ricky," said Trish.

Jaz turned to the dockmaster. "Thank you, Jim. Sorry we lied."

"I've always thought lies were like holes in a boat. Eventually, they'll sink you. Much better to tell the truth. After all, costs nothing."

Jaz and Trish slunk out of the office like naughty schoolgirls fleeing the headmaster's study.

Elated, Jaz clambered into her car. "Now we know George Campbell didn't kill Roger Mansell."

Trish agreed. "The same person could have murdered both George and Roger. Big chap, wears a hat, knows about boats, doesn't say much. Remind you of anyone?"

35

Listening to mindless radio babble, Trish waited for the kettle to boil. She'd promised herself a cup of coffee plus an afternoon nap, and while the two weren't necessarily compatible bedfellows, she prepared to give the combination a shot.

Almost two years had passed since Trish completed cancer treatment. All regular scans proved favourable, signs of her battle for life having disappeared. Hair thick and lustrous. Face purged of the gaunt telltale pallor of treatment. Brain and tongue sharp as her heels. Crushing fatigue no longer overwhelmed, but she'd become accustomed to an afternoon siesta. It remained her comfort blanket.

Trish had been busy since Jaz dropped her off. Paid a couple of bills, sown a row of beetroot in her small allotment, supervised the workman, who'd turned up to change the locks. He'd tried to keep the conversation light and frothy, explaining the merits of mortise locks, lever locks, and knob locks, but Trish was a tough audience.

"Any lock'll do so long as it works, doesn't break, and keeps out mad men with knives," she yawned.

With a nervous chuckle, he went about his work, not realising Trish was deadly serious. He was gone within the hour.

Trish made instant coffee and let it stand while idly processing a snippet about the dangers of fashion shoes. Her phone rang.

The shrill voice sounded panicked. "Trish? It's Maria."

"What's happened?" A dreaded ache churned in the pit of Trish's stomach.

"Terry's found her. He's outside banging on the door. He knows we're in. Saw Lynn at the window."

"Is she all right?" Trish heard banging and raised voices in the background.

"Think so. She's talking to him through the upstairs window. What should I do?"

"I'm coming over. Don't open the door. Whatever you do, don't let him in."

Trish slipped into her flattest shoes, grabbed her bag, and dashed out. She'd sold her car after finishing cancer treatment when doctors advised a year's break from driving. Not a burden. One benefit of living close to Lexford Park, especially in summer, was omnipresent taxi drivers plying their trade close to her front door.

Half-walking, half-jogging, Trish reached the taxi rank in record time. Two drivers picked at the remnants of lunch at the wheel of their cabs. Trish jumped into the back seat of the first taxi. Grimy. Torn upholstery and muddy footprints.

"Spring Road, please. Fast as you can, I'm in a hurry."

The driver crammed the last wedge of sandwich into his mouth while attempting to slot the plastic lid onto the empty lunch box. Struggling to connect the grooves, he turned the box around, repeating the manoeuvre from the other end. Still no luck. He twisted it around once more.

"Never mind the fucking lid. There's nothing left to keep fresh. Just drive the car, for God's sake."

The dishevelled sixty-something man, whose laconic demeanour suggested he'd never operated in life's fast lane, turned his head. He looked shocked, sandwich morsels spilling from his lips. "Do you mind? I don't want crumbs in my cab, thank you very much."

Trish screamed. "A few crumbs won't make a difference. I've seen cleaner cat trays. This cab's a sh—" Trish abandoned the profanity midstream. "Just drive. Please, drive."

Affronted by Trish's manner, but sensing her desperation, the man shrugged, tutted to show his displeasure, then discarded the box on the empty front seat. Finally, he drove off. Maria lived four miles away on the other side of town, but the roads were clear and they made swift progress. Swinging onto Spring Road, Trish pointed out the house. No sign of Terry.

The cab's meter read £8. Trish pulled a tenner from her purse, sliding out before it came to a halt. She stuffed the note into the driver's hand. "Treat yourself. Have a sandwich on me."

She pushed through the gate to the terraced home. The front door flung open and for a fleeting moment, she prayed she'd see Lynn. Instead, Maria appeared, worry etched on her face.

"They've gone!"

"What?"

"Lynn's gone with him."

"Gone where?" Trish was frantic. She stepped into the hallway.

Maria took a deep breath, using all her trauma nursing experience to stay calm.

"I don't know. He kept banging on the door, threatening. Saying he'd burn the house down and kill her if she didn't go with him."

"Why didn't you stop her? I was on my way."

"Have you tried stopping her? Lynn's *your* daughter, you know what she's like. Has a mind of her own. Said she couldn't stay now that he knew where she lived.

Wasn't fair to drag me into her problems. I would've kept the house bolted and called the police, but before I knew it, she was gone. They got in his car and drove off."

Trish slumped against the wall, slid onto her haunches, and covered her face with her hands. Tears welled, but she fought them back. She felt nauseous at the thought of losing Lynn again, but two years ago, she'd vowed never to waste a breath or shed another tear because of Terry. Biting back emotion, a burning sensation replaced the sick feeling, not unlike the one she'd experienced in her kitchen a few days before. The taste of hate was familiar. She stood up and wiped both eyes with the back of a sleeve. Her steely calm surprised Maria.

"I'm sorry, Trish."

"Don't be. It's not your fault. You've been a good friend to Lynn. I'm grateful for that, but this can't go on. Lynn won't live in fear. I won't have it. I'll sort that bastard out if it's the last thing I do." Trish slung her bag over her shoulder and strode outside.

"How are you getting home?" Maria shouted.

"I'll call a cab."

"No, you won't. Wait there." Maria ducked back inside, scooped a bunch of keys from the hall table, and pulled the front door shut. "I'll give you a lift home. It's the least I can do."

At the top of the road, Maria made to turn left but Trish pointed right, tone determined. "Let's sort him out now. I won't let Lynn spend another night with him. Do you know where he lives?"

Maria considered lying. Following Terry and Lynn would escalate matters, resulting in more confrontation. Much better to let tempers cool, she reasoned. Then she remembered. Trish didn't do cool.

"Lynn told me he's renting a house on the Manton estate. Ten Churchill Place. Easy to remember, for obvious reasons. Lynn described it as one of those new terraced boxes. Tiny, by all accounts."

"Okay. A couple of miles away. They can't be that far in front of us."

Maria knew arguing was pointless. A brooding silence lingered until they reached the housing estate. Barely into the complex, Trish spotted a sign for Churchill Place.

"Right, let's give the bastard hell," Trish said.

Maria gritted her teeth. Disturbing scenarios crossed her mind, none of them consistent with a pleasant day off. The car pulled up outside the house. Trish jumped out and pummelled the front door. No answer. She banged again. Loud. Urgent.

"Trish, you'll have the whole street out." Maria glanced around, expecting to see twitching curtains, curious faces at windows and doors, but spotting none. "They mustn't be in. If they were here, Terry's car would be outside, wouldn't it? There's no sign."

Trish ignored her.

A neighbour's door swung open and a bleary-eyed man stuck his head out. "Pack that in, will you? I'm on nights, trying to get some sleep. You're doing my head in."

"Sorry," said Maria.

"We need to talk to Terry," said Trish.

"Good luck with that. He left a couple of days ago. Saw him packing a van when I was leaving for work. Said he hated living around here and was taking off."

"Did he say where he was going?"

"Didn't leave an address, if that's what you mean. Going to live somewhere without nosy neighbours, he said. Charming, I thought. Not." The man closed the door.

Trish turned to Maria. "I'm going to the police."

36

A strange atmosphere percolated the office when Jaz returned from her trip to the marina.

The radio blared with the usual regional chatter. Jeremy talked incomprehensible sport with a contact on the phone. Alison and Angela debated the lot of the sexes with Jack and Pete. They were sitting so far apart they could have been married for years. The conversation was spiky, Angela in the chair.

"It's a man's world. A world made by men for men. It's plain to see every time you step out of your house. Open your eyes, Pete. About time it changed."

Pete guffawed. Not a wise move in front of an ardent feminist. He still wore a bandage around his head and was in danger of needing another. "How can you say that? Britain's had women prime ministers and parliament's full of women these days. Not as if women don't have the vote anymore."

Alison threw Pete an exasperated look. "Grow up, Pete. You don't know what the hell you're talking about. You can stick your vote up your arse."

"I was only—"

"You can follow that with your politics and prime ministers."

"I didn't—"

"Did you know Jacob Simpleton was one man campaigning against the vote for women in 1908?"

"I didn't."

"Do you know what he did for a living?"

"No."

"He was editor of the Lexford Journal and in his spare time, a professional shit-stirrer."

"I never knew that."

"Come to think, you're just like him."

"I'm not an editor."

"You're a simpleton and a shit-stirrer."

Visibly jolted, Pete took a step back.

"We're not talking about the vote or politics. We're talking about the ordinary things in life that privileged men take for granted, but discriminate against most women."

"Such as?"

"Supermarket shelves. Kitchen cupboards." Settling at her desk, Jaz earwigged the debate, wading in to show sisterly solidarity.

Pete laughed, shook his head, and turned to Jack. Jack shrugged.

Jaz went on. "Don't laugh, Pete. You're six feet tall. You don't have a problem reaching for the cereal on the top shelf, but next time you shop, watch how many women have to ask someone to hand stuff down. Who designs supermarkets? Six-foot men. Who does the shopping mainly? Five foot or thereabouts women, like me. You do the maths. Then there are studies that prove safety tests for cars don't consider women's measurements. The crash dummies used to test seatbelts are all men, with men's measurements, and crucially without women's contours. I read women were forty-seven per cent more likely to die in car crashes."

Pete looked away, searching for the nearest exit. He was no longer laughing.

"They make smartphones so a man can use them with one hand. Hey, guess what? Most men's hands are bigger than a woman's. Not so smart if you're a woman."

Angela took the baton from Jaz and ran with it. "And don't get me onto toilets."

"Oh, come on. Surely there's legislation that says there have to be as many women's toilets as men's."

"Have you ever stood in a queue for the ladies?" Angela's face had turned a curious shade of crimson.

"Funnily enough, no."

"There's a good reason women's queues are ten times longer than men's. Because men design toilets. Women are eight times more prone to a urinary tract infection than men. They need to go more often when pregnant and require at least as many cubicles as men have urinals. Do you know *why* they don't have them?"

"No, but I think I'm going to find out."

"You haven't been listening, Pete." Angela's anger grew with her exaggerated pronunciation. "Because who designs toilets? Wait for it. Men!"

Pete held up his hands in surrender. Angela sloped off down the corridor.

Jaz laughed. "I'd give up, Pete. You won't win that argument with Angela, or any woman, for that matter. Think yourself lucky the chat didn't expand to childbirth. Anyway, how's the head?"

"Okay. Throbbed last night, but much better now. I feel an idiot in this headgear, that's all." He pointed to the white bandage.

"Hmm, not the best look, but if it keeps the brains in, that's the main thing."

Jaz motioned for Pete to join her and told him what she'd learned at the marina. Pete listened intently. He'd grown to respect as well as adore Jaz over the past year. She didn't possess all the professional certificates, but her writing was clear, decisions sound, nose for news as sharp as anyone on the paper.

"So, what should we do now?"

"We need to know who rents that boat. Who sails it. What it's used for. All we know at the moment is a company named LSE rent it, but there's no record of that firm at Companies House. Not in Lexford, anyway. I've checked. An individual must have set it up with no paid employees. We need to cast eyes on the person or people concerned."

"You mean one of your infamous stake-outs?"

"Something like that. Me, you, and Trish, if you're up for it? For a couple of days. Dan won't wear us wasting too much company time, but after work, maybe? A scout around the marina, watching for some action early evening when people visit the boats."

"A surveillance team? Count me in."

Pete's journalist father had raised him on tales of daring escapades. Searching for elusive figures such as Lord Lucan and other high-profile criminals in foreign parts, in the days when national newspapers had deep pockets and huge staffs. Those days were gone, but Pete had always craved a piece of that action.

Jaz spent the rest of the day researching small companies in the area, hoping a clue to LSE would surface. She leafed through the local trade directory, telephoning several firms on the off-chance. Locksmiths. Loft conversion companies. Letting agents. Basically, any firm whose name or trade started with L. None fitted the profile, or admitted to renting a boat at the marina.

Frustrated, Jaz packed up for home. Before leaving, she telephoned Trish, immediately feeling a stab of concern. By nature, Trish was vivacious. Loud, blousy, full of fun and mischief. Invariably inquisitive, with an answer for everything. Not this time.

"I can't make it tonight." Trish's voice was hushed.

Jaz detected lethargy, a sloth of disinterest in Trish's tone. "Why not? You love a stake-out. We can have a good natter if nothing else."

"Sorry, Jaz. I'm not in a good place at the moment."

The hate for Terry no longer stoked Trish's inner fire. Instead, she smouldered in a more desolate place strewn with thoughts of recrimination and despair. Twice, Terry had wrenched her daughter away and no obvious route existed to finding Lynn, let alone freeing her from his control.

Recognising Trish's torment, Jaz teased the story of that afternoon's confrontation as delicately as she could, promising to help her find Lynn.

"Thanks, Jaz. Sorry about tonight. I'm sure I'll feel better in the morning. Need to wash today out of my system."

"No problem. Have a soothing bath, a gin and tonic, and a good night's sleep. Tomorrow, we'll make a plan."

37

Jaz and Pete pulled into a clearing, upstream from The Anchor car park above the river. Wooden tables and bench seats suggested the area served as a picnic spot, but at eight o'clock, picnickers were long gone.

Across the bank, they could see *Ride a White Swan* at the end of a row of boats in the marina with speedy access to the river. A line of swaying willows partially obscured the pub, but Pete pointed out a narrowboat hugging the bank, along with a couple of similar craft, where he'd slipped and gashed his head. He trained a pair of binoculars on the boats in the marina, reporting all quiet. No sign of movement on or around *Ride a White Swan*, although a few sailing types pottered on decks by the dockmaster's cabin.

"Okay, you take first watch. I'll catch the last of the light." Jaz reached into her handbag, took out *Northanger Abbey,* and reclined her seat to settle in for a few chapters.

She'd read a few pages when Pete nudged her with his elbow, motioning to his right. A cyclist in the distance weaved a drunken trail along the towpath in dire peril of making a splash. Compromising his balance, a cumbersome, black-bagged load strapped to his back, extending two feet on either side of his shoulders. Jaz reached for the binoculars. She couldn't make out the cyclist's features as his head leaned over the handlebars, face down, back hunched with effort, but the white ponytail gave him away. Charlie Brook.

"What on Earth's he carrying?" said Pete.

"Search me, but if he's not careful, he'll end up at the bottom of the river with his bike and load on top of him."

They watched as he trundled nearer, passing The Anchor, whose lights now shone through the trees, cloud cover hastening the gathering gloom. Reaching the mooring for the first narrowboat, Charlie stopped and planted his right leg tentatively to steady his load. He lowered his bike to the ground, letting it fall the last foot, twisting the handlebars so they pointed skyward at a crazy angle. He stepped out of the metal in the same way he might leave his pyjama bottoms and swung the load off his back, dragging it behind him down the boarded steps to the mooring. Reaching the side of the boat, he tossed the load on board. Jaz expected Charlie to follow, but he didn't. He turned around, picked up his bike and headed back down the towpath in the direction he'd come.

Jaz and Pete looked at each other.

"How do you know him?" asked Pete.

"Charlie's the guy who told me and Trish there was another boat on the river the night Roger Mansell died. He lives close to where The Artful Roger's moored. Quite a character. Used to be a millionaire but now lives in little more than a shack on the riverbank."

"Wonder what's in that bag. Could be a body." Pete was joking, but the bag was the right shape, probably explaining the nervous titter embedded in his laugh.

"Go and find out, but watch your step. We don't want you ending up in casualty again. I'll stay here to keep an eye on the boat in the marina."

Pete swung the car door open, half-walking, half-jogging down to the narrowboat. The bag was of hard-wearing duffle variety, tied with toggled cords not unlike a boxer's punchbag. Glancing around to ensure no one was watching, Pete stepped onto the boat, lifted the bag on its end and grappled with the cords. After several attempts to loosen the knot, he surrendered, instead prising fingers under the seam and into the small aperture to touch the contents. It felt like sackcloth. He let the bag fall onto its side, then headed back to Jaz.

"Well?"

"Nothing to get excited about. No dead body or anything. Felt like a pile of sacks."

"That's interesting. I think I know where they came from. The question is, what are they being used for?"

Jaz told Pete about the visit to Charlie's caravan and the plastic bins full of hessian sacks in his junkyard.

"Probably something and nothing," said Pete.

"Yep, I'm sure you're right."

Another hour and twilight fell upon Lexford, the only signs of life, the odd goose honking, combined with laughter and chatter from The Anchor carried on the breeze.

"Okay, let's call it a night," said Jaz.

As she fired the ignition, a light flickered on *Ride a White Swan* inside the cabin. Pete noticed first and grabbed the binoculars. Jaz cut the engine.

"There's someone on the boat, all right. I can see movement. A silhouette. Looks like someone big, but it's hard to tell. The cabin curtains or blinds are shut."

"What should we do?"

"Let's get round there. Come on, Jaz. It's the one sure way of finding out who's renting it."

Jaz revved the engine, and the car screeched out of the clearing, heading for Lexford Marina bridge. Jaz spotted the one flaw in her stake-out plan. She and Pete were on one bank of the river, the boat bobbed on the far side. The perfect view came at a cost. Reaching it across the marina vehicle bridge required a twisty two-mile detour.

Halfway there, Jaz realised another mistake. "Damn! I should have left you on the bank with the binoculars. First law of the stake-out—keep your eyes on the subject at all times."

"Never mind that. We're almost there."

They raced through the marina gates along the perimeter road. Regulation speed 10mph. Jaz clocked around 40, headlights on full beam. The car crunched into the gravelled parking area alongside the access boardwalk leading to *Ride a White Swan*, joining a row of half a dozen motors. Jaz and Pete jumped out and sped along the boardwalk by torchlight, which proved an essential ingredient in Jaz's stake-out kit. Close to the boat, a powerful engine fired up. The couple heard the catch of tyres on gravel behind them. A vehicle pulled out two cars down from Jaz's car and motored up the perimeter road. Too dark to see the driver or identify the make of the vehicle. Pete sprinted towards the boat. No lights. No sign of life. He banged on the cabin door. No answer.

Jaz joined him as they watched the car slide through the marina gates into the night. "Bugger. The swan's flown."

38

Propped on one elbow, her finger tracing words, Jaz lay on the bed reading the final chapter of her book. She read most nights, a habit from university when she devoured so many novels her tutor remarked if he turned her upside down, letters would shower like confetti.

Reading allowed Jaz's mind to breathe. Enthralled by the story of Catherine Morland, she didn't hear Dan climb the stairs.

"Burning the midnight oil again," he said, popping his head around the bedroom door.

"Yeah. Did you have a good night?" Jaz pressed her forefinger on the page to save her place and looked up, tossing Dan a cheery smile.

"Not especially. All turned sour."

Dan had spent the evening as guest of honour at a church fundraiser organised by vicar, Gerald Ford. Dan's role involved shaking hands with local dignitaries, sipping cheap wine, and delivering a talk about life as editor of a local newspaper.

"How did the speech go?"

"Fine, until a guy at the back stood up and called the Journal nothing but a muckraking tabloid."

"What did you say?"

"Said if there's muck to rake, the paper will rake it, as long as the story's in the public interest. That's what all good news is about, but you won't find it rooting through bin bags and rubbish skips for tittle-tattle, tapping phones, or paying nannies to spill the beans on wealthy employers."

"Good answer."

Dan went into the bathroom. "I thought so. Don't think I convinced the man."

"Why not?"

"He held up the front page from last week's edition, the one with the house of horror headline, and invited everyone to see what he called 'gutter journalism.' Then he scrunched the page in his fist and lobbed it at me."

"Did you catch it?"

"No, didn't reach. Hit the mayor on the back of the head, though."

Jaz chuckled. "How did it end?"

"Oh, usual procedure. The mayor looked affronted. The vicar called for calm and the paper flinger flung me two middle fingers and stormed out."

"You got away with it then."

"Yep."

Dan brushed his teeth, stripped off his shirt and slid into bed. "Finished your book?"

Jaz put her book on the table. "Just about. I'd forgotten how much I enjoy Jane Austen. I think it's the humour, the satire, the way she unpicks flaws in society. Always gives me a warm feeling inside."

"How did you and Pete get on?"

Jaz told Dan about Charlie Brook's bag drop, spotting the light on *Ride a White Swan* but narrowly missing identifying whoever had been on board.

"We're going back tomorrow. I still think the key to this whole thing is the boat, and I'll return the book to The Anchor at the same time."

"You make it sound like you're off to the library, not a pub."

"You should see Logan's book collection. It's impressive. Look." Jaz grabbed her mobile phone off the bedside table and flicked through her photo files. She showed Dan an image of the pub's study.

"See what you mean. Not many pubs with a built-in library."

Jaz pointed out *Little Women*, one of her favourites.

Dan spotted *The Complete Works of William Shakespeare* in a compendium. "What makes a classic? I mean, who decides? Reading is subjective. Is it done on volume of sales or universal appeal or longevity? What's the secret ingredient?"

Jaz paused. This was exciting new territory. Most days, she and Dan explored varied topics of conversation from journalist ethics to global warming to more pressing matters such as which firm made the best tomato soup. They enjoyed stimulating debate on politics and crime, even religion. No subject was taboo in the Armitage household, but never, until now, had they touched on her passion for literature. She found that puzzling, but its late arrival energised her.

"Those are big questions, but they label books classics for a reason. Invariably, they're written by the most inquisitive, astute literary minds of an era. It doesn't matter if classics are twenty years old, a hundred years old or, in Shakespeare's case, four centuries old. It doesn't even matter what genre they occupy. Nearly all the classics explore universal themes of love and hate, shared experiences and emotions, often shining a light on human joy as well as frailty and suffering. The language may sometimes appear archaic. The books may be of their time, but in the classics, the messages are as relevant now as the day they were written."

Jaz loved Dan for his sense of humour, loyalty, and compassion, but this new communion was beyond intriguing. She encouraged him to continue. "What's your favourite book?"

"Don't know. I realise that sounds weak and incongruous from someone who's made a career out of writing, but I'm not a big reader, unless you count newspapers and magazines. I was as a child. Devoured all the children's classics, especially Roald Dahl. Matilda. The BFG. The Twits. They were my favourites."

Jaz laughed. "Oh, Dan, how funny. I loved them too."

"I think they probably steered me towards journalism, but somehow I've lost the reading habit. Three or four books a year, that's my lot."

"Okay, what was the last book you read?"

Dan considered for a moment. "The Kite Runner, Khaled Hosseini. Read it before you moved in here."

"Powerful story, great choice. I suppose being set in Kabul, it had a special resonance for you."

"Yeah, you can feel the torment and disruption the Afghan people have endured over the years. In essence, it's a father-son tale, but you can taste the dust. Sense the feelings of guilt, the need for atonement. The power of redemption."

Jaz's eyes widened. He'd said it all right there, with an economy of words and natural empathy. Jaz thought Dan couldn't rise any further in her estimation. In that moment, he had. She snuggled up to his chest, bathing in the feelings of warmth and closeness while viewing the bookcase together on her phone.

Within minutes, she dozed, her eyes flicking back and forth across shelves of hardbacks. Suddenly, she sat up, grabbed the phone from Dan and pointed to the bottom right shelf. "Well, I never. They take me back."

"What are they?"

"The best works of Virginia Woolf. I did a dissertation on Virginia Woolf at uni and had to read Mrs Dalloway, To the Lighthouse, and The Waves. They were brilliant.

She was one of the first authors to use stream of consciousness as a literary device."

Dan grunted, eyes shut, sleep beckoning. "What's that? Sounds like Trish when she gets a bee in her bonnet and you can't shut her up."

"You're not far off. It's when an author expresses the flow of thoughts and feelings so that readers feel they are inside the minds of the character. The technique can exhaust the reader, but if done well, it allows characters the freedom to travel back and forth in time. Oh, I'm not explaining it very well, but Virginia Woolf used it all the time.

"She was quite a tragic figure, actually. Suffered from bipolar disorder, depression, and sexually abused by her half-brothers. Not much peace in her life, but maybe that was why she was such a creative writer. Suffering inspires art, don't you think, Dan?"

A grunt or a snore, hard to tell, came from deep inside the pillow next to her, followed by a slurry sentence. "Know nothing about Virginia Woolf except that she committed suicide. Wonder if she left a note."

Jaz smiled and kissed Dan on the cheek. She placed her phone on the bedside table, turned over, and waited for sleep, accompanied by a whirl of unconnected thoughts. She woke later with a start. Troubled. Dark broodings racing through her mind. Back in her student days, cramming for final exams, working deep into the night to finish her dissertation. Same day, same body of work, same fears and feeling of foreboding churning time after time.

The sepia image jolting Jaz into consciousness was equally disturbing. A middle-aged woman dressed in a long overcoat wandering towards a deep, fast-flowing river and, without breaking stride or changing her sorrowful expression, falling in, disappearing beneath the current, only to surface, gasping, 'Jaz!' before sliding back into the deep forever.

Virginia Woolf. That's who it is. My dissertation. The feeling of sadness Jaz experienced when studying one of Britain's esteemed authors of the twentieth century flooded her brain once more. As did Dan's slurry comment. *Wonder if she left a note.*

39

Jaz pulled back the sheets and padded to the kitchen. Down the years, in times of night stress, a warm slug of milk had proved her calming balm. She poured a measure and popped it in the microwave, then wandered through to the lounge to fire up her laptop.

She found a picture of Virginia Woolf, circa 1902. Long face, dark hair tied in a bun, youthful glow hiding sad eyes. Jaz reacquainted herself with the woman regarded as a pioneer of feminism but plagued by mental turmoil, who drowned herself in 1941 after stuffing rocks into her coat pockets then jumping into the River Ouse at Lewes. She was 59.

In the article, Jaz found a link—Virginia Woolf's suicide note—and clicked. She'd seen a copy of the handwritten note during her dissertation studies and although the content written in a spidery hand escaped her memory, she recalled being moved. Written to Leonard, Woolf's husband, Jaz remembered questioning her tutor on how someone could write so beautifully and rationally, yet behave in such an extreme manner.

Jaz studied the scrawl at the top of the page, confirming the note was penned on a Tuesday and addressed simply to 'Dearest.' The opening thoughts, written on an upward slant, revealed that Woolf feared she was going mad, hearing voices, spoiling her husband's life.

Milk forgotten, a tingle fizzed up Jaz's spine. Fine hairs on her arms and nape stood to attention. She gasped as she read a paragraph towards the end of Woolf's farewell note.

'*What I want to say is I owe all the happiness of my life to you. You have been entirely patient with me and incredibly good. I want to say that—everybody knows it. If anybody could have saved me, it would have been you. Everything has gone from me but the certainty of your goodness. I can't go on spoiling your life any longer.*'

Sure she'd heard those words before, Jaz was now wide awake. Taking care not to disturb Dan, she tiptoed into the bedroom to retrieve her phone, searching her photos until she saw the image she'd taken of Trish's notebook with Roger Mansell's suicide note.

"Fuck." Jaz didn't routinely swear, but this was big. Apart from one sentence, the rest of the prose was identical to Woolf's.

What does it mean? Who wrote it? Would Roger Mansell have copied part of his suicide note? Oh, God, have I been wrong all along?

Jaz's brain thumped. She needed to talk to someone and rocked Dan's shoulder. "Dan. Dan."

He stirred. "What? What time is it?"

"Three o'clock."

"What's the matter?"

"I need to tell you something."

"At three in the morning?"

"Sorry, but I can't wait to tell you."

Dan eased himself to a sitting position, back against the headboard, eyes sticky with sleep. He ran his fingers through tousled hair.

"Makes a change, I suppose. Usually it's my nightmares keeping you awake. What is it?"

Jaz related her discovery, the obvious conclusion being that part of Roger's note was a direct copy of Virginia Woolf's. She opened her phone, pointed to the relevant paragraph and read out the words. "I remembered those phrases because they were so beautiful and poignant. I told Cheryl Mansell as much when I met her in Cambridge. What do you think it means?"

Dan took a while to answer, pondering Jaz's discovery in his foggy brain. "Well, you told me Roger used that study as his workplace. He had access to those books and maybe a thing for Virginia Woolf. He was always quoting Shakespeare, so we know he had a penchant for the dramatic. Maybe he knew the sentiments he wanted to convey to his wife, but couldn't compose loving words of his own, so borrowed a few. It's quite touching when you think about it, and I remember Murph saying some suicide notes contain plagiarised passages."

"So you think the police were right, and this makes it more likely Roger wrote the note?"

Jaz looked at Dan, her eyes uncertain. The tilt of his head and non-committal shrug answered her question.

"Oh, I was so certain. I should have listened. I've wasted so much time."

Dan enveloped Jaz in a comforting hug. "Don't worry. You were right to investigate after we received that anonymous letter. You wouldn't have been doing your job if you hadn't given it the hard yards."

"Thanks, but I still feel a fool."

"That's no way to talk about your fiancé."

Jaz managed a weak smile, turned over, and tried to sleep. None came.

40

There was a limit to how long Dan could stare at a video of Bill's lounge. About 10 minutes, and that was when Bill was awake, which turned out to be rare. The camera Dan wedged in the Napoleon clock was movement activated, at least cutting down the snoring interludes, concentrating on the action. Even so, Dan had surpassed his limit by almost 10 hours over several days.

He'd watched June and Karen, busy at their jobs. Recorded half a dozen other carers come and go, saw one of them spill tea over the carpet, and seen Bill struggle to the door to answer the meals-on-wheels driver. The wallet remained on the sideboard, the Queen's head undisturbed, poking resolute from the top.

As Dan contemplated calling time on the operation, concluding he and Jaz were too suspicious by half, he sat up at his desk. A woman entered the room, head down, back to the camera, no carer's uniform. With slow exaggerated steps, she tiptoed past the sleeping Bill.

"Here we go," Dan muttered, watching the woman move towards the sideboard. There she fidgeted for a few moments, glancing to ensure Bill was still asleep, her body shielding her actions from the camera. "Come on, turn around," hissed Dan.

When she did, the wallet was gone. As she tiptoed back past a snoring Bill, she looked directly at the clock and into the camera.

"Oh, God, no." Dan jumped up and knocked on the office window, beckoning.

Jaz came in and watched the video footage in silence. When it clicked off, she paused for a few seconds in deep thought. Then, "What the hell shall we do? This'll destroy Bill."

41

Jaz rang the bell and waited for Bill to Zimmer his way along the hallway. Dan knocked next door.

Tell the police, don't tell the police. Dan and Jaz had agonised over the ramifications of the video footage countless times and decided against involving the Lexford constabulary.

The woman removing Bill's wallet was Pat, his next-door neighbour and late wife's best friend. The woman with the sweet smile who Bill clearly adored. While Jaz gently broke the news to Bill, Dan confronted Pat.

"Hi, Bill, I'm here again. Can't get rid of me, can you?" Jaz's voice was a touch too cheery as Bill opened the door.

"What did you have for breakfast? Happy pills? You know it's not my birthday until next week, don't you?"

"Of course. Thought I'd check up on you. Brought you something to help the day go by." Jaz took a jigsaw puzzle from her bag and laid it on the coffee table.

Bill picked up the box and gazed at the countryside scene, including a distinctive windmill. "I used to love doing jigsaws when I was a kid. Do you know who invented the jigsaw puzzle?"

"No."

"An Englishman called John Spilsbury. In the eighteenth century, he made a map of the world out of wood and cut around the countries to help local schoolchildren with their geography."

"That's nice, and interesting."

"Died young though. Had a special tribute on his tombstone."

"What did it say?"

"Rest in pieces."

"That's terrible, Bill."

"Not my best, I'll grant you. Tell me where you're up to with the dead landlord."

Jaz's mind whirred with ways to tell him about Pat. She stalled, making a cup of tea, revealing Trish's worries about Lynn. She also told him how she'd staked out *Ride a White Swan* with Pete. Bill seemed engrossed, but Jaz steeled herself, deciding there was no easy way to spill the truth.

"Bill, we know what happened to your watch and missing money."

"Really."

Jaz nodded, a sympathetic catch in her voice. "I'm sorry to tell you it was …"

Five bangs on the door. Loud. Urgent.

"Now that sounds like a copper," said Bill.

Jaz flung the door open. Dan and Pat stood side by side, anxious looks on their faces.

"Have you told him?" said Dan.

"No."

"Good."

"Dan? What's going …"

They traipsed into the lounge, Jaz detecting a tremor of false jollity in Dan's voice.

"We've solved the puzzle, Bill."

"What puzzle? Haven't got it out of the box yet."

"The watch. Remember the Rolex that went missing?"

Dan went over to the sideboard and opened the top drawer. He took out a small display box, then the wallet with two notes poking from the top pocket. He held the box in one hand and wallet in the other, gesturing to Pat.

"I'm sorry, Bill. It was supposed to be a surprise for your birthday. You're always complaining about your watch, never keeping time, so I sneaked in when you were asleep and had it mended at that kiosk in the market. Said it was a dodgy spring. I put it back a couple of days later. Was going to tell you next week."

Dan flicked the box open to reveal the watch.

Pat continued. "I also saw the wallet, and it looked too tempting with all the people you have visiting these days, so I put it in the drawer, out of sight."

Bill looked bewildered. "So, there's no thief about, after all."

"No." Jaz and Dan in unison.

"You were wrong all along, Dan."

"All right, Bill, don't rub it in."

"And you're a good neighbour, Pat. Thank you."

Jaz remained silent, thankful she hadn't accused Pat, who made an excuse about leaving the oven on and made a hasty exit.

"We'll be off too, Bill. Let's get together for your birthday," said Dan.

On the way back to the office, Dan glanced at Jaz. "We're not doing too well at this detective lark, are we?"

"Not this time, but Bill's little escapade proved what I've been trying to tell Inspector Cross."

"Go on."

"You may have heard this before, but things aren't always what they seem."

42

Jimmy Munro had a careworn expression. Years ago, his kind face, caring manner, and listening skills landed him the front of house job at Lexford police station. Back then, Lexford was a small market town. Not much bother. The odd fisticuffs between rival farmers at closing time on Friday and Saturday nights, but the friendly day sergeant was tucked up in bed by then.

All that changed when the government's relaxation of building regulations allowed vast housing estates to spring up, sucking whole communities to Lexford's picturesque rural villages to escape the tyranny of London's property prices. The cut and thrust of life on the frontline of law and order had become depressing, stressful, meaning Jimmy now dealt with as many complaints and allegations in a day as he used to face in a month. Enough to wear any man down.

Trish was his first complainant of another sultry day. She'd been waiting for the door to unlock at opening time, eager, babbling, but Jimmy struggled to tune in to her wavelength.

"Okay, Mrs Parker, have I got this right?"

"Ms."

"Pardon?"

"Ms Parker. I'm not married. Divorced. Parker's my maiden name."

"Sorry, I stand corrected. You're telling me you want to report that your daughter's missing and is in danger?"

"Yes."

"Taken by the man she was living with."

"Yes. She'd left him a few days ago and went to live at her friend's, but he turned up and forced her to go with him."

"Was she hurt or harmed in any way?"

"No."

"Did she go of her own free will?"

"Well, she unlocked the door and got into his car, but only because he was causing a scene in the street."

Reaching for a pen and notepad, Jimmy took details. "What's her name and how old is she?"

"Lynn. She's twenty-one."

"Have you any idea where she is now?"

"No. It could be Cromer. That's where they used to live. Or it could be Lexford. They could have even gone to London, but he abducted her."

Jimmy's brow knitted. "Abducted? That's a serious allegation, Ms Parker."

Exasperation tugged at Trish's tongue. "He told her to get in his fucking car or he'd burn the house down and kill her. Is that serious enough for you? Sounds like abduction to me. He's a complete shit. I should know. I lived with him long enough."

Jimmy's expression remained neutral, but in his head, alarm bells clanged. He sensed the murky world of domestic abuse, fraught with claim and counterclaim, an area police forces find challenging. Full of he-said-she-said allegations, tons of emotion, but rarely an ounce of hard evidence.

"What's this man's name?"

"Terry Marsh."

"Has he ever struck your daughter?"

"She's in fear every fucking day."

"Ms Parker, calm down. And, please, no need for that sort of language."

"Sorry, but he controls her every move, like he did with me. She's not allowed out of the house, not able to use her phone or get in touch with me or her friends. He's forever putting her down. He might not hit her, but he threatens to harm her. Anything to keep her under his thumb. Terry doesn't care about anyone."

Sensing genuine agitation in Trish's scattergun delivery, Jimmy assumed a concerned, sympathetic air.

"It's psychological torture," said Trish.

"What you're describing, we call coercive control. That's an offence."

"I know. That's what I've been telling you."

"The problem is, often the victim doesn't want to press charges. Many women think involving the police will make things worse. That's not to say we can't do anything, merely to warn you that sometimes taking another avenue can gain more beneficial results. Has Lynn heard of the National Domestic Abuse helpline?"

"She doesn't need a helpline with a do-gooder on the end of the phone. She needs someone to keep this bastard away from her. He's bat-shit crazy."

"Has she thought of taking out an injunction?"

"Are you saying you can do rock all?"

Jimmy's eyes developed a steely glint, patience teetering and ready to snap. "Ms Parker, your daughter's a grown woman who left a safe, locked house of her own free will to join a man she'd been living with until a few days ago. A man you admit hasn't physically abused her. You do not know where she is. I will happily take a statement, but we can't do much unless your daughter gets in touch or we at least have an address."

"He threatened her with a gun." Trish clutched in desperation at the emotive phrase, hoping to jolt the sergeant into a proactive stance.

"When was this?"

"You had him in for questioning a few days ago."

Jimmy paused, sucking the top of his pen while scrolling down his computer screen. "I thought I remembered that name. Here it is. He's the guy we picked up in connection with a car crash fatality on Cambridge Road. Had a cast-iron alibi, checked out on CCTV too. From what I recall, there's no evidence on the question of a gun."

"Whose side are you on?"

"It isn't a question of taking sides. It's a case of following facts and evidence. As far as I can see, from what you've told me, yours are dubious on both counts."

"Thanks for nothing."

Trish strode from the station into a wall of heat. Not yet 9:30am, but mercury hurtling towards 35 degrees matched only by the rage in Trish's boiler. She stepped into an alleyway a few yards away on Lexford High Street and screamed. Then again, this time louder, more piercing, the noise bouncing off walls, exorcising a portion of Trish's mental trauma over the past few weeks. She didn't know where to turn. Her mind a blizzard of confused thoughts, Trish resorted to what she always did in such circumstances. Phoned Jaz.

"Oh, Trish, I'm sorry. Can't talk now. I'm working in the office, but going to The Anchor tonight. Come with me, we can talk it through. Pick you up at eight?"

"Okay."

Jaz clicked off, returning to her computer screen. She'd tossed and turned all night. Hitching a ride into the office with Dan, she still wrestled with the revelation of the plagiarised paragraph, but more pressing was the feature on suicide and why it was more common in males and prevalent in recent years in Lexfordshire. She consulted her notebook, trying to make sense of the scribbles she'd made of her meeting with Murph.

One verbatim passage jumped out at her. *You'd have a heart of stone if the phrases referring to his wife didn't touch you. They come across as genuine.* Murph had picked out Virginia Woolf's words from Roger Mansell's suicide note and correctly identified them as real. *Well done, Murph. Still got it after all these years.* That Murph hadn't endorsed the rest of the note nagged, but Jaz put it to the back of her mind and busied herself creating an informative, nuanced article. She quoted official statistics for the region, inserting comments by experts in the field, one of whom revealed that every 40 seconds a person worldwide commits suicide.

All the while, she could see Dan and Thomas Henry deep in conversation in Dan's office. Their meetings had proved edgy of late. This one appeared more amiable, filled with smiles and nods of approval. Jaz made a mental note to ask Dan about it at home.

She finished her feature and filed it into the copy folder to be sub-edited and revised, then went to Pete's desk. He greeted her with a cheery grin, a less intrusive dressing having replaced the bandage around his head.

"Are we messing about with boats again tonight, Jaz?"

"I don't think that'll be necessary." She explained about part of the suicide note being plagiarised from Virginia Woolf's original.

"Who the hell copies a suicide note? That sounds sick to me. And who's Virginia Woolf?"

"A brilliant, creative, extraordinary writer, Pete. Not to everyone's taste perhaps, but she did as much for women's emancipation as anyone."

Pete still nursed scars from his man's world chat with Angela. "I'm not getting into that again. I'll take your word for it. Are you sure you don't want me to keep tabs on the boat? Be good to know who's renting it. Could still have something to do with George Campbell's death. Square the circle, so to speak."

Jaz's voice was weary. "No thanks. I'm going to the pub with Trish tonight. We'll take a look. No point in spoiling everyone's night." She picked up her bag and was about to head for the stairs when her desk telephone rang.

"Is that Jaz?"

"Yes." Jaz recognised the soft, refined voice but couldn't place it.

"It's Cheryl. Cheryl Mansell. Remember—"

"Of course. How are things?"

"Oh, soldiering on. Still feel numb, but trying to keep busy with the children."

"What can I do for you?"

"Nothing. I've just been thinking about what you said at the church. About Roger maybe being mixed up in something dubious. And you're right. If Roger's death wasn't suicide, perhaps it had something to do with some of the dodgy characters who drink or work at The Anchor. Some of his old cricketing mates. Oh, I'm probably wrong, but like you, Jaz, I'm not sure all is what it seems."

"Cheryl, I think you should tell this to the police."

"I will. I will." Cheryl rang off.

Jaz replaced the receiver, striding out of the office with renewed purpose.

43

Ominous clouds rumbled and a jagged flash in the distant sky caught Jaz's eye as she drove into the clearing by the river.

She chose the same spot she'd taken with Pete the night before, applied the handbrake, but left the engine running. Both she and Trish wore light cotton short-sleeved blouses. Trish thought Jaz's vibrant yellow number a tad luminous for a stake-out, but for once kept her opinion to herself as they enjoyed the refreshing draught of the car's air conditioning against their skin. A scorching day had built into a sticky evening. Even the branches of desperate willows on the bank below strained towards the cool of the river. A bumblebee thudded into the windscreen, an air of foreboding lingering.

"Can't take much more of this heat," Trish moaned. "Can't sleep, can't think straight. It's so bloody hot."

Jaz pointed to her left, where the sky had turned a creepy shade of black and purple. "Looks like we're in for a storm, though. Hopefully should freshen things up a bit."

In the time it took to drive to The Anchor, Jaz had relayed the content of Cheryl's phone call and Trish had blurted out the latest developments in the tumultuous tale of Terry and Lynn. The fracas at Maria's house, the frustrating visit to the police station. Seething anger and cold, considered hate tumbled from her lips, followed by feelings of despair and helplessness. By the time Trish finished, Jaz's ears felt assaulted, but she was also strangely proud and secretly envious of the number of profanities Trish could shoehorn into one sentence.

"So where do you think they are now?" said Jaz.

"I don't think they've gone back to Cromer. That doesn't make sense. Lynn was adamant that Terry returned to Lexford because there was a good job and money to be made, although she didn't know where or how. He always hated London, so I don't think that's likely either."

Jaz tried to sound encouraging. "That's good. They shouldn't be too hard to find if they've stayed in Lexford. I'll ask Pete. He could help. He has lots of contacts."

"Thanks, Jaz. Right, what are we doing tonight?"

Suddenly, Trish sounded eager and unburdened, her mood changing in an instant, like she'd flicked an emotional switch. The trait never ceased to amaze or impress Jaz, who told Trish about staking out *Ride a White Swan* and failing by seconds to discover who rented it.

"We know someone's visiting the boat, maybe even living on it, so we'll keep our eyes peeled." She reached across to the glove box, grabbed a pair of binoculars, and handed them to Trish.

"Such a lazy river, rolling on, minding its own business," said Trish, unfolding the binoculars and taking a casual look down the Lex to adjust the focus.

"True, but rivers are like people."

"How?"

"You never truly know what's hiding beneath the surface. I'm going to return my book and ask if anyone at the pub knows who might use the boat. Shouldn't be too long. Call me if you spot anything."

Jaz grabbed *Northanger Abbey* from the back seat and popped it into her handbag. Another growl of thunder echoed in the distance. "Don't like the sound of that."

"Me neither. Thunder gives me the creeps. Always has done, ever since Dad told me thunder was dead people banging on the doors of Heaven. What a bloody stupid thing to tell a little girl. He was that sort of dad."

Jaz rolled her eyes. "Dead man's thunder? Never heard of that before."

"Maybe it's Roger Mansell," sniggered Trish.

Jaz shivered. "Don't. You okay if I switch off?"

Trish nodded and took a bright folding fan from her bag. Like a geisha, she waved it in front of her face.

"Good for you. You came prepared."

Jaz killed the engine and wandered down the dirt path from the clearing, bushes and trees hiding it from the road. Leaves rustled, branches flailing in the spirited breeze.

It was a quiet night in The Anchor. A few couples at tables in the lounge, three regulars propping up the bar. The snug was busier. A darts match in progress, a bunch of young lads whooping encouragement whenever an arrow fixed its intended target.

When the swing door opened, Jaz glimpsed Victor, or maybe Joe, sat on the wooden bench under the window, pint in hand. She crossed to the bar, where a barmaid with cascading black hair chatted with a regular.

"Hi. Is Logan around?" Jaz asked.

"Not working tonight." The girl returned to her conversation.

Jaz regarded books as precious artefacts. Leaving one with the barmaid didn't sit well, especially one forming part of Logan's classics collection. She felt a responsibility to return it to the hands of its rightful owner.

"Is he here? I have something for him."

"I'll go see," said the girl, who seemed pleasant enough, despite a vacant expression.

Logan appeared, a smile as warm as the night radiating from his eyes.

"Hello, Jaz, how lovely to see you!"

Jaz immediately felt comfortable. Logan had that effect on people. A genetic gift, Jaz mused. Blue eyes, high cheekbones, lips curling upwards at the edges, a relentlessly optimistic outlook on life. Natural warmth.

Logan clocked the book in Jaz's hand and beckoned her to follow him into the living quarters. He turned left, and Jaz expected the shot of pleasure. Another chance to appreciate the collection. Walking into the study, she heard pots and pans clanking at the end of the hall. Presumably, kitchen staff clearing up. She handed Logan the book.

"Did you enjoy the read?"

"Loved it. That sumptuous feeling of immersing myself in those long, descriptive sentences. Simple and clear, yet infused with complex nuances. You care about the people as if they're real. That's the genius of Jane Austen."

"That's the secret of any good book, isn't it? Characters with depth and feeling readers can relate to. Hear their voices. You don't need to like them all, but you must believe in them and ideally they should stir something inside you."

Logan returned the book to its home on the top shelf. "I'm glad it aroused such warm feelings. Feel free, anytime. Logan Sharp enterprises at your service."

Jaz took a step back to study the bottom shelf and quickly alighted on the works of Virginia Woolf in the bottom right-hand corner. "Tell me, Logan, did Roger read your books and, if so, any in particular?"

Logan looked perplexed. "Not that I know of. Unless you're thinking of Shakespeare. He always picked out this one." Logan reached over and touched *The Complete Works of William Shakespeare*. "Went through it for little lines he could memorise from different plays. He'd recite them to customers at the bar like some sort of literary aficionado. Got on my nerves. He never read the actual play, hadn't a clue what the quotes meant, but they were good sound bites and he trotted them out like jokes from Christmas crackers. To be fair, that was more his literary level."

Jaz recalled Cheryl quoting Roger's favourite lines from *Henry IV* outside the Cambridge coffee shop, although she appeared to value his party trick, accepting it with appreciation and grace.

"So he wouldn't have been into Virginia Woolf?"

"Roger? No way. He was a philistine. Wouldn't know what to make of moral dilemmas, idiosyncratic language, Woolf's stream of consciousness. Whatever you say about that lady, she knew how to write. Roger wouldn't have had the patience for Woolf, and he certainly didn't have the nous to work it out."

"Logan." A man's voice sounded down the hall. Deep and vaguely familiar.

"Be just a minute." Logan motioned for Jaz to stay and browse the bookcase.

While waiting for his return, Jaz paraded in front of the bookshelves, marvelling once more at the variety of classics on show but also trying to picture Roger Mansell at his desk studying Shakespeare. On a whim, she reached for the book Logan had pointed out, prising it from one of the lower shelves and placing it with a thud on the desk. The book must have weighed several kilos. She threw the pages open to find a bookmark reserving a place in the middle of *King Lear*.

The passage held no relevance, but the bookmark intrigued her. A piece of white A4 writing paper, The Anchor's logo and address, embossed in the top right-hand corner. The paper was blank, apart from Roger Mansell's signature, Christian name only, written in ink, complete with distinctive swirls towards the bottom right-hand corner.

Jaz's heart thumped, her mind exploding with a hail of permutations. She'd seen that signature once before. On the photo of the suicide note on Cheryl's phone. Written on a piece of paper with the pub logo. *Why would Roger's signature be on a blank piece of paper?*

She heard Logan returning and quickly closed the book with the paper inside.

"Had a good browse?" asked Logan, his manner easy, smile even more welcoming. He noticed the gap in the bookshelf and clocked the Shakespeare book on the desk. "Been looking for Roger's party tricks, I see."

Jaz managed a weak smile. "Yeah, I quite like Shakespeare. There's so much of it. You're bound to find something you appreciate, eventually. When you lift a book such as that, you wonder if he wrote by the pound."

Logan chuckled. "By the ton, more like. I enjoy talking to you, Jaz. Don't get much chance to chat books with the darts crowd."

Jaz endeavoured to make her next remark sound unforced, but it tumbled out awkwardly, anyway. "Did Roger do all the ordering for the bar?"

"Sorry?"

"I mean, did he do all the admin, writing to breweries, that sort of thing?"

"Why?"

"Just interested in how the stress of the job got on top of him."

Logan's smile remained, but his eyes looked guarded. "He attended to most of the admin, but sometimes when he was away or snowed under, I'd help him out. He'd leave a few cheques signed so I could pay for beer, food, and other essentials. Roger was organised like that."

Jaz edged a few steps away from the bookcase, standing on one side of the desk nearest to the door. The writing side of the desk, with Logan on the other. She felt safer that way.

"Did Roger sign blank sheets of writing paper, too, so others could order?"

"You ask a lot of questions."

Logan's jaw jutted. His eyes fixed on Jaz, trying to disguise the frown replacing his sunny disposition, but Jaz scrutinised every move. She noticed his eyes narrow, tension stiffening shoulder and neck muscles. She also spied another piece of paper on the desk in front of her. A scruffy hand had scribbled an indecipherable note, but the logo heading appeared crisp and printed in a pleasing blue font. LSE, the first letter of each word highlighted. *Of course. Logan Sharp Enterprises.*

Jaz heard the rumble of thunder and, for the first time, a tingle of fear sent shivers oscillating between her shoulders. *Run into the heat of the sultry night. Jump into the safety of the car with Trish. Head for home, into the arms of Dan.* Jaz's brain implored her to do all those things, but the terrier, or Rottweiler growling inside, wouldn't be silenced.

Jaz swallowed her fear, summoning her sweetest smile. "Oh, look, aren't they cute?" She picked up the photo of Roger's children, holding hands in the pub garden, the little girl dressed in a pink summer dress, daisy in her hair, blowing a kiss into the camera. "How he must have loved them."

Logan nodded. "Yeah. Jenny and Tobes were his life."

For one paralysing moment, Jaz couldn't breathe. Her sympathetic system signalled red, caught in that no man's land between fight and flight as she assessed the situation, an innate reaction to fear common to all mammals. The cute move? Act dumb, smile sweetly, store the information for another day.

She averted her eyes from Logan's gaze, but an involuntary spasm of panic contorted her features as she recalled Cheryl saying only Roger ever called his son Tobes. Her mouth dropped open, eyes widened, mind screaming with suspicion. *It's Logan. He killed Roger. He wrote the suicide note.* She almost blurted out the accusation but somehow held back, saying nothing, biting her lip hard until sure she'd drawn blood.

The silence lasted a few seconds but felt interminable and all the while Jaz sensed Logan's eyes boring into her soul. When she looked up, the cold glint behind that fake smile confirmed her fears. He knew she knew.

44

Logan laughed. A deep bray, Jaz thought insincere. "What's the matter, Jaz? Looks like you've seen a ghost. Anything you want to share?"

The laugh turned into a sneer. Logan picked up the Shakespeare tome and wedged it into the void in the bookcase. When he turned around, he was flat calm. "I think we both know you have something on your mind. All the visits. All the questions. Sure, you like your books, but come on, tell me why you're really here and don't tell me you're doing a feature on suicide."

Jaz's mind switched to overload, screaming to compute the information. *Solving crimes never happened like this in the movies.* Strung out in tidy fashion, clues developed slowly, affording time to deliberate and review, allowing an experienced detective to build a case and nail the suspect with adroit words of wisdom in the last scene. Clues weren't supposed to arrive in a blizzard of confusion piled high by a heavy duty snowplough. The Virginia Woolf quote, the signature on blank paper, Tobias's shortened name, the LSE headed paper. Jaz's mind was a blur. She yearned to phone Inspector Cross and pass on the information. Let the experts solve it.

"I should be going. Trish's in the car waiting for me." Jaz stepped backwards.

"You think I killed Roger, don't you?" Logan's stare pierced, his voice verging on a whisper.

At last, it was out in the open. Jaz's conundrum? Agree or deny. For an instant, she contemplated denial, but wasn't adept at lying and Logan had sucked her into a debate demanding a reasoned response.

Despite turbulent thoughts, Jaz kept a measured tone. "That piece of paper hidden in the Shakespeare volume proves someone close to Roger printed the suicide note above his genuine signature. My bet is, there are more of those order slips around here. They throw doubt on how he died. If the signature on the note wasn't written in ink and verified by his wife, the police wouldn't have been so easily convinced that he committed suicide."

Logan shrugged. "Lots of people work here, drink here, deliver here, pass through the pub every day. If you're right in saying someone killed Roger, any of them could have got Roger's signature. Anyone in the bar. Do you want to interview them all? Be my guest, Agatha Christie."

Jaz seethed, her fight response kicking in. Logan's apparent indifference, scornful words, patronising tone, along with that infuriating smile, chipped at her sense of justice. Something snapped.

"Anyone *could* have done it, but only one person did and, yes, Logan, I believe it was you. You murdered Roger. You're the only one here with a specialist knowledge and appreciation of Virginia Woolf. Was it some sort of catch-me-if-you-can game? Mess with the police. Have a bit of fun. Slip a paragraph from Woolf's suicide note into the one you wrote for Roger and see if anyone could work it out. Pretty sick if you ask me. And we know Roger was earning a small fortune on the side from something dodgy. What was it? Guns? Money laundering?"

Logan's face reflected a strange mixture of anger and bewilderment. "You think you have all the answers, don't you?"

"No. Not all. I don't know how someone with so much going for them—intelligence, education, good looks—could kill someone in cold blood. I would never have suspected you, but the clincher came just now when you looked at that photograph." Her voice rose as she pointed to the image of Roger's children.

"Jenny and *Tobes*. No one calls Tobias that. Apart from Roger. Cheryl never shortened his name and hated anyone else doing so. But someone close to Roger, say someone who worked with him every day, would have known. They could have planted Tobes in a suicide note to make it seem real. Cheryl was adamant. Roger was a kind, generous family man at heart who loved his kids more than anything."

They glared at each other, an accusing silence rending the air. A thunder crack sounded, shaking the building, a flash forking through the darkening gloom.

Logan clapped his hands. Slow, deliberate. "Well done, Jaz. Got to hand it to you. You're sharp and you've made a strong case. You're even convincing me, but I didn't murder Roger."

"What do you mean?"

"I *was* on his boat that night."

"On his boat?"

"I went to see him after I'd sorted the pub meals. Took the boat down for a late sail. We were arguing on deck. He took his shotgun and told me to get off or he'd blow a hole in me. He would have done, too. At times, Roger could lose it. Didn't handle stress well, not like me. I tried to grab the gun. We wrestled with it for a few seconds, then I let go." Logan sensed disbelief in Jaz's eyes. He laid his palm flat on his chest. "I'm not an idiot. It was getting dangerous. I turned around, jumped on my boat and sailed away with Roger's curses ringing in my ears."

"Why didn't you tell the police this?"

"You don't understand."

"If what you say is true, you can still go to the police. Or I will."

Logan shook his head, frustration mounting. He hadn't known Jaz long, but sensed an unshakeable resolve. The terrier in her. Not the sort to let this scrutiny drop.

"Wake up, Jaz. What do you think's going on here? It wasn't a barney between a landlord and barman. I couldn't give a shit about Roger and his pub. Roger's problem was that he was thick. Plain stupid. He thought he could take the money in the good times and bale out whenever he liked. It's not that sort of club, Jaz. It's serious, with evil people. You can't jump on a twenty grand a month bandwagon and saunter off whenever you like. That's not how it works."

"What are you talking about? What club?"

"Do I have to spell it out? The FLC club. Fentanyl-laced cocaine. Drugs. Hard drugs. Dangerous. Highly addictive. The sort you hear about on the telly. That's what your kind, generous, loving, butter-wouldn't-melt-in-his-fucking-mouth family landlord was dealing. Or at least helping to transport."

As much as Jaz didn't want to believe it, if only for Cheryl and the children, Logan's words rang true. The deposit of unexplained cash into the children's bank accounts. That Roger believed he was about to hit the big time and could abandon the pub to save his marriage. The pieces slotted into place.

If Jaz was to believe Logan, and she couldn't think of a reason not to, The Anchor was the base of an organised drugs network. A sizeable one, too, considering Roger alone earned £20,000 a month.

"What were you arguing about?"

"When?"

"On The Artful Roger."

"I've told you. He wanted out. No way I could let that happen. The syndicate wouldn't allow it. Only one way he could leave, and that was the way he did. His death solved a problem for me, but I swear I didn't kill him."

Jaz wanted to believe Logan, but it didn't matter. She knew she had to tell the police. As did Logan.

"I'm going now, Logan, and will phone the police to tell them about our conversation."

Though Jaz's heart hammered against her chest, the words somehow emerged calm and measured. She half-turned to make for the safety of the bar, surprised that Logan made no move to prevent her, when thunder struck and all went dark. Disoriented, Jaz felt someone yank a hood over her head and tie it from behind. She tried to scream, but no sound came.

Meaty arms wrapped around her, lifting her in a bear hug, stealing the last dregs of breath. Through the hood, she could smell garlic mixed with the stench of stale sweat. A big hand slammed against her mouth. Her phone rang in her handbag. That would be Trish. *If only she'd called five minutes earlier.* Jaz wriggled to a standing position, but the man jerked her close against his body, his bulk overwhelming her efforts to escape. She felt a sharp object pressed into her side.

"Make another sound and so help me. I'll knife you here and now." The voice was raspy, familiar, but with the hood over her head, rain battering against the window, and acid fear rising in her throat, Jaz couldn't place it.

"Okay. Out the back and stick her in The Swan. I'll be along shortly to decide what to do." Logan's voice was calm, but urgent.

"Remember, not a whimper." The rasp followed by a sharp jab in Jaz's kidney.

Terrified, Jaz felt herself being swung into the air, thrown over a shoulder, and carried out into the deluge.

45

When Jaz didn't answer her call, Trish sensed danger. She'd watched the storm swing in, a few drops at first, followed by an insistent pitter-patter on the car's roof. A downpour of such ferocity followed, Trish imagined the vehicle floating off its picnic perch, launching like a new ship into the River Lex.

No way Jaz would leave The Anchor anytime soon. Not in a skirt and flimsy blouse. But why didn't she answer the phone? Must be the atmospherics. A storm of this magnitude could deactivate half the national grid, let alone the local telephone mast. That'd be the reason. Nothing for it but to settle back and wait until the storm passed.

If only Jaz had left the car keys. Trish no longer drove, but would have driven the short distance to pick Jaz up. If only. The story of Trish's life. She snuggled down, made herself comfortable in the passenger seat, thinking of Lynn. Immediately, Trish blamed herself for hitching up with Terry in the first place and bringing a loser into their lives. Tolerating his coercion. Not doing enough to rescue her daughter when Lynn fell under his spell, even though Trish was fighting her own life battle against cancer.

As a rule, Trish didn't embrace self-hate, but she couldn't help herself. An ocean of guilt and self-recrimination persisted, washing over her, each wave subtly different in its recollections but generating the same desperate feelings of words left unsaid. Actions unrepaired. It was almost a relief to spot watery headlights across the riverbank moving in her direction.

Trish reached for the binoculars but wretched visibility remained, even though the deluge had eased from its monsoon beginnings. With no keys, Trish couldn't use the car's wipers. Eyes strained, she fiddled with the focus on the individual lenses and wiped the windscreen. She captured a watery image of the car pulling up alongside the decking leading to *Ride a White Swan.*

A big man clambered from the driver's seat. With wide shoulders and lumbering gait, he wore jeans and a dark anorak, hood up against the downpour. He strode around the back of the car, yanked open one of the rear doors, and dragged out a hooded figure. Rain lashed, the night pitch dark, save for the few marina lights dotted around the site, one of them conveniently in range. As the man half-lifted, half-dragged the figure along the boardwalk onto the boat, Trish glimpsed a vivid sunflower shining amid the bleak surroundings. Jaz's blouse. *Thank God she wore that yellow number.*

"Oh, fuck. Mother of God, what's going on?" Transfixed, Trish watched the two figures disappear into the narrowboat cabin. She reached for her phone, fumbling fingers jabbing at her contacts list. Panic rising, Trish searched for composure.

Trish hit the call button. Six rings. Nothing. Then the answer phone clicked in. "Dan, I think Jaz's in danger. We're at The Anchor and I've just seen a guy with big arms frogmarching her onto that boat we were watching, that Ride a White Swan at the mouth of the marina. I'm going to see if I can help. Please, hurry."

Now, the dilemma. Should she run to The Anchor for help or walk upstream to the pedestrian bridge over the river linking the marina with the residential side of Lexford? The latter would take longer, but Jaz had come from The Anchor. If Trish went there, she could walk into the same danger.

Trish chose the bridge, but first reached behind to the back seat where Jaz had left a light blue summer rain jacket. Trish wriggled into it, pulled up the hood, and pushed the door open when the thought occurred that she should phone the police. *What an idiot. I should've done that first.* She called 999 as another thunderclap exploded overhead. The screen flickered. No signal.

"Shit-shit-shit."

Trish tried again. No joy. Jamming the phone into her handbag, she set off for the bridge, thankful that she'd ditched her habitual high heels for sturdy walking shoes. Wind gusting, thunder in surround sound, the strangest of nights wore a sultry cloak, defying the usual cooling aspects of rain slicing in at a 45-degree angle.

Trish had reached the apex of the butterfly bridge when she detected activity to her right. Lights flickered on one narrowboat, hugging the bank next to the outer limits of The Anchor car park. She heard an engine splutter, the gentle chug as the choke depressed. Somebody was readying to sail.

What a filthy night for a boat trip.

46

Darkness. Total. Unyielding. That's why Jaz shivered. The wet blouse sticking to her skin didn't help, but the blackness, even with her eyes wide open, made her body shudder.

As a child, Jaz always insisted on a night light. Her mother reckoned she suffered from an overactive imagination. Jaz feared robbers would steal her toys or kidnappers would carry her off into the night. Doctors never confirmed a potential diagnosis of nyctophobia, but as the years passed, she learned to live with the unlimited frightening possibilities her brain equated with darkness.

This was beyond frightening. Dragged onto the boat by a faceless assailant, hood still in place, hands tied behind her back, bundled into a tiny wooden hatch at the prow with the door snapped shut and not a word of explanation. Her head felt hot and damp inside the hood, but she could smell cleaning fluid and paint mixed with the damp odour of weed and river water. She felt rough material at her back. Hessian sacks. Most likely a storage compartment, with enough room to sit but not stand or even kneel. Jaz was small-boned, double-jointed. It proved an easy manoeuvre to slip her hands underneath her, and tuck her legs inside the V-shape formed by her arms to balance her body. She pulled at the hood, fumbling for the knot, surprised how easily it loosened. The air against her face was cool.

Jaz tried biting the duct tape, but her abductor had tied it in criss-cross fashion, making it difficult. The darkness presented an equal challenge. In the nyctophobe's world, once the lights extinguish, fear spreads like a virus. Jaz knew that. She breathed deeply, trying to calm her fevered mind, recalling her mother's take on horror movies. 'The good ones never show the monsters, Jaz, because lots of people have imaginations like you. Makes things much scarier than a film director ever could.'

Breathing became easier. She tried pushing her feet against the hatch door, realising it was heavy with a solid lock and anyway, there wasn't enough room to aim a powerful kick. No chance of escape.

Oh, God, how stupid was I to get involved? Why didn't I take Trish to the pub with me? Why didn't I suspect Logan? LSE, for Heaven's sake. It's obvious now. He had the opportunity. The means. The motive.

She heard a noise close to her head on the other side of the compartment. A knock. Soft at first, then louder, more persistent.

Finally, a voice. "Hello, who's that?"

A young woman's tone. High-pitched and familiar, yet Jaz couldn't place it.

"My name's Jaz. Who are you?"

"Jaz! Thank goodness. It's Lynn."

For a moment, Jaz felt a surge of relief, expecting Lynn to open the hatch and lead her to safety. Then cruel reality dawned.

Lynn's voice, weak and plaintive. "I've been in here hours. Terry's a heartless bastard. Every time he goes out on a job, he makes me stay in here. It's hot, cramped and I can't see a thing. It's worse than a prison. I have to get away from him, this time for good."

Lynn's hatch was a mirror image of Jaz's. Two compartments-cum-cell blocks spanning the seven-foot width of the boat separated by a thin, wooden dividing wall.

"How long have you been on the boat, Lynn?"

"I've lost track of time. Don't even know what day it is, but I've been here ever since Terry came to Maria's. He said we were going to live on a boat. Have a taste of luxury. Some fucking luxury this is."

Jaz's mind engaged at the tale of Lynn's ordeal, the symptoms of nyctophobia buried once more into a recess of her brain. Lynn's presence provided focus. Someone to fight for other than herself.

"Tell me, Lynn. Do you know what Terry's mixed up in?"

"I know he's driving for someone. Not taxi work like in Cromer. He has to load stuff up at night from one of the other boats, then he's gone for hours. Some sort of haulage, I think."

"Have you seen him with that gun again?"

"No."

"Where's the other boat? The one he loads up from."

"Across the river, on the opposite bank. Moored up near to the pub. He uses a small rowing boat to reach it."

"Listen, Lynn, I came to the pub with your mum tonight and she's waiting for me in my car. When she realises I'm not coming, and can't get in touch, she'll come for us, hopefully with half a dozen cops."

Jaz knew Trish would have been monitoring Ride a White Swan through the binoculars. On any other night, Trish would have seen the man carrying Jaz on board, but Jaz couldn't be certain. The storm was wild, visibility poor, and she'd taken the car keys. Trish had no wipers. *What a fool.*

Jaz put her mistakes on hold and in between pumping Lynn for more information, once again tried chewing her way through the duct tape. It wasn't working, at least not quickly enough. The sound of heavy boots resounded on the decking. Two men, one much heavier than the other. They didn't come into the heart of the boat but stayed at the entrance to the cabin, near the wheelhouse, sheltering from the downpour. The boat stretched to 70 feet long, and the compartment was too distant to hear what the men were saying. Jaz detected Logan's voice, the chat urgent, heated.

Minutes later, the hatch swung open. Jaz blinked at the light and saw Logan on his haunches, blue eyes sparkling, usual grin in place. Rain dripped from his black waterproof jacket.

"I hope you're pleased with yourself. You've caused me no end of bother." Logan's voice was full of composure.

"From where I'm sitting, I'd say I'm the one in bother."

Logan chuckled. "You're a smart one, Jaz. That's for sure."

"Did you kill George?" The question had troubled Jaz for some time and she didn't know whether she'd get the chance to ask again.

"Crime. Poor old Crime." Logan shook his head, deliberating whether to answer. A naturally chatty manner, large ego, and genuine respect for Jaz proved too formidable to silence.

"Crime was much misunderstood. A decent guy. Kept himself to himself. Rented this boat out for an honest price and didn't ask questions. Had no problems with him. A few weeks ago, he found out Roger had his nose in the trough and that all changed. There had been some animosity between them going back years—to do with cricket, I think—and Crime thought Roger was a prat for breaking up his family."

"So, you did kill George."

Logan ignored Jaz's accusation. "He started giving Roger a hard time and when Roger died, he wasn't exactly upset. But Crime knew about the club, discovered his boat was involved, and word was, he'd sent an anonymous note to the cops or the press, or both, pointing the finger at us."

Jaz recalled her excitement at reading that note in the editorial office. Not from a nutter after all, although its sparse and cryptic content hadn't exactly fingered anyone.

"We needed to frighten him enough to keep him in check. He'd become a problem. If he was half as good a driver as he claimed, he'd be sitting in the pub right now nursing a pint. It's not my fault he wrapped himself around that telegraph pole."

"You were chasing him?"

No denial. Logan looked away.

"What happens now?" said Jaz.

"Thanks to you, our little money-spinning operation's dead in the water."

"Like Roger Mansell, you mean."

Jaz's lacerating sarcasm provoked a lip curl and shake of the head from Logan.

"I'm off to a new life. There are some who would've preferred you to disappear, Jaz, but I'm not that sort of guy, whatever you think. Bob Marley, remember? That's me. Go with the flow. Don't worry about a thing. So, I'm going to disappear instead. I'm sure people knew you were coming here, and I'm sure you've voiced your suspicions to your sidekicks. That means you'll have to stay here a bit longer while we sort a few things out."

Jaz thought the matter-of-fact tone surreal. Logan had assumed the manner of a hotel manager informing a guest her room wasn't quite ready and could she take a seat in the lounge? He made to shut the hatch, but Jaz jammed her foot in the door. She needed to know.

"Logan, why did you quote Virginia Woolf in the suicide note?"

"Don't know what you're talking about." He looked Jaz in the eye, his gaze steady and honest. "I read Virginia Woolf years ago and studied her style, but haven't opened one of her books for ages. Roger gave them to me, but they're not my cup of tea. You can believe that or not."

"Give yourself up." Jaz's tone beseeched, a plaintive appeal driven by desperation. "You've so much going for you. Well-read and sensitive, not a hardened criminal. You shouldn't be hooking up with a loser like Terry Marsh. You're young. Don't waste your life. Think of your future."

Logan chuckled. "I live for today. You must realise that by now. Let me tell you something my dear old mum once told me." He swallowed, striving to recall the precise wording of a long-lost saying before fixing Jaz with an earnest gaze. "Yesterday is history. Tomorrow is a mystery. Today is a gift. That's why they call it the present." He paused, bowing his head for a moment as if the words demanded sacred respect. "Now, if you don't mind."

His smile dazzled even brighter, and Jaz instinctively smiled back as he eased her foot out of the way. The door slammed shut. Imprisoned with fate unknown, terrified beyond belief, yet Jaz still found something endearing about this handsome, fey, enigmatic barman. It didn't mean he wasn't a killer. History's laden with charming serial killers. Charm facilitates the trust required to seduce their victims, she reasoned.

Darkness returned. Jaz bit ferociously at the duct tape around her wrists. If Logan and his accomplices realised their time in Lexford had expired, Jaz calculated they wouldn't hang around.

"What's happening?" Jaz heard Lynn's whimpered question through the dividing wall.

"I think they're cutting and running while they still can. We're going to be okay, Lynn. Hopefully, Trish has called the cops. Help's on its way, I'm sure."

Jaz sensed boots on the deck above. A flurry of activity and a couple of sharp, high-pitched shouts, indecipherable amid the squall of wind and rain.

"That sounds like Terry," Lynn shouted.

Jaz pressed her ear to the hatch door. Footsteps approaching inside the cabin, then a swishing sound as if someone was shaking bottled water. Violent. Up and down. Side to side. Then the smell of fumes permeated the hatch door.

Jaz shuddered, fear radiating up her spine, as the pungent scent of petrol nuzzled her nose. In the blackness of that compartment, she screamed. A frantic, visceral shriek of abject terror.

47

"**I** knew you'd come through, Cathy. I owe you."

"I've heard that before, Dan. It's becoming an annual ritual. Like Glastonbury or the running of the bulls in Pamplona. Hey, it's July. Roll up, must be time to save Dan Armitage's arse again."

Dan chuckled. His phone beeped, showing another caller waiting, but he ignored it. The current call held his undivided attention. The one he'd yearned for.

"Okay, Cathy. Hilarious."

"I'm not joking. You'll pay for this. We'll want our pound of flesh. You can forget taking Jasmine on any exotic holidays for a year, at least."

Dan was elated. The *Times* board had approved his audacious plan to train two young journalists at the *Journal* for the next five years. Two per year, starting with Pete and Jack. The *Times* would pay the wages, but in return the board expected Dan, as a former journalist of the year, to host a dozen reporting seminars at a variety of the company's outlets. Pete and Jack's jobs were safe.

"Cathy, you don't know how much this means to me. Can we meet next week at Joe's Joint to go through the details?"

"Only if you ply me with fine wine again."

"You're on."

Ringing off, Dan saw a new voicemail. Trish, her voice muffled, intermittent. He pressed the phone to his ear. The message made no sense, but the tone was urgent. Piecing together the fractured phrases, Dan's stomach churned. Hot, nauseous, his breath quickening. He recognised the signs. The same panic he'd experienced half a lifetime ago when police informed him a drugged-up driver had run down and killed his wife. The same desperation he'd felt when witnessing his best friend incinerated in Iraq.

Dan grabbed his coat and car keys, bounded down the apartment block's stairs, and dived into his car, oblivious to the downpour. Even in dark, filthy weather, Lexford Marina was a short drive. He stomped on the accelerator. The car wasn't the only thing breaking the speed limit. His mind was too. *Should have gone with her. Christ, I called it a House of Horror. How could I let her walk in there? If any harm comes to her, I'll never forgive myself.*

Dan gulped air. Stemming panic, he jabbed numbers on his car phone.

A calm voice answered. "Which service, please?"

"Police, and ambulance. Lexford Marina, near The Anchor pub. Armed man. Woman in danger—" The phone cut off. "Shit!"

Dan slammed his hands against the steering wheel. The self-help group he attended for his PTSD had taught him various techniques to relieve such feelings, but none of them computed what to do when the love of your life was in mortal danger. How could they? So, he made one up, roaring at the top of his voice, screeching through puddles, leaving a frantic vapour trail of spray in his wake.

Dan knew the marina. He played there as a boy when it seemed bigger but much less grand. His father had moored a small rowing boat. Summer after summer, barely a weekend passed when his mother wouldn't pack sandwiches, prepare a flask of coffee, and set off with Dan and his brother in search of a river adventure. He could use those distant thoughts as a source of comfort and distraction. Concentrate on the good times. Keep calm.

Hurtling towards the marina gates, Dan controlled the car between the twin pillars with an expert slippery-surface slide, revving again, touching 50mph in the 10 zone and speed-restriction humps. The car rode the first two, grounded on the third, a fountain of sparks piercing the night air. He narrowly missed an oncoming vehicle, then he was there, at the gravel lay-by next to the decking, the car's tyres fighting for grip, throwing up a hail of stones then sliding to a halt.

Dan stumbled from the car into the harsh, slicing rain. He bounded up the four steps onto the decking, sprinting along the boardwalk to the mooring, when a thunderous blast and shock wave knocked him off his feet. He went down, head slamming into the wooden decking. For a few moments, he lay stunned. *A freak clap of thunder? A lightning strike?* Lifting his head, he saw a huge fireball rising from the boat at the end of the dock, shaping into an ominous mushroom cloud. The biblical night served up a staggering crescendo.

"Oh, God, no. Please, no. Jaz. Jaz. Jaz!"

Devoured by the elements, Dan's shouts went unheeded. Rising to his feet, he sprinted towards the flames, hoping beyond hope.

48

Think, Jaz, think. Cramped in the confines of the compartment, Jaz waited for the whoosh of the ignition, scores of wild thoughts surging in her mind.

She tried tearing at the duct tape with her teeth. It frayed, but there was no hope of tearing it loose in time. A story came to mind. One she'd filed earlier that year about a man who lifted a medium-sized car to free one of his children in the driveway. Hysterical strength, she recalled. The reaction of the body's nervous system to fear and intense pressure. Energy and muscle power, otherwise inaccessible, released in a burst of sustained action bordering on the superhuman. That's the theory. Worth a try.

Jaz hitched backwards. Bracing her spine against the solid wall of the compartment, she recoiled both legs as far as the cramped space would allow. Not enough, she feared, trying anyway, gulping deep and flinging all her weight behind a double-footed kick at the entrance to the compartment.

The hatch door flew open without resistance and Jaz realised Logan hadn't locked it. *An oversight in his haste to flee? Or had Logan manufactured an escape route knowing what was coming?* Jaz preferred to believe the latter, but right now she didn't care. Squirming from the compartment, she fumbled to find the bolt securing Lynn's prison. A sudden whoosh of combustion solved the problem. A wave of heat enveloping the cabin, instant fire spitting and crackling at the wheelhouse, blocking the escape route but at least supplying light. Jaz slid the bolt and Lynn crawled out. Sobbing, she threw her arms around Jaz.

"I'm scared, Jaz."

"Me too. Is there any other way out of here?"

Smoke billowed down the cabin. Lynn made spluttering noises.

Despite her tied hands, Jaz grabbed a cotton shirt and a dish rag off a bench. "Wrap this around your mouth," she shouted over the roar of the flames.

At the galley end of the boat, Jaz spotted a sink and a washing-up bowl. She searched for cutlery and handed Lynn a vegetable knife she spied.

"Quick. Cut the tape."

Lynn sawed at the tape, freeing Jaz's hands. Black smoke filled the cabin, swirling along the roof, billowing in toxic waves, flames still confined to the back section.

"Lynn, please think. Is there any way out?" Jaz's voice was frantic, her composure rapidly fraying. Stinging tears from the smoke ran down her cheeks.

Frozen in shock, Lynn looked blank as she held the shirt over her mouth. She knew Terry had secured the foredeck doors the day she arrived. Locked and barred. Then she remembered. "The Houdini hatch."

"What?" Jaz struggled to hear over the snap and crackle of the flames.

Lynn pointed at the roof. "The ventilation window. A skylight. It's an emergency escape hatch."

Jaz reached up, blindly. Her hand touched the glass window and wrapped around a lever. She pulled. It didn't budge.

"Let me. I've seen Terry do it." Charged with purpose, Lynn pushed Jaz out of the way. She grabbed the lever, swivelling it anti-clockwise. The skylight raised and slid, smoke funnelling out, rain flooding in. Lynn coughed and choked, persevering with the lever until the skylight almost retracted.

The boat's cabin headroom was generous, but Jaz and Lynn were short. Jaz felt around, searching for something to stand on. Her hands touched a wooden box full of electrical items. Dragging it under the skylight, she pulled Lynn close to her body.

"You go first."

The skylight space was tight, but both women were slight. Lynn wriggled up, using her elbows to get a firm hold on the cabin roof, then clambered out with ease.

"Lynn. Lynn. Over here."

Lynn knew that shout, but couldn't make out where it came from. Then she spotted Trish's astonished face on the boardwalk. Lynn was the last person Trish expected to see emerging from the burning boat. Trish had resigned herself to losing her daughter, perhaps forever. Now relief surged with terror as she watched Lynn scramble across the roof, silhouetted against the flames.

"Mum, I'm coming!" Lynn shrieked through the blaze.

Lynn slid down the side of the narrowboat perched on the gunwale and leapt onto the boardwalk. She ran to Trish, mother and daughter sobbing and hugging. Watching anxiously over Lynn's shoulder, Trish saw Jaz inching along the slippery roof.

As Lynn had done, Jaz aimed to slip onto the gunwale. She was ready to sit when the blast came, catapulting her high into the air.

49

Ride a White Swan carried two propane gas cylinders. The fire had reached one of them, thrusting it into orbit in a spectacular inferno. Fortunately, the cylinders were stored on the aft deck, the cabin housing affording Jaz protection from shrapnel. Unfortunately, the blast threw her clear of the foredeck and into the river.

Ears ringing, but otherwise unhurt, Jaz surfaced several metres from the boat to a scene of carnage. *Thank God Lynn made it.* Jaz spotted Trish and Lynn hurrying along the boardwalk to meet a man running the other way. It looked like Dan. *It is Dan.*

Swollen from the thunderstorm, lethal current swirling at the confluence of marina and river, the mighty Lex snatched Jaz. A capable swimmer, she'd learned sea safety while body-surfing on Manly beach during her gap year in Australia. Even owned a certificate to prove it. This was different. She thrashed out for the bank, quickly realising she wasn't making progress. The river was choppy, but not overly wild from above, despite the thunderstorm. Still, Jaz felt the undercurrent wrenching at her legs, sucking her strength, forcing her mid-stream.

Seconds of effort in fresh water's fragile buoyancy and already Jaz felt exhausted. Stress of the past hour had exacted a mental and physical toll. She recalled the expert advice, flipping onto her back, feet pointing downstream.

Keep calm. Ride the current. Go with the flow. Don't take in water.

She saw The Anchor's lights shining through the gloom to her right. Even recognised her car in the clearing next to the car park. As she floated past the narrowboat nearest to the pub, the one sitting low in the water, she spotted shadowy figures loading sacks into a van. Logan's blond hair stood out, even though the rain made it lank, bedraggled. He passed sacks to Brian, the pub chef of enormous arms and girth. A face hidden under a baseball cap completed the three-man line. Round shoulders gave him away. Unmistakably Terry, packing the spoils before fleeing the scene of the crime.

Without warning, the current jagged to the right, forcing Jaz closer to the bank. She had an instant to gamble. Flipping onto her front, she struck out diagonally for the bank, using her last thread of strength. She didn't quite make it. The current dragged her under. Taking in air and grungy river water, Jaz fought to the surface. Her lungs burned. Peripheral vision detected blue lights flashing on the bank and sirens wailing, but comprehension proved beyond her. Too intent was she on her battle for survival.

Treading water, Jaz was in danger of slipping under again when a flailing hand brushed against the ropy fingers of a willow tree. A flimsy port in a cataclysmic storm, but she clung onto one branch, hold tenuous, yet enough to ease the burn in her arms and legs. Wolfing another lungful of air, Jaz concentrated on riding the current. Too weary to stretch for the bank, too fatigued to fight anymore.

She thought of her mum and David, the past love who'd taught her to surf and instilled the dangers of water in Sydney half a lifetime ago. Then she thought of Dan. As the inevitable dawned, her limbs relaxed, her hazy mind floating into a whirlpool of submission.

Instead of slipping away, she rose from the water, a meaty hand clamped onto her upper arm. Looking up into the black of night, Jasmine Sharkey saw the blurred image of a huge man in a cowboy hat, with a grip of iron and a steely expression. She didn't know if she was safe. Too exhausted to care, Jaz closed her eyes, succumbing to the comfort of oblivion.

Dan was frantic. He'd learned from Trish that the blast had thrown Jaz into the river, sweeping her away. Sprinting down the boardwalk, he'd crossed the bridge to search for her downstream on the pub side. Screaming Jaz's name, numbed by panic and fear, Dan scoured the wildness amid the white noise of a rushing river, oblivious to three men on the slipway loading up a white transit van in the incessant downpour.

50

L ogan Sharp's wide, anxious eyes glanced over his shoulder as he packed the van. "Did the girls get out, Terry?"

"Who gives a fuck? They're nothing but trouble. I warned Lynn she'd cop it one day and that nosy reporter had it coming."

Logan swivelled to catch another glimpse of the fireball engulfing the boat, and his stomach turned. A plug of vomit rose in his throat. He had no time for Terry Marsh—the last person he wanted covering his back. Too slippery. Wouldn't trust him to pull a pint, but the syndicate's powers-that-be had different ideas, insisting Logan make Terry the wheelman in the Lexford area.

Logan's instinct favoured ditching the narrowboat's cargo, fleeing the scene, and taking Brian with him. Terry wanted to load up. He'd been out all day delivering, returning to the mayhem at the marina in a punchy mood.

"You couldn't run a piss-up in a brewery." Terry didn't hold back on the venom when he learned of Jaz's accusations.

"I think you'll find I've made a success of doing exactly that for the past two years."

"Well, not anymore. Let's get out of this place. It's a shithole anyway, but we're not leaving without the gear. We'll load as much as we can, then torch the boats. Cover our tracks."

Terry volunteered to do the honours, leaving Logan and Brian to load. While Terry transferred fuel into containers, Logan grabbed the opportunity to slip the lock on Jaz's compartment. He didn't trust Terry and knew Jaz was resourceful. Chances were, she and Lynn would make it. When they'd loaded the van, Terry jumped aboard the boat to set the fire. As he clambered into the driver's seat of the van, the windows in the boat's cabin blew, sending a plume of flame and smoke into the sky.

"Good riddance to Lexford." Terry pressed metal to the floor, lurching the van forward. Halfway up the slope, three police cars emerged at the top of the slipway, blue lights flashing, full beam headlights illuminating the scene.

"Shit!" cursed Logan.

Terry hit the brakes. "Let's ram the bastards."

A high-pitched cackle from the driver's seat led Logan to suspect Terry had sampled the boat's cargo. "Terry, this is insane. You'll get us all killed."

"I'm not doing time. They're only local bobbies. Let's go for it."

Terry revved, jabbing the gearstick into first. The engine screamed as he targeted the tight gap at the top of the slipway between one of the police cars and a concrete bollard. The van almost made it, would have done if Logan hadn't grabbed the steering wheel, deflecting it off course, bumper bar ramming into the front left wing of the police car, scraping along the concrete, gouging and screeching. Metal crumpled, the rear wheel shearing off as it took the full force of the bollard. The van shuddered to a halt.

Logan and Brian stayed put, accepting the inevitable. Terry swung the driver's door open and made a run for it.

"Armed police. Stop now!"

Ignoring the warning, Terry stumbled down the bank, heading for cover of the wooded area by the pub car park.

"Stop now!"

Three policemen gave chase, two of them carrying machine guns. Running, Terry fished inside his jacket and pulled out a black pistol. He'd reached the bushes when he slipped on sodden grass and tumbled down sloping ground with a jolting thud. A police searchlight at the top of the bank tracked him. Staggering to his feet, he did something hopelessly reckless. Even in the mad, miserable life of Terence Marsh. He pointed his gun at the police. Two shots rang out. Slumping to his knees, Terry stared into the searchlight, mouth agape, features fixed in a maniacal grimace. Face first, his lifeless body collapsed into the grassy bank.

Even over the wail of a siren, Dan heard the shots. Twenty years in war zones had attuned his ears to the sound of gunfire, but he wasn't concerned. He stumbled around the riverbank in front of the pub, smoke from the boat fires offending his nostrils, flaring flames casting ominous shadows. No sign of Jaz. A blind search was useless. Mind numb, Dan turned and headed for the pub. He needed to persuade the police to launch a systematic search. The pub may have a dinghy. Hell, there were enough boats in the marina, the majority packing powerful searchlights.

He sprinted up the bank, turning left towards the pub entrance. Quite a crowd. Under the shelter of the pub's awning, the darts players from the snug and a few couples watched the raging fires. A bunch of paramedics, with orders to keep their distance until police declared the scene safe, milled around.

Dan's gaze focused beyond them to a man appearing out of the blackness from the bank downstream of the pub. A man with a lumbering gait. *Joe.* Wearing a cowboy hat, he carried a lifeless figure, pale legs dangling, head lolling. Though drenched and torn, the yellow blouse was unmistakable.

"Jaz!" For an instant, Dan's world stopped spinning. He remembered the first time they'd met. Arriving at Jaz's door to take her for cancer treatment, when she collapsed in a hypoglycaemic faint. He'd caught her in his arms and ever since, their lives were entwined. He owed her his life. She'd persisted in looking for him and summoning help when he wandered into the world of a crime gang two years ago, yet, when she needed help, he wasn't there.

Two paramedics ran to Joe before he reached the crowd of onlookers.

Dan arrived at the same time. "She's my fiancée. Is she …? Is she …?" He couldn't bring himself to say it.

The paramedics didn't answer but carried Jaz the short distance to the ambulance.

Dan clambered in after them. "Is she?" he tried again.

This time, a medic replied. "Is she alive, and will she be fine? Yes, to the first question. We'll let you know about the second in a few minutes."

Dan closed his eyes in thanks.

The ambulance crew busied about their work. Stripping off sodden clothes, checking vital signs, swaddling Jaz in a hypothermia wrap and hooking her up to a rehydration drip as core temperature had fallen to a dangerous level. The ambient mercury read 25 degrees Celsius, but the deluge had soaked Jaz on the way to Ride a White Swan and she'd been in the river for a prolonged period. Classic causes of heat loss.

As her vital signs improved, Jaz's eyes flicked open.

"I'm here, Jaz." Dan took her hand in his.

"Is Lynn safe?" Jaz's concerned tone was weak.

"Yes, she's with Trish."

A faint smile. "I need to write a story for the print edition, Dan. Now I know for sure. Roger Mansell was murdered."

"Never mind that now. Let's get you to hospital. You can tell me all about it later."

"Dan?"

"Yes?"

"I dreamed a cowboy pulled me from the river and saved my life."

51

Jaz hated hospitals. She didn't mind visiting; it was the staying she disliked. Too noisy to sleep. Too many germs. If airborne bugs didn't catch you, MRSA hiding in nooks and crannies would.

That was why Jaz woke before six that morning on Lexford Infirmary's observation ward and tuned in to County Radio. The incident outside The Anchor led the main news. Shamelessly, the reporter had lifted his story from the *Journal's* website without attribution. When Dan left Jaz at the hospital the evening before, he'd driven into the office and worked through the night. He established marksmen had shot dead one man and arrested two more, although it was too early for police to release names. With Trish and Lynn's help, Dan had also pieced together the chronology of events. There were quotes from paramedics and a police spokesman, plus a rehash of the tragedies associated with The Anchor in recent weeks.

The print edition now waited for the full story. Jaz was determined to be involved and, with a midday deadline, she needed to write, which was why, when a nurse asked what she'd like for breakfast, she asked for toast, a pot of jam, a spare laptop, and some peace.

For the next two hours, Jaz tapped out the stories, filing them via email to her account at the paper. By 10, she'd convinced the consultant she was strong enough to be discharged. Dan picked her up and wanted to take her home, reasoning she required rest and recuperation, but Jaz insisted on travelling to Lexford police station to make a statement. Dan knew better than to waste time arguing.

"What's the capital of Burundi?" Dan fired out the question.

"What?"

"See. Proves my point. You're not ready for questioning. You could have delayed brain fade."

"Burundi. Yes, landlocked country in East Africa. I remember, the capital city is Gitega, if you mean the political one, but Bujumbura is the biggest city and economic capital."

Dan shook his head. He didn't know if Jaz was right, but he'd learned not to doubt her knowledge of the world, nor her capacity to retain useless facts.

When they arrived at the station, the desk sergeant ushered them through to Inspector Cross's office.

"Miss Sharkey, we meet again," Cross said, stopping himself from calling her the duck lady.

Jaz shook the inspector's hand, detecting a more agreeable tone than when they'd last met. Cross nodded at Dan, while his young sidekick sat beside the desk, notebook in hand.

"I believe you were part of the excitement last night. Would you like to tell me exactly what happened?"

Jaz composed herself and steeled her mind to relive the ordeal. "Kidnapped, locked in a shitty compartment, almost burned alive, and left for dead. That do for starters?"

"We need to sort through the details. We're about to charge Logan Sharp and Brian Snape with possession of Class A drugs with intent to supply, but perhaps we can do better than that. So, if you don't mind and are feeling up to it, the details would help."

Jaz recounted the story of the night before, images sharp and clear from the point when the hood was pulled over her head.

"What a dreadful ordeal, Miss Sharkey. Quite a story."

Dan knew why Cross's smile bore a trace of smugness. Once they'd charged Logan and Brian, reporting restrictions would apply and by law, the *Journal* could only report bare facts. The charge, names, addresses, ages. The rest, all the meat and colourful action, would need to wait for court. Dan would have bet a year's salary on charges being brought before the paper's print deadline.

Jaz fixed Inspector Cross with a determined glare. "I don't care about the drugs. What really matters is what Logan told me. He admitted being on the boat and wrestling over a shotgun with Roger Mansell the night he died because Roger wanted to get out of the drugs trade. He as good as admitted killing George Campbell."

"When did he tell you this?"

"In the compartment not long before the fire. He also had an opportunity to fake the suicide note."

"How could he write Roger Mansell's signature? After all, his wife verified it."

Jaz told Inspector Cross about the signed blank order paper, the bookmark in the Shakespeare book.

"What about George Campbell? Did Sharp actually say he ran him off the road?"

"No, but he admitted he wanted to frighten him because he knew about the drugs network at the pub. And he knew Campbell had sent an anonymous letter to the paper." There was frustration in Jaz's tone.

Dan cut in. "Just how big was this drugs network, anyway?"

Inspector Cross paused before answering. "Well, this will form part of the charges, so I can report it. This morning, police officers, some from the Met and the National Crime Agency, removed around two tonnes of illegal Class A drugs from the van at the scene and from the shell of a boat. All high-grade stuff."

Dan whistled through his teeth. "*Two tonnes.*"

"A street value of, who knows, we haven't put a figure on it yet, but it'll run into tens of millions."

"Where did the drugs come from? Why Lexford and why The Anchor?" Dan's news nose twitched.

"It's early days. We don't know all the answers, but it seems they arrived on a shipment from Holland and the boats were used to transport en masse to towns and rural communities nationwide."

"Are you sure? Narrowboats to transport drugs? Seems like snail mail to me."

"And your surprise, Mr Armitage, proves the point. Who would suspect a tourist boat trundling down rivers and canals during a long, hot summer? The perfect cover for large quantities to reach the heart of communities. Like a mobile library van that no one ever notices. We suspect The Anchor was one of the drop-off points to unload drugs for distribution at speed and in smaller quantities along the motorway routes. Problem with drugs, we only ever catch the grunts, the small fry like Sharp and Snape who take the risks. The real criminals stay under the radar in their fortified mansions using anonymous offshore accounts to rake in millions."

"What about Mr Mansell's murder?" Jaz wouldn't let the matter drop.

"All in good time, Miss Sharkey. I'll put the relevant questions to Sharp, but don't get your hopes up." The Inspector leaned forward, his tone earnest and appreciative. "I believe what you've told me and there's every chance this Sharp guy was involved in Mr Mansell's death, and that of George Campbell, but all we have is hearsay. I doubt we'll get an official confession and the situation remains as it was. No concrete evidence."

Dan turned to Jaz and mouthed, "What about the money?"

She knew what he meant. The cash transferred into the bank accounts of Roger's children that Cheryl had made Jaz promise not to mention. Jaz shook her head.

Inspector Cross rose from his chair.

"What about the dead man? Can you confirm it was Terry Marsh?" Dan said.

The inspector nodded. "That's not for immediate publication. We're informing relatives and an inquiry is under way, routine in any police shooting, but we'll release the name later this morning."

As Dan and Jaz left the station, Trish rang. Dan had already spoken to her twice. Once the night before, when he'd given an update on Jaz's condition and early that morning. She wanted news on the dead man.

"How's Jaz?"

"Ask her yourself. She's right here."

"First, have you heard yet? About the guy police shot and killed?"

"You were right. It was Terry. The police have confirmed, although won't release the news until—"

The line went dead. Dan thought he'd lost the signal and waited for Trish to call back. In reality, Trish had dropped her phone, then threw her arms around Lynn. Weeping, mother and daughter, estranged and controlled by Terry's evil for so long, clung to each other, satisfaction and relief pulsing through their bodies. Freedom at last felt sweet. When they broke away, they looked into each other's blurry eyes.

"His name was written on a bullet, after all, Mum."

"Yes. We may not always find what we want in life, but in the end, we usually get what we deserve. If that's true, then that bastard should have no complaints."

52

"**S**urprise!"

Jaz and Trish screamed as Bill struggled to open his front door. They sang *Happy Birthday* and Dan and Murph joined in.

"My God, you lot are a sight for sore eyes."

It was the first time the gang of five had been together since their meeting on Mount Snowdon. Dan and Jaz had called for Trish, then collected Murph. At first, he was reluctant, but when he realised Trish's talons weren't taking no for an answer, he grabbed his hat and coat.

"Don't worry, Murph, if you need to go, there's a toilet downstairs. I know that's your number one requirement. For your number two requirement, please go upstairs." When it came to calls of nature, Bill had never spared Murph's embarrassment, and the banter slotted in where they'd left off months ago.

Bill had followed the latest developments at The Anchor in *the Journal,* and he and Murph wanted the details. Dan told them what he could, playing up Jaz's heroism but scaling down the scarier aspects of her ordeal. No one mentioned the death of Terry. There was a cosy feeling in Bill's lounge as Jaz and Trish busied themselves unwrapping a cake and dressing it with candles. Lots.

"Steady on. Are you trying to make me feel ancient? The candles must have cost more than the cake. I'd forgotten I was that old."

Dan lit the candles and everyone sang *Happy Birthday* again, then Jaz said, "This time, make a wish before you blow them out, Bill."

"Okay."

"Well, what is it?"

"I wish I could remember who you all are."

53

By the time Dan and Jaz reached St Anne's, mourners crammed the church, many in an overspill standing like living statues against stone walls.

Reverend Ford had reserved pew space for Dan and Jaz three rows from the front. Two weeks since the explosive night at the marina and finally, Roger's funeral could go ahead. The turnout was a testament to his popularity as a landlord, as well as the interest in the case of the body in the river.

Heads turned as Jaz walked down the aisle. She exchanged knowing smiles with Trish and Lynn and waved to Charlie Brook, who'd convinced the police he knew nothing about drugs and his hessian sacks were part of a legitimate business. She slipped her hand into Joe's, who sat on the end of a pew with Victor and recalled visiting his farm with Dan to offer gratitude the evening after nearly drowning. He'd made a cup of tea and they chatted for an hour. Jaz was careful not to mention she'd initially thought he could be an accomplice. Mixing him up with big Brian, charged alongside Logan with drugs offences and false imprisonment, wasn't complimentary.

Half the *Journal* staff swelled the congregation, including Sharon Mercer and son Johnny, who'd become something of a celebrity among his schoolmates since finding Roger's body in the murky River Lex. Pete Rainford and Jack Ashton hovered in a professional capacity, Pete writing a colour piece on what had evolved into Lexford's newsiest story of the year. Jack hung around the church entrance, snapping photos.

Lexford Journal proprietor Thomas Henry also attended. He'd called Dan into his office that morning to relay the latest circulation figures. "Up ten per cent and still rising. We may have turned the corner. Shows the public are still prepared to pay for hard news, meticulously gathered and well displayed."

"Are you saying the body in the river may have kept us afloat?"

Thomas threw Dan an admonishing glance, but secretly congratulated himself for landing an editor capable of steering *the ship*, as he liked to call the paper, through troubled times. Dan and Jaz took their seats. Rev Ford escorted the funeral cortege into the church, led by Cheryl Mansell, flanked by Jennifer and Tobias, all holding hands.

The usual introductions and exhortations from Rev Ford followed over a coffin adorned with an anchor tribute of wild roses in white and red. More flowers spelled DAD. Roger was a talented man, insisted the vicar, a man loved by many. God is full of mercy and compassion, and may he forgive any of Roger's transgressions. There followed two readings read by family members and a rendition of *The Lord is my Shepherd*, then Cheryl rose from her pew and walked past Roger's coffin to the lectern.

Grief, or at least the trappings of mourning, enhanced Cheryl's bearing. She suited black, and her lacy dress, just below the knee, showcased her statuesque frame to full effect. With head held high, slightly frizzed auburn hair cascading onto her shoulders, dark glasses conveyed an air of mystery.

No notes. As if composing herself, Cheryl scrutinised the congregation, searching for a face on which to fix. She alighted on Joe, probably because he had distinctive features, and was in the middle of the church at the end of an aisle. Theatrical, she pointed to a sculpture set into a cornice. The Archangel Gabriel rising on a cloud. When she spoke, her tone curiously combined warm and cold, her words filtering through a mixer tap of emotions.

"My husband was not an angel. He loved his cricket. Enjoyed a pint, more than he enjoyed serving them, if the truth be told. He was easily led, hopeless with money, at times, too generous for his own good. He was stubborn too, and we didn't always see eye to eye, not in the last two years, anyway.

"But he loved Jennifer and Tobias more than anything, and that's how I want to remember him today. Giving Jennifer piggybacks in the garden. Playing football with Tobias and pretending the ball had gone in the net when it hadn't. Laughing and joking with his regulars and quoting Shakespeare, even if he didn't always know what play the quotes came from. I want to remember Roger Mansell the dad, because Jennifer and Tobias were the best things he ever made. At least that's something we could always agree on."

Cheryl nodded to the congregation and returned to her pew.

Rev Ford stood up. Surprised by the brevity of the eulogy, he added a few words of his own, including an anecdote about Roger supplying communion wine at short notice one weekend when the church ran out. "Best Merlot I'd ever tasted. Roger came to the vicarage that evening and we finished the bottle."

The church resounded to polite chuckles. The congregation sang *How Great Thou Art*, Rev Ford administered a final blessing, and pallbearers carried out the coffin to the tune of *Dreadlock Holiday*. Roger didn't *like* cricket. He *loved* it.

The mourners emerged into the brilliant sunshine. Dan and Jaz broke off from the main procession and chatted on the gravel path leading to the church gate. A dark blue vehicle and a white police car pulled up in front of the gate. Dan's brow knitted as he watched a stern Inspector Cross climb from the first car, accompanied by his young sidekick. Two uniformed police officers emerged from the marked car. They strode up the path and approached Cheryl, who had her back to them, talking to relatives.

"Mrs Mansell?"

Cheryl spun around to face Inspector Cross. "Yes?"

"I arrest you on suspicion of the murder of Roger Mansell."

54

Inspector Cross read Cheryl Mansell's rights, but nobody heard. Dan and Jaz stood open-mouthed. One of Cheryl's elderly relatives staggered, requiring two sturdy mourners on either side to steady her. Jennifer and Tobias clung to their mother, unaware of what was happening, while the main body of the congregation spilled from the church.

Police officers stood on either side of Cheryl, who displayed no emotion and offered no denial. She stooped to comfort her children. "Don't worry, everything will be fine. You go with grandma. I have to help this gentleman with some questions, and I'll see you later." She hugged them before being led away, leaving a murmur of shock and disbelief in her wake.

Dan caught the eye of Inspector Cross, who motioned for him and Jaz to join him.

"What the hell's going on?" hissed Dan, reaching the gate and turning left behind the church wall, out of sight and hearing of mourners.

"I'm sure there's a Bible reference somewhere that would sum up what's going on, but things aren't always what they seem does it for me." Cross looked at Jaz. "You were right all along, Miss Sharkey. Roger didn't commit suicide and don't think I didn't listen to everything you've said these past few weeks. I did, but the weight of evidence wasn't there. That's changed since we interviewed Logan Sharp. Not that Roger's death had anything to do with the drugs network. Not directly anyway."

Jaz's face was a study of bemusement.

"This is all off the record."

Cross fixed Dan with a stare. Dan signalled his agreement, then Cross turned to Jaz. "Okay. I'll share a few facts with you. Wouldn't normally do this, but you were adamant Mr Mansell didn't commit suicide. I admit that was one reason I took another look at the case. You were also instrumental in bringing Logan Sharp and Brian Snape to justice.

"As you said, Sharp visited Roger that night on the river. He's given an official statement to that effect. They had a heated argument on the deck of The Artful Roger. Sharp told Roger he was too involved to opt out of the drug deals. They even wrestled over a shotgun, as again, you already know. Sharp left, warning Roger he'd be *brown bread* if he defied the syndicate."

"What happened next?" Dan was eager to hear the conclusion.

Inspector Cross flashed him a reproachful look. "What Sharp didn't know was there was someone else on board the boat, below deck, listening in. We believe that was Cheryl. Roger and Cheryl had been trying to patch up their marriage for the sake of the children. According to Sharp, they'd even planned a couple of days away, but when Cheryl overheard the drugs talk, I'm guessing she flipped. When Sharp left, there was an altercation on deck. We know that because Charlie Brook heard a high-pitched female voice. More like screams."

Jaz frowned. "He didn't tell us that."

Cross wore a weary expression. "Perhaps you weren't asking him the right questions. Charlie can be a contrary fellow, but when we brought him into the station, it concentrated his mind. He remembered a woman screaming after he'd seen a second boat departing, although it was drowned out by wildfowl on the river."

Jaz recalled her chat with Charlie in his caravan. "Oh, wait a minute. Charlie did say the geese were screeching like his ex-wife. At the time, I thought nothing of it."

"Anyway, we believe Cheryl snatched the gun. A struggle ensued, and I think you can guess the rest."

Jaz inhaled, exhaled, and still looked bewildered.

"A crime of passion, then?"

"You could say that, although I think it was more frustration on Cheryl's part that Roger got himself embroiled in another mess he couldn't fix when they were trying to patch things up for the kids' sake. It's hardly surprising that she snapped. I'm confident Cheryl will fill in the details down at the station. There's nothing forensic tying her to the gun or that boat, but the thrust of evidence's too compelling to ignore."

Jaz was still unsatisfied. "But why did Cheryl phone me saying she was going to tell the police she no longer thought it was suicide, when the Lexford constabulary had decided it was?"

"Good question," said Dan.

"And there's a good answer. And you, or at least your newspaper, are part of it."

"How?" said Jaz.

"Because, you're right. After telling you she didn't believe it was suicide, Cheryl rang us and slid down the list of suspects. She's clever. Streetwise. She knew, in any unexplained killing, those closest to the deceased are always prime suspects. I call it the sheep syndrome."

"Why sheep?" said Dan.

Cross puffed out his chest, much as he'd done when demolishing Jaz's duck test weeks before.

"The sheep spends its entire life fearing the wolf, only to be eaten by the shepherd."

"What are you saying? Cheryl's the shepherd?" said Jaz.

"In this case, yes. It's a fact that a victim's nearest and dearest, those who love them the most, are most likely to kill them. We began investigating Cheryl, interviewed her. She was a prime suspect in those early days. She knew that, and either panicked when she rang you, or purposefully tried to hide under a blanket of confusion. By pouring doubt on the suicide notion she'd concocted, she hoped to deflect attention away from herself as a suspect. After all, what murderer would invite an inquiry into their own crime? She probably also wanted to unmask the drugs ring and the dodgy goings-on at The Anchor. There was no love lost between Cheryl and Logan Sharp, that's for sure."

"But what about the suicide note?"

"We believe Cheryl wrote that herself, probably on the boat on a laptop, then went back to the pub to print on an order slip with Roger's signature. She used to do the ordering so that wouldn't be a problem. As you discovered, there were order slips already signed by Roger."

"And the Virginia Woolf quote?"

"You may not know this, Miss Sharkey, but Cheryl graduated in drama. She also trained to be an actress, although never pursued the career professionally."

"Actually, I do know."

"Well, did you know, after leaving university, she also wrote a book? Not that it enjoyed much success."

"What was the book called?"

"*The Peculiar Life and Times of Virginia Woolf.*" Inspector Cross savoured his revelation.

"So that's what clinched the case for you?" said Dan.

"It helped. As did my little chat with Sharp, but the clincher was money. Always follow the money. That's what they say, don't they?"

"If you're Woodward and Bernstein, maybe."

Looking perplexed, Cross continued. "The morning after Roger's murder, someone cleared two of his online personal bank accounts. Where did the cash turn up? A newly opened account in the name of Cheryl Mansell. She must have been worried that his drug cash would be impounded. After all she'd been through, she wasn't missing out on that. Not exactly the actions of a grieving widow. We also found large amounts paid into the children's accounts, which we believe Cheryl must have known about."

Jaz flashed Dan a sheepish glance.

"It's taken a while for it all to come together, but I'm confident we have the bones of the real story," said Cross.

Jaz looked sad, her mind fizzing with events of the past few weeks. She felt manipulated and deceived by Cheryl, the budding actress, especially regarding the suicide note. Cheryl must have known Logan called Tobias *Tobes*. It was a significant clue, subtly laid to deflect suspicion away from her and onto the only other obvious suspect with daily access to the pub office. She'd skewed the investigation and Jaz had fallen for her deception.

"I'm shocked. Cheryl seemed classy, sensible, good-hearted."

"She'd been through a lot, though, Jaz," said Dan. "Not an angel, easily led, stubborn. Hopeless with money. Not a eulogy I'd be proud of. Roger won't be getting a soppy memorial on his tombstone."

They thanked Inspector Cross for his impromptu briefing, nodded when he reminded them everything remained off the record, and wandered back up the path. Reverend Ford had departed for the crematorium with the cortege. A few mourners lingered amid the ancient tombstones. Dan and Jaz strolled among them, reflecting on the passage of time.

"What do you want on your tombstone, Jaz?"

"Something traditional, hopefully about enjoying a long, happy life. That I always tried to be kind and gave people the benefit of the doubt, although in Cheryl's case, I'm wishing I'd made an exception. What about you?"

"Something alternative, maybe. Don't know what exactly."

They spotted Trish and Lynn waving, waiting patiently by the turreted bell tower, eager for news. Dan persuaded them the church grounds weren't a suitable venue for high-grade gossip, so they piled into his car and drove to the Three Tuns pub.

Over lunch, Dan and Jaz related the gist of Inspector Cross's revelations, skirting around details they believed he'd given in privilege. A unanimous decision determined that Roger was tragic, Logan misguided, Jennifer and Tobias unfortunate, Cheryl manipulative but a damned good actress, and Inspector Cross a first class plonker, but a half-decent detective.

"Blimey, it's like one of those murder mystery films," said Lynn.

Trish had one question that troubled her about the stormy night two weeks before. "Dan, how come the police sent a squad with machine guns to The Anchor that night? I mentioned nothing about weapons when I left a message on your phone. I hadn't seen any."

"Sure you did, Trish. You said one of the men was armed."

A trademark Trish cackle echoed around the Three Tuns. Heads turned, eyebrows raised. "No, I didn't. I said the man had big arms."

Everyone laughed.

"Well, that seals it. This is definitely the craziest funeral I've ever been to. I didn't realise what was happening when we came out of church with all those cops around. I thought, bloody hell, this is a day that can only get better."

Dan turned to Jaz, who'd been quiet over lunch. "You okay?"

"Yeah. I'm fine."

She wasn't. Her mind was in turmoil. Jennifer and Tobias were without a dad and mum. Roger had gone to his final resting place. Cheryl may face a considerable stretch in prison. Terry Marsh was dead. All because she'd pursued a hunch. Thoughts weighed heavy. Her phone trilled. She called voicemail and heard Logan's voice. Light, engaging.

"Hi, trouble. Do me a favour. Look after my books until I get out, will you? Feel free to read any you like." The message clicked off. Jaz placed the phone on the table and folded her arms.

"Who was that?" said Trish.

Jaz shook her head in disbelief and wonder.

"Bob Marley."

"Who?"

"I'll explain later."

"We'd better be off," said Trish. "All this excitement's left me knackered."

After hugs all around, Trish declined Dan's offer to drive them home. "Thanks, but we'll walk. Get some air. We've lots to talk through." She and Lynn waved goodbye.

When they'd left, Dan turned to Jaz. "It was Logan on the phone, wasn't it? What did he want?"

Jaz nodded, sad eyes, finger twirling her handbag strap. While strangely pleased the barman had phoned, annoyance lingered that her first impressions of him proved so wrong. Dan didn't expect her reply.

"Have you ever read Othello?"

"No."

"There's a character known as honest Iago. Everyone likes and respects him at first. He's charming, but not what he seems, manipulating and deceiving everyone he meets, spreading death and mayhem."

"Sounds like an evil so-and-so. Does he work in a pub?"

"No."

"But he's a psychopath?"

"Sort of. Put it this way, he and Logan have a lot in common, although I don't think Logan is evil. Iago wouldn't have let me escape."

Dan drained his glass. "I must brush up on my Shakespeare."

"Funny you should say that. As the great man said, 'Make use of time, let not advantage slip.'"

A baffled look crumpled Dan's features. "Meaning?"

"Follow me. I know exactly where to find the complete works."

ABOUT THE AUTHOR

A journalist by profession, Frank Malley worked as a columnist and deputy sports editor with the Daily Express for 15 years. As chief writer with Press Association Sport for 17 years, Frank covered Olympic Games, football, and rugby World Cups, and top events in golf, tennis, and motor racing.

Shortlisted for Columnist of the Year in the Sports Journalists' Association awards, Frank began writing books after turning freelance five years ago.

www.frankmalley.com

If you enjoyed *If it Looks Like a Duck*, the author would appreciate a quick review on Amazon, Goodreads, or your favourite book website. Reviews are vital – a few words matter.

ALSO BY FRANK MALLEY

Living on the Deadline
(Pitch Publishing 2014)

Simply the Best
(Pitch Publishing 2017)

When the Mist Clears
'The first Lexford Town Mystery'
(Whisper Publishing 2020)

Available in paperback and Kindle formats
from Amazon.

THE FIRST LEXFORD TOWN MYSTERY

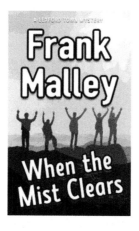

Released worldwide on 15 May 2020

One former war correspondent. Four brave strangers.
Will they live to keep a promise?

When Dan Armitage leaves his job as a war correspondent, he meets four brave strangers battling for their lives with two weapons. Hope and humour. Defiant against a life-threatening illness, the wise-cracking group quickly becomes friends, promising to meet again in a year if they're still alive.

As the friendship deepens, light-hearted shifts to sinister, when Dan's digging draws him into a criminal web and he's held captive by a murderous gang.

Can Dan's new friends save him? Will they live to keep their promise? Find out in the warmth of this feel-good story as humour and romance collide with intrigue and crime.

If you like stories bursting with remarkable characters, bags of laughter, and a splash of sweet romance, then you'll love Frank Malley's absorbing cosy mystery.

Available in paperback and Kindle formats from Amazon.

ALSO BY WHISPER PUBLISHING

Released worldwide on 10 November 2021

Two mysteries to solve. Who can Keira trust?

Keira Brody's Roman holiday isn't living up to the hype until mysterious compatriot Leo Callinan walks through her door. Journalist Keira smells a big story.

Enigmatic Leo is charming and fun, but why the secrecy about his trouble with the local authorities and why is one particular policeman hostile towards him?

Determined, Keira vows to help Leo. Will the decision make her career or break her heart?

Available in paperback and Kindle formats from Amazon.

ALSO BY WHISPER PUBLISHING

Released worldwide on 10 September 2021

What happens when fortune makes a shy bachelor eligible?

Harold Pettigrew leads a sheltered life. Nearing 40, he's never had a girlfriend, rarely left his hometown, and a strict father and possessive mother have kept him in line. Harold's job at the public library is his only escape. Then, things change.

A vast lottery win finds Harold on a luxury cruise with six women as companions, but what are their motives? Do they know of Harold's secret fortune? Does his eligible bachelor status arise from wealth or genuine attraction? Who is not the happy holidaymaker they seem?

Board the Lottery Loveboat and live a warming story of romance, revelation and intrigue—with one petrified millionaire.

Available in paperback and Kindle formats from Amazon.

ALSO BY WHISPER PUBLISHING

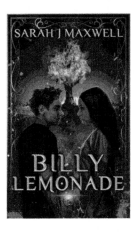

Released worldwide on 20 January 2021

When a broken-hearted girl befriends a desperate boy, the secrets haunting them may tear them apart …

Jane Smith is too lonely for words. Ignored by her grieving mother, uncaring teachers, and peers, the distraught thirteen-year-old can't find any solace after the deaths of her father and sister. Resigned to an empty, isolated existence, Jane can hardly believe her luck when she meets a poor, older boy. Taunted, scorned, and stuck with a despised nickname, he is happy to be her friend.

Sensing the boy identifies with her pain, Jane finds hope as their friendship deepens over drifting summer days. But, when she suspects he's hiding a terrible truth, Jane fears the skeletons in his closet will pull them both back into the dark.

Will Jane make the ultimate sacrifice to release despair and take them to a together forever place?

Billy Lemonade is a beautifully crafted standalone YA story. If you like real, raw characters, authentic drama, and a dash of supernatural suspense, then you'll love Sarah J Maxwell's compelling journey.

Available in paperback and Kindle formats from Amazon.